Realignment

Bibi Heartsglow

Realignment

A Korpsigin Story: Book 1

Production copyright FurPlanet Productions © 2025

Text Copyright © Bibi Heartsglow 2025

Cover Artwork © Eight-Stroke 2025

The Korps Universe © Karen King 2024, and used with permission

Published by FurPlanet Productions
Dallas, Texas
www.FurPlanet.com

Print ISBN 978-1-61450-674-4
Electronic ISBN 978-1-61450-675-1

Table of Contents

This book contains depictions of: Queerphobia, Misgendering, Deadnaming, Parental Abuse, Violence, Blood, Vomiting, Electrocution, Kidnapping, Ableism, and Arrests.

For everyone fighting for a better world, for all those who cannot fight for themselves, and for all we've lost along the way.

FOREWORD

BY KAREN KING

Nearly seven thousand years ago, an event shook the world. An arrival of something ancient: the merging of humanity with the world of the beast, the eruption of superpowers, and the proliferation of the supernatural. In the modern day, this world appears much like our own but for the pantheon of species that occupy it and the extensive presence of superheroes and supervillains alike. While many states have their own super-powered forces, a vast variety of independent actors exist.

Among the most prominent independent supervillain groups is an organization known as the Korps. As far as most are aware, the Korps is an organization dedicated to world domination, led (in theory) by the shadowy Overlord. This sinister being has tried to wrap their vicious claws around the planet, time after time, since the beginning of recorded history.

The truth, of course, is significantly more complex.

Led by some of the world's strongest superpowered beings, the Korps sees itself not as a state-in-waiting, but a governance method — seeking to depose repressive state-based hierarchies to install systems more capable of effectively distributing resources to those in need. It sees state actors — "Heroes," police, paramilitaries — mete punishment out on innocents, yet go unpunished in turn. It knows, — for all the cartoonish pretensions of the supering world — that this is the true evil. It knows, too, that this cannot go unchallenged.

Operating a number of covert front companies and satellite operations for many decades, the Korps has dedicated a great deal of resources to outpacing the world's greatest scientific, engineering and medical minds. Korps medical technology in particular is extremely advanced, allowing its members to essentially build their preferred body from scratch — and permitting this capacity at scale. The Korps has learned well that monocultures become stagnant without personal expression, which it fiercely encourages in its members — a reality at odds with the widespread public perception that they are nothing more than brainwashed drones.

One of the most useful and distinctive tools at the Korps's disposal are Rose-Coloured Glasses, or "RCGs," a high-capacity communications tool, heads-up display and computer-brain interface so powerful they can be used directly as a VR headset. RCGs can function as an assistive device or therapy tool… but the nature of the technology means they have the power to directly access and even alter one's thoughts. Alternately viewed with relief, mistrust, or fear by the supering world, it is known that wherever they are worn, the Korps is not far behind.

Having emerged in the wake of the Second World War, the Korps has gradually spread its influence, eventually emerging fully into the public consciousness in the 1990s. With increased visibility and emphasis on immediate action, however, comes ever more entanglements…

The Korps began as a big pile of superhero and supervillain tropes that I'd built up a love of through various types of media, like the James Bond movies. While I originally just threw it together as an action playset of stock characters, over time, it began to morph into something very different. Using stock pop culture antagonists to take swings at the injustices unfolding around me began to carry more and more emotional weight.

In an era when information became more and more readily available, we were able, at any time of day, to pull out our phones and view some kind of great injustice unfolding, live in front of the world — to see police forces with the budgets and capacities of small militaries crushing peaceful protestors, to watch the deceptions of nations exposed constantly but slip by unpunished, to see the suffering of those in need, on our feeds, 24/7 …

It became increasingly clear to me, and to many, that the status quo is not a state of normalcy, but something imposed by force. Equally, to many, the concept of rallying the villains — those who challenged the status quo — and giving us a context in which we can, in some sense, strike back against it all… It struck a chord among those of my generation. In a world where fighting back seems so hard, an entity like the Korps is something compelling.

I am now sitting here writing the foreword for an actual, published work about it, and my mind is reeling. Giving the Korps as a set of narrative tools to the wider community feels like it has uncorked a flood: a need to right wrongs, a need to highlight injustices, a need to tell intimately personal stories, stories of love, and stories of redemption... rushing out onto countless pages, from countless perspectives.

All I have ever wanted to do is to help give people a community, and the tools they need to create, and to build the stories they need. It is an honour and a privilege to introduce this story to you — one of love, one of breaking free, one of deep wounds beginning to heal...

— Karen King

CHAPTER 1

IDOL PLAYTHINGS

Early 2017

"Don't you appreciate any *modern* Heroes, Austin?"

Volta cast her eyes aside and scratched at the underside of her muzzle. It wasn't that she didn't *know* other Heroes. It was just that True North II was *cooler* than any of them.

"Like Chris Marcotte?"

The lemur gave a sympathetic frown. "Any Heroes who *aren't* a True North? ...But I mean, the regeneration thing is cool, I guess."

Volta shrugged. "He's not really my favorite, anyway."

"I'm actually surprised — I thought the legacy appeal would be worth more to ya!"

Legacy. Right. Volta took a deep breath, then let it out in a huff.

"Okay, so the heavies he goes against are way more extreme, yeah, but also this means he puts nothing on the line himself, and that's just not as cool." It was an opinion that she'd carefully considered for a while. "He's not *bad*, just. I dunno. Doesn't catch my interest, I guess...?"

Luke leaned in and popped open his lunchbox. Festooned in orange and black, with a few "witty" puns emblazoned along the sides, it was pretty clear who the lemur's favorite was.

*Even **I** don't carry my True North II lunchbox around, and I'm embarrassing enough as it is.*

"All right — Supersonic, then. She's got speed, she's not invincible, and she looks *great*. Honestly, if I were a villain, I'd wanna fight *her*."

Volta considered that. Luke, the Fanboy Villain: powerless, scrawny, and more than a bit of a dweeb.

Not like I'm any different, Volta thought. *If I didn't shoot lightning out of my hands, I'd probably be just like him, only... bigger. I only even work out because I want to be a Hero some day; I wouldn't even have that going for me. I'd just be a bigger, redder Luke.*

It was an uncomfortable thought.

"Supersonic's... *cool,*" she admitted. Her eyes focused on her muzzle as she tried to make eye contact... and not look like she was sweating. Still, she had to change the subject. Something about the cat's shape in that bodysuit was... well, Volta always felt faintly gross thinking about her. *Like one of those creepy guys on the forums that don't realize nobody wants to read a two-paragraph description of what they want to do with her.*

"Golden Gavel, though," the red wolf tossed out. He wasn't her favorite, by any means, but...

"We both know he's overrated," said Luke, shaking his head, "and I said *modern.* He's been retired for a while now."

Still, that didn't stop half the boarding school from chattering on about him every time Heroes were brought up. Volta had eventually learned not to mention True North around most of her classmates. Hearing her favorite get dismissed in favor of "Uncle Adam" was the fastest way to ruin any momentum a good mood might have had.

"No, no, no," Luke continued around a mouthful of sandwich, "all those Heroes, working for the government? Or with big teams that have basically been around since the Bronze Age?"

I know where this is going.

"No, no, you want a Hero for the *people.* Everyone's Hero!"

Please don't.

"Lawful Neutral! With the Everyone's Hero Agency!"

Luke pulled an action figure out of his backpack. Her outfit matched the orange and black of his lunchbox. "Look — she's not invincible, but she *always* wins anyway! Not because of some boring power like *super-speed* or *regeneration* or *her-dad-spent-a-lot-of-money-training-her-with-his-superhero-buddies* —"

"— Hey! —"

"— but because she's just *that funny!*"

Volta made a face. Lawful Neutral was... well, funny wasn't the right word. Puns weren't *funny.* When she had come home with a Lawful

Neutral trading card one day, her parents had frowned, and asked if she thought superheroes were meant to have fun. Volta hadn't been sure how to answer that — surely heroes should enjoy their work as much as anyone?

But that had only gotten her a lecture about hard work, pride, and the importance and solemn dignity of *duty*. The occasional one-liner was fine — heroic, even! — but it was agreed upon that Lawful Neutral took it *way* too far, even *if* her powers seemed to rely on her comedic "talents."

"Besides," Mrs. Travers had said, "the way she dresses is *hardly* appropriate."

Volta had wanted to object to that. A spandex bodysuit was hardly *unusual* hero attire, but her mother wasn't about to comment on the reason Lawful Neutral — by all accounts a small-time Hero working for a small-time agency self-importantly comparing themselves to *Bradley Group*, of all Hero teams — had risen to more fame than her station necessarily deserved. The *reasons*, in fact. Likely the same *reasons* Lawful Neutral probably couldn't see her own toes without leaning forward.

Volta would have suspected Luke of having the same reasons for liking her, if not for...

"Did you catch her latest fight?" Luke practically bounced in his seat. Volta didn't have the heart to tell him that she only watched YouTube compilations of the demimorph's fights once a month, at most. Mostly so that people didn't think that *she* was the sort to record it and then play it back in slow motion.

"No, but that means you get to tell me about it?" She wanted to be supportive, after all, and a good friend would be supportive. Like Luke was, when she wanted to talk about True North II. Sometimes.

"Okay, so she squared off against that villain that's been making a name for herself over there — Stampede, that villain that just charges people and flattens 'em? Lawful didn't even use her *powers* for the first half of it — she was just dodging around and heckling her the whole time!"

Volta raised an eyebrow. "Isn't that a bit dangerous? If she'd landed a hit..."

"*That's what makes her so cool!* So, Lawful Neutral tricked her into charging into the wall —"

"Ouch. Wait... did she go through?"

"Oh, yeah! Horns got stuck and everything. So then Lawful grabbed her by the horn and said, 'If you're a sheep who likes to charge, does that make you a… *battery ram?*' and I *lost* it! Funniest shit I've ever seen."

Volta snorted and shook her head. "She's gonna get herself killed some day if she doesn't start taking this seriously." She knew she was just parroting her parents… but they were right, weren't they?

Luke didn't seem nearly as concerned. "She'll be fine. She's *super* quick, and she's *really* powerful, if you think about it!"

"I guess." Volta pondered the action figure in the lemur's hand. Lawful Neutral *was* pretty approachable; she was a B-tier Hero with A-tier charisma, at least. Plus, demi folk like her weren't exactly common, even though anyone could be born with it.

In extreme cases of demimorphism, they looked almost like ancient humans, the kind that showed up in cave paintings and computer recreations from skeletons thousands of years old. The biggest differences were the only clear links to their modern lineage.

Almost all had at least a pair of ears and a tail matching their species, but many other people with demimorphism had additional features that would have given the action figure manufacturers at least a *somewhat* easier time, but not her. The only other foxy features Lawful Neutral boasted were a set of canid teeth and tongue inside her too-short, furless muzzle, and deep brown eyes that glinted like fire when they caught the light.

The factory that manufactured those action figures had been forced to make an entire new mold to accommodate her decidedly un-vulpine features. The cost of creating a one-of-a-kind mold had been so prohibitively expensive, in fact, that the figures barely made pennies of profit apiece.

Volta had only learned that while looking up information about vintage Arthur Simonds figures, and she didn't want anyone to think she'd been looking so far into Lawful Neutral merchandise that she'd learned information *that* obscure about her.

After all, if she knew that the nine button-activated voice lines for her action figure were provided by a hired voice actress and not the superheroine herself, what were the odds that she *didn't* know the agreed-upon speculation as to her bust size?

"Austin. *Austin*. Look at me." She hadn't even noticed that Luke was holding up the figure. "Look —"

"*In the Name of the Moon… I'll PUN-ish you!*" came the tinny voice. Luke's thumb pressed the button at her hip again.

"Look at me."

"*I can vix it!*"

"One more — look at me."

"*Anyone can be a hero!*"

"There it is. That's what I like about her. She's not just some glory hound or something! She's doing it to *inspire* people, to… *help* people." Luke turned the figure over in his fuzzy hands. "I dunno. It might sound stupid because I don't have any powers like you, but…"

Luke let it hang. It took Volta a moment to realize that Luke was waiting for her to take the cue. *What does he want me to say? I can't help him with that. But I have to say **something**.*

"Do you… *want* to be a Hero?"

"I guess not." He sounded a little dejected. "I mean, maybe in the metaphorical sense? It would be nice to have someone be proud of me. Besides my parents, anyway."

Volta cleared her throat, and Luke did too. "Anyway. Just. I guess, when you're a Hero, if you ever team up with Lawful… can you tell her she's really important to me? T-to a lot of people, I mean…! But, you know, you can use me as an example."

God, she felt awkward. But still…

"Redline and Lawful Neutral, on the same team?" asked Volta.

*With my powers even I should be at **least** a tier above her. Especially if I get in at the TPA Academy — she'd be lucky to manage "sidekick" at that level. Luke won't want to hear that, though.*

"If I meet up with her some day, I'll let her know."

Chapter 2

New Heights

August 2017

The dress clung to her body in ways that made her usual skin-tight bodysuit feel modest by comparison, but at least she wasn't alone. The arm of a tall, middle-aged English Foxhound stayed hooked under her arm as she was paraded from one group of chattering socialites to another. Ellen couldn't help but feel like she was not being escorted but *hauled*.

She was still getting used to fashionable attire; outside of work she tended towards easy and comfortable. The last dress she'd bought had come from a Walgreens end cap. She wasn't sure how much more expensive her current attire might be, but if she had to guess, she'd have put it at least two figures higher — and with half as much material.

"Have you met Ellen?" asked the dog beside her, snapping the vixen out of her meandering train of thought as she was swung to a halt in front of the latest clique of semi-celebrities. "She's my proudest find."

Jack was practically *glowing* with self-satisfaction. Ellen was still trying to figure out how to carry herself, but the smile on her face was, at least, infectious enough to make up the difference.

"Pleased to meet you!" she found herself saying for what felt like the twentieth time in the past fifteen minutes. Yet another hand squeezed her own, and yet another set of eyes slid inevitably away from hers toward her employer's. She could never tell whether she found that to be demeaning or a relief, but at least they weren't sliding down to her cleavage.

It was supposed to be a fun event; Arthur Goldstone had recently finished construction on a tower filled to the brim with lavish apartments. The party commemorating the occasion, high in his penthouse suite, hosted only those with the kind of funds to stay there — and their plus-ones, of course.

All told, Ellen felt entirely out-of-place, but at least her parents had trained her to be polite. She worried that it might have come off as stiff... but better that, than to embarrass Jack in front of potential investors. Her grip was firm, not crushing; her smile was easy, and mildly interested. Her Lawful Neutral accent was present — people *expected* it of her, after all — but subdued enough to not be so cartoonishly over-the-top. She was forgetting names as quickly as Jack spoke them, but that part was probably fine. She was hardly getting more than a couple of sentences out before she was rotated to the next cable news anchor or retired footballer.

It wasn't long before Ellen found herself in front of a well-groomed man somewhere between Jack's age and her own. She wasn't entirely sure who he skewed closer to, but the big red wolf's solid posture would have made him look younger than he was regardless.

His handshake was like a vice, and his claws dug into the back of her fleshy hand. Ellen's grip was strong, but she felt the bones in her palm squeeze inward, just for a moment, and suppressed a wince.

"Ah, Lawful Neutral." He cleared his throat, as if considering what to say to her for a moment. "So, you're one of those 'demo-morphs?' Huh. The camera doesn't do you justice, young lady."

Through great force of will, Ellen forced her ear to keep from twitching. She'd heard far worse than "demo-morphs" before — it was close enough, anyway, and from what Jack had prepared her for, it could have been a lot worse. James Travers was *Texan* old money, after all.

"I appreciate it," she said with a just-barely-too-forced smile. "Jack tells me you're in the property business?"

"Oh, yes," he said, waving off the topic as quickly as it had been raised — though the upturn at the corner of his lips suggested he appreciated her having done her research. "I wouldn't want to bore you with the details, though."

"You know," his red wolf wife chimed in from beside him, her tone conspiratorial, "our Austin developed superpowers as well."

"...Austin, *Texas?*" asked Ellen.

"Our *son*, Austin Travers," corrected James.

The red wolf squared his shoulders and puffed out his chest, as if his figure wasn't macho enough already. "We have *high* hopes for him."

"Ah."

Ellen wasn't certain what to say to that. The child's existence as a super of unspecified powers charged the air with an awkward, expectant energy, both of the wolves staring at her with inscrutable intent. Jack, beside her, emanated an aura of equally mysterious urgency until — finally — James cleared his throat.

"So, did you always want to become a comedian, or was Hero really your first choice?"

Ellen shifted on her feet; the tension had relaxed in the same way that a bow might, having merrily sent its arrow of social discomfort squarely into Ellen's corner.

"I was actually intending a career in biology, sir," she managed, "but life had... other plans."

"So why Hero work, then?"

"As a proud Wisconsinite, I've always considered myself part of the first line of defense, sir."

His brow furrowed. "Against...? Oh, the Korps?"

"Not exactly, sir." Ellen's face went deadly serious, her voice grim. It was Ellen's turn to puff up; her shoulder-squaring was vital to offset the heft of her chest — especially in this getup — in front of a former Miss America. "*Canadians.* It's been over two hundred years since their last attack, but the Midwest remains vigilant."

That got a good chuckle, and James gave Jack a clap on the shoulder so hard that the Foxhound's knees buckled. The pair exchanged a significant look, and Jack pointedly cleared his throat.

"Ah — Ellen, I think I have some business with James to discuss. Keep Hellen company while we find a good, quiet corner to talk numbers."

He brushed past her, patting her bare shoulder as James broke off to accompany him. Ellen watched them go, then turned her eyes back to the remaining lupine.

The woman was *gorgeous.* She'd seen plenty of Hellen Travers on magazine covers when she herself was barely in kindergarten. With what she was wearing, Ellen was seeing plenty of her now, too — and she knew for a fact that, back home, her sister Vixie had an ancient copy of Esquire still wedged beneath the mattress that showed even more.

In Ellen's imagination, the former Miss America always seemed taller — but then, everyone was a giant when she was a kid, and she'd never really updated her mental image to match. The eight-foot tall woman in her mind simply didn't match up to the more reasonable reality.

At least, in real life, she didn't have to crane her neck.

Hellen's white eyebrows rose almost imperceptibly slightly, her gaze dipping low for a fraction of an instant before returning to Ellen's. It was a given that she would look up to Hellen — but she hadn't expected the face on the other side of that coin to be looking down its muzzle in return.

"I'm glad to have met you, actually," the wolf said, her voice sweet and sharp. "I have always found black to be slimming, and now that I've seen you outside of your uniform... well, the color palette makes sense, I think. After all, if one wishes to be taken *seriously*..."

She let that hang in the air like a cabbage fart in a crowded elevator, and slipped past her with all the grace of a runway model who had just left a cabbage fart in a crowded elevator'. Ellen was left alone to wrinkle her nose in the cloud of self-consciousness and disappointment. She'd heard of never meeting one's heroes, of course, but she supposed one should avoid meeting their sexual awakenings as well.

Maybe she could find better company elsewhere. Ellen scanned over the party; there were plenty of other folks chatting with each other in tight circles and loose collectives... but not a single one she knew. Jack's breathless introductions hadn't given her time to find the first spark of chemistry with any of the people here. She'd hardly hobbed more than the first whiff of a nob since she'd arrived, when one got right down to it. She frowned, left alone with the thumping sounds of generic Top 40 satellite radio. That was hardly unexpected, but she'd been hoping not to get abandoned so swiftly.

Oh well.

Left to her own devices, abandoned by the one she'd come to the party with for a taller, wealthier man, Ellen did what any self-respecting Wisconsinite did when times were tough:

She made a beeline for the bar.

There, a marmoset in a well-made suit slung beverages with a stylish flair to a smattering of partygoers who were largely there to pick up some drinks for their friends, aside from a couple chatting each other up and a lone mongoose forlornly nursing a drink.

Might join you soon, if Jack doesn't pop back up real quick —

"Oh, Jesus *fuck!*" the mongoose yelped, a sharp, crackling *pop* had made everyone bar side leap, but none more so than Ellen, her Hero instincts soaring into a blaze. By the time she realized what exactly had happened, she had one hand on the mongoose's shoulder, eyes darting between her, her suit, the counter, and the floor. Her tail wasn't the only one that had gone bushy, but when Ellen's gaze finally took stock of the crowd, she realized she was the only one who'd sprung into high alert.

"You okay?"

"Yeah," Ellen said, hissing as she accepted a towel from the barman. She was splashed with what had once been an old fashioned, judging by the muddled remnants of orange and cherry in what remained of the glass. She reached out to pick a shard from the mongoose's suit, grimacing sympathetically. "What happened?"

"You know how it is," said the mongoose, with far too much confidence in Ellen's knowledge of how it was. "Rich *fucks* will spend thousands on the prettiest glasses, but don't give a shit if they pop under the slightest pressure."

Ellen blanched. Mingling with the guests was easy when everyone was self-absorbed — all she had to do was offer a few vague compliments and express the barest interest — but no one had prepped her for one guest expressing anti-rich sentiment. Was she supposed to agree? Would smiling and nodding be too sympathetic?

"Sorry," the mongoose finally grumbled when Ellen failed to respond. "Diane. Uh, if that's important to you. I'm Diane."

"Ellen!" Ellen ellened, with her trademark Ellen-thusiasm, extending her hand out to meet the mongoose's gloved paw. "Lawful Neutral, when I'm in costume."

"Yeah?" Diane cocked an eyebrow. "Never heard of you, but hey, maybe someday I will." She raised the jagged base of the glass in a mock toast. Ellen raised her empty hand to meet it and took an exaggerated swig.

Diane just stared back at her. "I'm not doin' that."

"Yeah, I realized it too late," Ellen grimaced. "Well, uh, hey — I think I'm gonna circle back for a drink later. The whole 'broken glass' thing kinda put me off of it for a minute."

"Funny," said the mongoose with an unreadable expression, "I think another old fashioned should help me forget about the first one."

Ellen rose, chuckling jocularly and flashing a winning grimace and a pair of finger guns — but as she turned to leave, the mongoose rapped her knuckles loudly on the table, phewing to a putter.

"Couldn't pay me to go in there," the other woman huffed, eyes locked on the wide-open glass doors and the partygoers beyond. Part of Ellen agreed with her; the mood out there was certainly *jubilant,* but she could hear people's nerves all the way from the bar area. Just looking up into the balcony pool's glass bottom from the street had made her breath catch in her chest.

Ellen forced herself to shrug it off. "Probably no more dangerous than a roller coaster."

"Still. If you think a regular pool's got a lot of piss in it, that thing's probably 50% terror urine."

"Mm." Jack had been *very* enthusiastic about Ellen making the most of the opportunity to try new things, and she'd been trying to amp herself up to at least dip her toes since the moment Jack had told her about this place. "Still."

A new drink in a fresh glass slid onto the bar, and Diane raised it half-heartedly to Ellen.

"Hey," she said, taking a swig, "it's your funeral."

Don't look down 'til you're out there, the fox had told herself, but it was hard to take her own advice. She had never in all her life been more grateful for the size of her prodigious chest than she was now. The borrowed orange-and-black one-piece squished her breasts together in a way that Ellen found faintly *ridiculous,* but anything that obscured her view of the street down below was a boon she wouldn't dream of turning away.

At least the other bodies in the water gave her *plenty* of options to hold her attention. She'd never been so thankful to be bisexual; men and women with expensive exercise plans made for many a trim physique, even if they weren't a great majority. Nobody she saw quite made her *burn*, but that was good — just enough to distract her from thinking too hard about the street below, not enough that she'd find herself aching to get home and relieve some tension.

She was a *Hero*, after all... even if eyeing a well-built man's shoulder made her feel a little less like one.

When she realized that her gaze had slipped away from her, only to finally surface somewhere within the plunging halter of Hellen Travers's swimsuit, she felt somehow lower than even a *villain*.

Worse still: Hellen had noticed.

The corner of the red wolf's narrow mouth twitched; she tore her attention from the socialite she was speaking to and toward Ellen. Once again, she felt uncomfortably *seen* by someone decidedly above her on the social ladder and immediately wondered whether it would be gauche to see if anyone would laugh at a pun about vanishing from sight.

"I wouldn't expect *you* of all people to be jealous," Hellen sniffed, "but of course, I'm used to it. I *do* have that effect on people, after all."

Ellen forced a sheepish chuckle. She couldn't resist folding her arms under her own pair, feeling suddenly and horribly like a woman in a piece of hacky erotica, as she tried to make shrugging her shoulders (and her O-cups) look casual and disinterested.

"Sorry," the fox muttered. Excuses flicked through in her mind — "I was just spacing out," or "I got nervous and my eyes settled on the familiar," or "I needed something steady to stare at and I figured those things had enough plastic in them to work" — but for a variety of reasons, Ellen couldn't bring herself to speak them aloud.

The lupine's muzzle wrinkled in distaste, and she returned to her conversation with her friend. Ellen was grateful, at least, that the wealthy matron had nothing more condescending to say. Taking a deep breath, she finally gathered up the courage to look down. She was amazed; she'd expected the water to obscure the view, but it was nearly as transparent as the glass beneath, save for the shine of the sun on the surface. She could see the ground past her feet; distant, so distant, yet... somehow, uncomfortably, close.

She was glad that when the pit of her stomach dropped, it at least had the glass bottom to catch it.

This isn't so bad, she lied to herself, hoping to find it truer than it was.

As if in answer, the pool *groaned* around her.

Fear spiked; the hackles of her tail rose, her heart quickening and breath going thin.

The glass creaked, almost *hummed*, and Ellen could feel it thrumming against the bottoms of her feet. She desperately hoped that it was just the wind, but the way everyone else was taking note of it, everyone who'd been there longer than she had, and *presumably* would have gotten used to the wind by now...

Oh no.

She wasn't sure who started screaming first, but pretty soon it was nearly everyone, desperately splashing through the water to get back to the penthouse. Her ears perked; for the second time that day, she snapped into focus.

The groan gave way to a very thick-sounding *crack*, and the floor beneath them buckled. An ugly white scar ran instantly up the length of the pool all the way to its zenith at the far end of the pool, so, *so* visible through that perfectly clear water.

Ellen knew they weren't gonna make it. *She* wasn't gonna make it. She had to do something — *now*. She whirled and caught movement. Hellen Travers and her friend, fighting the water's resistance as they ran in desperate slow motion. Ellen gasped at the sight. It was a long shot. It was *stupid*. If she was wrong, her last words would be from a popsicle stick.

But she had to try. She grabbed Hellen's arm in a vice grip, hoping against hope that she was the right choice as she wrenched her down to Ellen's level, forced her so close that she could feel the fur of her forehead against her eyebrows.

"Hellen!" she barked; the supermodel struggled, but didn't tear her face away. *Good.* She had her attention, despite everything. "Why did James throw a clock out the window?"

And then the weight of it all broke through; the glass bottom shattered into enormous shards, and the water and the glass and the people all fell.

Ellen felt the glass fall away from her feet and start twisting in the wind, even as she fell with it. Her breath froze in her chest as they picked up speed, but she hadn't lost Hellen. She grabbed her by both arms now. Wind rushed up as the street rose to meet her. Civilians stood far below on the ground; they wouldn't be out of the way fast enough.

She had *one* chance.

Deep down, she knew it all came down to Hellen, not her. The wolf inhaled to fill her powerful lupine lungs, and Ellen cut in just before she could reverse the flow:

"*To see time fly!*"

Hellen stared back at her in furious disbelief; the skin of her nose tightened and folded into an enraged heap of wrinkles, and she *screamed* in toothy, impotent resentment that the last words she would ever hear were nothing more than a mediocre child's *joke.*

Ellen only barely heard her start before it suddenly stopped. Her face froze like that — *all* of her froze like that, and so did her friend, a few feet to one side, and everyone else. The glass, the water, all falling like deadly rain, had *stopped.*

But no, not 'stopped,' not quite. Hellen's fur still moved, slow as a sloth surgeon, and she still drew inexorably toward the city sidewalk, but as if through molasses. Whatever sound she was making was coming out at such a slow frequency that Ellen could no longer hear it — or much of anything, for that matter.

Ellen had stopped falling, too, but not for the same reason. The energy within her grew buoyant and strong; it rose with her breath, it filled her lungs and spread through her body like oxygen through her bloodstream.

Okay.

She had everything she needed now, and time to think, but she had to be careful. Time was slow to *her,* but the impact would still be very real if — or *when* — they hit the ground.

She willed herself downwards. The time-slowed water fought her for every inch, but she tore through it and out the other side, past the transparent panes, and lowered her momentum as she approached the asphalt that she would have broken against any other way.

A few careful nudges got those on the ground moving. They'd stumble, some would even likely be thrown, but she'd be there to catch them later. With another deep breath and a force of will, she forced her energy *up* and took to the air once more. Despite herself, Ellen flew back to the falling lupine first. She couldn't *stop* her in midair — not without causing almost as many problems as the asphalt would another thirty yards down — but if she just applied enough careful pressure to slow her down...

*Am I saving you first because you're familiar, because you're hot, or because I need a practice dummy and you're **very** rude?*

Whatever the reason, the vixen laid her palms against Hellen Travers's back, waited for her weight to settle down into her as she fell, then left the older woman where she was, her fall slowed but not stopped. Another swimmer was waiting for her, and another, and another, and another...

This would take careful, deliberate work, one by one, then all over again until they finally reached the ground, but she could do it. No one would die today — not on her watch.

She felt more like a Hero, a real *hero*, than she ever had before, and the feeling made her blood come alive inside of her like nothing else could.

Seconds later, the situation was well in hand.

The glass had been redirected to the street, its shards spraying harmlessly against the curb. The partygoers' descents had been carefully controlled until they were lying, gently, on the sidewalk. Their heads fell the last few inches onto pillows and balled-up clothes that Ellen had retrieved from the changing room. For Ellen, it felt like she'd left it behind minutes prior, but as she dragged a dangling civilian back up and over the edge onto the safety of the penthouse, she saw that the dry partygoers were still only just beginning to react to the apparent imminent demise of their friends and partners — and, perhaps, the whirling streaks of orange and black that saved them.

Hellen's rage had been *intense*. At this rate, a bullet would have moved through the air no faster than a bowling ball tossed by a child, if Ellen had to guess. God, if only she could can that sort of reaction to power her ability — Pun For All, as she called it, much to Jack's dismay — the Color Guard would be knocking her door down with a recruitment offer…

Ellen swung the energy in her body upwards and ascended over the crowd, her ears brushing the ceiling as she scanned faces and body language. It was *possible* that the pool had simply had too many people in it, but that was the *convenient* answer, the answer that lined up with her anxiety going into the glass bottom pool in the first place.

But it didn't make *sense*. This was no corner-cutting amenity in an apartment Goldstone Investments had built for *poors*, it was the private penthouse of the real estate mogul himself. He wouldn't dare construct a pool this high up unless it was made to last, or at least, not made so poorly that it shattered the first time it was used. Something — or *someone* — had to be responsible. But who?

Those nearest the pool were gasping, shrinking back, screaming, *horrified*; those further back were mostly still turning and realizing what had almost happened, and those past the bar island were only barely starting to figure out what direction all the screaming was coming from. Almost all of them were rooted to their spots, except a couple of quick-reactors who had been scrambling to help those who had reached the edge in time, and Ellen had nudged them back once she'd taken care of their charges.

That was everyone, except…

Bingo.

One mammal had their back turned, their legs hustling fast enough for Ellen to see them moving. Straight toward the exit, even, apparently weaving through the crowd, their fingers inching the hem of a glove up over their furred wrist.

Ellen floated over the crowd toward them, eyes furrowing. There hadn't been a bomb, or an impact, or anything — it had been *gradual,* or as gradual as breaking glass could be. Somehow, they'd managed without.

She swung down and grabbed them beneath the armpits, hauled them up into the air and toward the off-limits master bedroom through the thickness of time. She needed a place to maneuver, to figure out what powers she was dealing with, away from everyone else.

Diane's eyes were widening already. Good — Ellen had the element of surprise, then. She put her down and frog-marched her into a bedroom the size of her own apartment, kicked the door behind them as they passed, and pinned her to the wall by the shirt, brow furrowing.

Best be careful. I think I know how she did it, but if I'm wrong...

The door slammed shut as the world sped back into time, shutting out the quieting screams as they turned to noises of relief and confusion. The mongoose groaned, disoriented from sensory whiplash.

When Ellen spoke, it was with a single word through bared fangs:

"Why?"

The mongoose's expression told her she was right; Diane wasn't confused, but *angry*. Defensive.

Caught.

"Bite me," she growled.

"Who *are* you?"

"The fuck do you care?"

Ellen huffed, she clenched her fists around the fabric of Diane's shoulders and bit back her impulses. Deep breath.

"Fine. It's not my job to find out, anyway. You could have *killed* them."

"A Hero *and* a detective? Shit, do you juggle, too?" Ellen's eyes narrowed, but the mongoose only cackled. "Look, *Hero*. Ain't a person who can afford to be here who didn't deserve it. Fuck, if there were any bystanders below it was *still* worth it."

"How can you *say* that? *Every* life has worth!"

"You think those people believe that?" Diane snapped, nostrils flaring and hackles raising. "You think your *boss* believes that? Rich fucking assholes only think people's lives are worth what they add to their own goddamn wallets," she snorted. Ellen couldn't tell if the mongoose found it *funny*, or if she was pissed.

Both, probably.

"Shit, your boss is probably wringing every dime he can out of *you*, too. He'll squeeze you 'til you're dry and throw away the husk, just like the *rest* of them." She grinned. "If he's not a splatter on the pavement, anyway."

"He's not," growled Ellen. "*No one is.*"

For the first time since she'd started talking, the mongoose was speechless.

"I saved every last one of them. You're caught, and if I've figured out how your powers work — they're not exactly combat-oriented, are they?"

"*Fuck* you! You're lying! You just don't want me to have the *satisfaction* —"

"I'm not a liar," Ellen hissed, leaning in flat nose to pointed muzzle. "I'm a Hero. *Everyone's* Hero."

Jack's hand had found its way back to her shoulder and hadn't let go since. Ellen's hair was still wet, but she didn't have much to complain about given what else could have happened.

Diane — if that was her real name — had been carted off in zip ties by the police fairly quickly. The handcuffs they'd tried to clap on her at first had, after a minute, shattered to pieces and led the mongoose into a fit of manically exasperated cackling, but there had been nowhere for her to run. Any fondness that Ellen had formed for the poor woman holding a shattered glass at the bar had vanished when she'd tried to turn Ellen into road pizza.

A small crowd of partygoers and news teams had formed around them, as EMTs supplied blankets to the shaken-but-otherwise-fine swimmers. A collie held a microphone between them. It wasn't quite a press conference, but that didn't stop Ellen's boss from treating it like one.

"I'll tell you this," Jack declared, a wry grin spreading across his muzzle. "If I didn't have my Plus One open, I think the news today would be very different. Thank God for my divorce and thank God for Lawful Neutral!"

Ellen buzzed with a thick layer of pride; she'd done such a good job that when the EMTs arrived all they'd had to do was help Goldstone's staff pass out towels to the shaking swimmers.

Jack was beside himself, too. With a save like this, the Everyone's Hero Association had just found its way onto the map, with Lawful Neutral as its shining star, front and center.

CHAPTER 3

BEAT YOUR HEROES

June 2020

Volta brushed the brick dust off of her knuckles and rolled out her shoulders. This kind of job called for a heavy, and she was happy to fit the description. Eight feet of rippling muscle and jiggling flesh constituted what was now the villainous Redline, eyes and visor both agleam in the midday sun.

Her job was simple: open a hole in the building, stand watch, and deal with any Heroes that showed up, while the other Korps agents located and extracted the cargo. Medicine, if she recalled correctly, but her part of the plan didn't really rely on a thorough understanding of it. She didn't have a lot of time to ponder, though. As she turned back around, agents entering through the breach behind her, she locked eyes with someone who hadn't been in the van.

Barely waist-high, in an orange and black bodysuit. A flat, furless face and long, reddish-brown hair. A very familiar smirk, and a pair of raised fists.

"New Korps heavy-hitter?" asked Lawful Neutral. "Not every day they send a big bad wolf to fight me. They trying to throw me for a loop-ine?"

Volta snorted. "Haven't heard of me yet? That's all right. I'm new in town... but I know *you*. Lawful Neutral. Powers: making shitty jokes. Origin: bitten by a radioactive dipshit. That about right?"

Lawful Neutral's mouth pushed up into a pout. "Aw, c'mon. Your mom is a lot of things, but her nuclei are *perfectly* stable." Before Volta could process how to feel about that, the fox hero grinned. "Your mom isn't a horse, right? Because that would have been hilarious if she was a horse."

"She's... not a horse," said the wolf, gesturing towards her own wolfish-ness.

"Oh, good. Although it would make sense that you gravitated toward being... *Korps-ralled.*"

"I'm Redline," sneered Volta, "and I gotta say, I'm disappointed. People told me you were funny."

"Aww." The fox wagged a finger. "Don't believe everything you hear. Did you hear the rumor that Supersonic ran away from a fight so fast she left her trousers behind?"

Volta raised an eyebrow.

"Yup — she was so scared, she speed her pants!" The wolf tried to scoff, snorted instead, and ended up sounding like she had sneezed in the end. *That's so fucking stup —*

And then she made a rather different sound, as the hero's elbow collided with her abs at a hundred and fifty miles per hour.

"HWOOF!!" Volta stumbled back. Her entire midsection was suddenly sore, she could feel it in her *back*. "Dammit, ow!"

So fast!

Electricity surged to her fingertips, and she dropped into a low stance to protect her middle from a follow-up attack.

It didn't do much. Volta saw an orange blur, heard "Over here!" and before she could turn to look, she felt a knock in the head from the other direction. She stumbled and snarled, cracking off a streak of lightning toward where the shot had come from — but of course she was almost a full *second* too late, and by then, she felt a kick in her calf.

That one hurt the least, actually, but it still might be a bruise the next day.

Wait. If that shot had been just a little higher, she'd have kicked my knee in! And that abdomen shot earlier, too...

The wolf stumbled to the side, kept her back close to the wall as she clutched the deep ache in her middle. Sure, Volta was a one-ton wrecking machine, but at the speed this Hero was hitting her, one half-decent blow to the kidney would leave her a one-ton mattress. She could hear rapid footsteps. If she just focused, surely, she could...

She found herself stumbling to the side, clutching her ear after a loud, sudden clap. Her hackles rose, and she shook herself to keep herself from hunching too much. Had Lawful Neutral seriously just clapped in her ear?

Rapid footsteps, again. It was still hard to tell the direction — she shot off another bolt, but the fox was zig-zagging, her blur now just a field of orange in front of her. "Dammit — hold *STILL!*"

Thunder clapped — this time, not from a bolt from Volta's fingertips, but an all-encompassing *CRACK*. Electricity surged out in a wide, snapping burst, and Volta panted as she rubbed away the ache in her jaw.

"Yeah, what, are you faster than *lightning*, dipshit?"

Lawful Neutral hadn't been close enough to get zapped, but she was still on the ground, groaning as she rubbed at her eyes. Volta was sure she wasn't going to get up too quickly...

...*But why take the chance?* With a smaller *crack*, Lawful Neutral was spasming on the ground. From Volta's experience, she was going to have a hard time seeing anything for a minute or two, and her hearing would be accompanied with a high-pitched ringing for a while.

Her big, meaty paw closed around the Hero's hair, and she lifted until Lawful Neutral was half-standing, half-crouching on her quaking legs.

"Hey. Got a message to pass along. There's a guy in Texas named Luke. He says you're a *real* inspiration to him." Volta grinned, and with a swing of her leg, sent the fox skidding across the pavement, clutching her middle. "He asked me to pass that along, if I ever saw ya."

"Hvvrn... hnngh," came the elegant, teeth-grit response from the floor.

"What was that?" sneered the wolf, squatting down.

"Hv-v-v rrr... 'Redline,' huh?"

"Don't you forget it, now."

"Are you gonna stay close to me?"

Volta blinked. "I'm... no, that's —"

"Red, red, liiiiiiiiiine... *Stay close to meee-heee-heee...*"

And at that moment, Volta knew that they would never, ever fuck.

"Hey, *Hero*. How are you gonna be a comedian when you can't even... *standup?*"

The Hero gave her a shaky pair of finger-guns, then collapsed completely. "Heh... good one..."

Chapter 4

A Supervillain Korpsigin Story Part 1

July 2022

The gymnasium doors flew open, an imposing figure silhouetted against them. Eight feet high and rippled in equal parts muscle and curves, as the villainous Redline stomped across the gym floor, the lights glinted off of her long, sharp teeth and her sleek leather jacket.

"This is a dumb choice of locale, even for *you*, Standup," the massive red wolf sneered, looking down her nose at the woman who'd summoned her here.

"I thought maybe it had been a while since you last got schooled, Red."

Lawful Neutral stood three feet shorter. The fox was clearly athletic, but her musculature was much less impressive, and her outfit... well, there was a reason that orange-and-black spandex with a half-tailsleeve had never exactly come into style.

Redline raised an eyebrow beneath her magenta visor. "You bring me all the way out here just for that, or do you have more shitty jokes?"

"I mean... I *do* have more jokes," LN said, clearing her throat. "Good ones!" The larger woman crossed her arms impatiently, shooting a bemused look at the floating Everyone's Hero Association camera drone hovering over the bleachers.

"Let's get it over with," grinned the wolf. "It's no fun kickin' your ass if your ass ain't even super yet."

"Yeah, yeah," chuckled the vixen, stretching out her furless arms. "I don't need a joke this time — *I* visited a genie!"

Redline glowered, eyes narrowing. "Uh-huh."

"She gave me the ability to resist lightning — and all I had to do was *rubber* a little!"

Redline buried her muzzle in her meaty mitts, shaking her head. *"Why are you like this?"*

But it was too late. The vixen's skin, and the bodysuit that clung to it, were already rapidly growing glossy and black. Lawful Neutral tried to rub her hands together excitedly, and found the friction stopped her entirely.

"Perfect," she grinned, even her pointed *teeth* were rubber.

"You forgot somethin', Standup."

"Did I?" she asked, putting up her fists.

"Sure did."

And then Redline *charged*. Half a ton of lupine muscle squeezed into just-barely-enough Korps attire pounded the ground beneath her boots, hot pink sparks flying off of her calves. She closed the distance in a second, and before LN could react, the wolf's enormous fist slammed into her stomach.

"I'm still a GODDAMN FORCE OF NATURE!"

With that, the rubber foxgirl was off her feet, flying across the gym. She had gotten used to the way she had to adjust her body mid-air after one of the wolf's attacks to avoid being horrifically injured on impact with a wall — it *happened* to her often enough, after all — but this time... well, she wasn't quite so fragile anymore, was she?

LN hit the wall, feeling the force impact her shoulder and ripple down to her feet in an instant. She came rocketing back at the hulking villain, who barely had a moment to register her surprise before she leapt aside.

"Holy *shit*, Standup," she chuckled, watching the Hero's momentum fade as she skidded across the floor, squeaking with each bounce. "I'll admit, 'Extra-Large Chew Toy' is a direction I wasn't expecting!"

Lawful Neutral pushed herself back up onto her rubber soles, sparing a quick glance over her shoulder at the gymnasium wall. "Yeah, yeah, you're a big dog, I get it," she said, shaking her head a bit to force the world to balance again. "Sorry to tell you, this chew toy bites back!"

Redline snarled, shaking her head as LN started moving toward her, picking up speed. *"Lame.* You just sayin' shit to say shit, now?"

The rubberized heroine closed, and Redline didn't even rear back. Instead, she abruptly jolted her knee upright and sent the fox flying up into the ceiling. When she bounced back down, it was with a cascade of broken glass.

"Standup, if you just wanted to *play*, you coulda *asked nicely*. Got a few friends back at base that would *love* to toss you around, after their run-ins with *you*."

"I could say the same to you," LN grinned, still airborne after her second or third bounce, trying to angle herself to land on her feet. "C'mon, I *know* you can hit harder than that."

Redline raised her brows, snorting down at her. She considered for a long, excruciating moment…

Then, she shrugged. "Nah."

"Nah?"

"Let me guess — I kick you so hard you put a dent in that wall over there, then you bounce right off and hit me just as hard."

The hero shifted awkwardly on her seat. "I mean. That… I don't see how that would work."

Eight feet of wolf nestled down into a comfortable squat as Redline rested a cheek on her fist and looked the prone Lawful Neutral over. "Heroes ain't supposed to *lie*, Standup."

"You're right — justice never sleeps!"

The foxgirl's foot jetted upward, but Redline was quick to tilt back, and all Lawful Neutral got was a combat boot in the ass for the trouble, sending her skidding across the floor. "You *are* out of good ideas," she grinned, straightening up and rolling out her shoulders. "Fine. I'll give you the *mangling* you're begging for, so I can get on with my day."

LN was already on her feet. "I've heard jail time can really put a crimp on your evening plans," she prodded.

"I've heard being an *unfunny twerp* can keep you from *having* evening plans."

The rubber vixen deflated like a slashed tire. "*Ouch.*"

"See? I can still hurt ya," grinned the villainous wolf.

And then she punted Lawful Neutral square in the solar plexus.

LN went flying, hands clutching her middle. Even with the rubber replacing much of her flesh and bone, the wind had gone right out of her and it was hard to regain it as she bounced head-first off of the far wall, chin knocking against her collarbone. Or what passed for it in rubber form, anyway.

"*Huogh,*" she mouthed as she passed Redline, who helpfully swatted at her back to *really* get her spinning and knock out what little air she'd managed to suck down. She felt something hard and oddly-shaped hit her a moment after and realized with a frown that it must have been the EHA camera drone.

Bet that's coming out of my salary.

Lawful Neutral struck the ground and bounced at a weird angle, her stomach roiling as she raised one hand to cover her mouth. She held an arm out to steady herself, but it was another three bounces off walls and floors before she skidded to a stop on her knees.

She held up one polite finger to the villain, belching into her opposite fist as Redline plodded her way over. "H — urrf... hold on."

"Curl up a bit, will ya? I bet we could get you football-shaped if you really tried," sneered the villain as she loomed over Lawful Neutral.

"Gim... *hoooo*... gimme a minute," pleaded the Hero, desperately trying to steady herself.

"Nah," said the wolf. Lawful Neutral barely had time to look up at Redline's short running start before she felt the impact of a boot driving into her stomach, and she was flying faster than she'd thought possible. It was barely an instant after she felt wall hit her back that she felt the floor against her knees.

It was too late; she couldn't put her limbs out to try to control her bounces. It was all she could do to keep her lunch down, and even that seemed like a losing battle.

"I... I'm gonna...!"

She whizzed past Redline's ear, feebly reaching an arm out to grab on, but far too late. It was another few bounces before she was anywhere near her, and by *then*... by *then* she was a whirling top spewing half-digested spaghetti and bile across the floor, across the backboard of the basketball hoop, across...

"My jacket!!" snarled Redline, shaking off vixen puke as she ran to take cover under the bleachers. "This better not stain, or I'm gonna wring your fucking neck!"

But Lawful Neutral couldn't hear her over the sound of her own body squeaking off of her surroundings. Finally, she forced herself to reach out, to slow her momentum; without Redline's 'help' she finally rolled to a stop, panting, groaning on all fours.

The sound of heavy boots on the gym floor let her know that the massive wolf was coming back. There wasn't much the Hero could do; it would be hard to deliver puns while dry-heaving, so all she could manage was to turn her head and look up, up, *up* at the statuesque lupine that was her nemesis.

"Look, usually I like to brag about our little encounters, but I think I'm just gonna let this one go. That was gross."

"*You're* gross… *huuughgh*… foul villain," wheezed LN.

"Sure. Clean yourself up good before you come after me again, Standup."

The Hero felt a boot against her side.

"N… nghhgh… nono*nono* —"

But her pleading fell on deaf ears. With a quick *shove* and a wet *splush*, the Hero known as Lawful Neutral fell into a stripe of her own vomit. She groaned and let her eyes close. She just needed a moment's rest. She heard Redline walk away and open the door, and heard the door finally close a while later.

"I'm… rubber… you're… glue," she breathed. "Whatever you say… bounces off me… and *I shoulda thought that one through*…"

"I-is she gonna b-be okay, M-Miss?"

Ellen groaned, as the familiar voice spoke to the doctor outside her door in the medical ward. Their voices quieted, and Ellen listened to the hushed sounds of their conversation from the bed.

She hadn't actually been hurt *too* badly. She was resting in a hospital bed more for protocol than anything, the rubber had harmlessly absorbed the brunt of each impact. Aside from a crick in her neck that simply would *not* go away no matter how she stretched it, and some pretty strong dehydration, she was feeling pretty good.

'Aside from dehydration,' of course, wasn't leaving room for a lot of 'asides.' She was plugged into an IV and had a glass of water that was being *very* attentively filled by one of the nurses. A fan, she'd gathered, he had insisted that she tell him whatever happened to Stampede but had been *equally* insistent that she wait until she was better hydrated. She could have told it right then, though; it was a pretty short story, after all.

The door finally opened, and Ellen's sister stepped through, crossing the distance in a flurry of little steps until she was at the bedside. Vixie was... *short*. Ellen was short at five feet, but her twin sister was six inches shorter still — though between her mass of messy red-brown hair and the pear-shaped curves of her figure — they likely shared a similar mass.

The other woman didn't speak, she just stared at Ellen with widening, wettening eyes, and the beginning of a whimper in her throat. Ellen took a deep breath and gave her a big smile.

"I'm okay, Vix. Just a bit sore and under-hydrated. Doc says I just need some rest and some water, and I'll be back in fighting shape in no time!"

She had tried to sound chipper, but the look on Vixie's face only worsened; her lip quivered, and her eyebrows bunched up and rose in the middle.

"That was a figure of speech, Vix," Ellen hurriedly assured. "I'm not going toe-to-toe with Redline until I've given my next one some thought, okay?" She shifted in her hospital bed, propping herself up on her elbows.

"Y-you're all I h-*have*," whimpered Vixie, her scared, soft brown eyes locked onto Ellen's.

Ellen froze; the only movement she made was the sinking of her heart. "Vix..."

"I kn-*know*," she said. She was... *shaking*, slightly. "A-and I know y-you're just doing your b-best for me — f-for *us* — b-but, Ellen..."

"I know, Vix."

"Sh-she's *dangerous*, Ellen!"

"I *know*."

Ellen took another deep breath and turned her head. The tree outside her window obscured most of the view this time of year, but even just the wall of leaves was a more welcome sight than Vixie's worried face. She already knew what that looked like, after all; she could see it whenever she closed her eyes.

But Heroing paid the bills. Well, it paid *most* of the bills. And now there was… an *expectation*. She wasn't just Ellen, sister to Vixie, struggling to provide for both of them; she was Lawful Neutral, Hero, at least to those who found the Bradley Group and its equals to be an unattainable ideal. LN was *relatable*, a symbol to those with lesser powers, or none at all. She had risen to some measure of regional popularity and success despite her genetic condition, with only a convoluted and unwieldy superpower to use against the forces of evil.

What would it say if she quit because it was too hard?

What would it say if, one day, she finally overcame even *Redline?*

Ellen turned her head back. Vixie had finally taken a seat, her hands laid on the arm rest beside her sister's elbow; hesitant to touch, but eager to offer. Ellen rolled her arm towards her sister, and immediately felt Vixie's fingers wrap around it.

"Hey, enough about me. How about you? How was work?"

The other demimorph's forehead lowered until it was pressing down on Ellen's arm, ears drooping. She didn't have to see Vixie's tail to know it was following the trend.

"M-Mister Kasten y-yelled at me again." Her head rolled to the side so that she could face away from Ellen. "I d-don't like the w-way he looks at m-me."

Ellen didn't know what to say to that.

Vixie's work history was… *fraught.* Not as fraught as her schooling had been — the fox had been on the verge of failing fairly consistently. Teachers had called her "unteachable," "useless," and *worse*, sometimes in front of the entire class. One had gone so far as to staple a failed test to a spatula, with a note that she'd be better off practicing burger-flipping than trying to learn algebra. It hadn't gotten particularly better when she'd moved from high school to the workforce.

"What does that old cat have against you?"

"W-well, a c-customer asked m-me if I could h-help him g-get a b-binder off a high sh-shelf… a-and I tried to c-climb it, b-but then some boxes f-fell on the customer and I f-fell on the floor…"

"Oh, jeez. Are you okay?"

Vixie tilted back again and gave a quick, reassuring nod. "M-my butt's a little sore, a-and the customer was okay, t-too."

"What did Kasten say about it?"

Vixie avoided Ellen's eyes.

"H-he said I sh-shoulda used a l-ladder. A-also a *l-lot* of other s-stuff."

Ellen reached out to the end of the arm rest and curled her fingers around the back of Vixie's hand, though she felt the pinch in her own. The IV was rather uncomfortable, but it beat the hell out of the alternative.

"If you want, I can try to get you a job somewhere else?"

Vixie's eyelids drooped until her eyes were nearly closed. From what Ellen could see of her iris, she was looking away again, but it wasn't enough to hide the glossy tears that coated her eyes.

"E-Ellen... do you ever f-feel like your b-best is only half as good as e-everyone else's worst?" Her voice wavered. "I-I try so hard t-to be *g-good...*"

Ellen drew in a deep breath, and let it out as naturally as she could, with her heart breaking.

Vixie was sweet. She had *always* been sweet. She'd never tried to hurt anyone or make others feel bad; even when they picked on her, she had never lashed out. Ellen had always done her best to protect her — verbally, mostly. *Mostly.* She supposed the exceptions had been what had started her on the path to Hero work.

Vixie wiped her eyes before the tears could fall, and Ellen reached out to scratch her behind the ear. "It's okay, Vix. Tomorrow's another day."

She looked up at Ellen, eyes still shining. The cogs of Ellen's mind whirred to desperation; *anything* to get her out of that pit.

"Hey. Hey. Do you know where these things go to college?" Ellen asked, pointing at the needle in her hand.

Vixie blinked back at her, a look of confusion on her face. "W... w-where?"

"*IV League* schools...!"

Vixie stared at her blankly for a moment, then frowned. "...I-I don't get it."

"It's okay," said Ellen with a soft smile. "I know you don't have very much updog."

Ellen held her breath.

"W-what's updog?"

CHAPTER 5

A SUPERVILLAIN KORPSIGIN STORY PART 2

July 2022

Lawful Neutral grinned wide, her pointy white teeth gleaming in the paneled lighting and flash photography as she shook the hand of one Mr. Ed Kasten. He was a cat of impressive stature — broad in the shoulders, waist, and tail, and standing at just over six feet. One of those thick-furred types, so it was hard to tell exactly what his physique might look like under all that shag, but Ellen supposed it didn't matter so long as he kept signing Vixie's paychecks.

That was why she was there, actually, dressed in her official EHA uniform that looked annoyingly similar to a spandex onesie, posed beside the big cat in front of rows and rows of hammers and light fixtures. She badly needed to make sure Kasten wasn't having any thoughts about hanging a "Help Wanted" sign over Vixie's register.

"When I need good materials at a fair price, I *always* come to Kasten's — where the service is solid as steel!" Kasten couldn't help but let out a flattered chuckle, leaning down and wrapping an arm around LN's shoulder as she spoke. "After all, not just any shop is good enough for my very own sister to work at!"

She turned her plastered-on smile to Vixie, whose eyes widened in surprise — but with a quick crook of LN's finger, she obediently hustled into the shot, offering a meek smile of her own as the cameras flashed for another round.

Try firing THAT.

The Everyone's Hero Association wanted their representatives to be every bit as heroic as their more-established cousins. But where the other registered Hero organizations were banking on obvious ability — cool-headed, good-looking folks with big, flashy powers like super speed, strength, heat vision, whatever — EHA aimed for the... *creative.* "Not everyone can be a Hero," Jack Phillips had said, "But I, for one, am willing to bet a *lot* more people can be Heroes than our competitors expect."

It was a risky enough investment, but Mr. Phillips had shown the ability to grow a brand time and time again, as CEO of various different companies over the years. With his investment, they were quickly raking in cash for security details, government contracts, advertisements, merchandising...

Why, in just seven short years, the Everyone's Hero Association had grown from a local group of burglar-busters to taking down *proper* supervillains — due in no small part to Ellen's once-unstoppable winning streak against scoundrels formerly assumed to be above her weight class. Lawful Neutral had become a household name, even if it didn't command the same respect as, say, True North, or Sunburst, or Lady Lorica. Hell, Lawful Neutral had even cameoed in a few of those licensed cartoons — which felt a little odd, hearing the nothing-like-her voiceover next to the soundalikes playing more prestigious Heroes — and she'd been added as DLC to the latest version of HeroClash after a fierce campaign by her fanbase. As a ditto fighter, sure, but still; none too shabby, she figured. She'd visited Can D's place to take a look when it had come out a couple of years back, and *that* voice actress wasn't half bad, honestly.

With all the fame, she was beginning to hope that, *maybe,* this year or the next, she'd be getting a raise. The EHA seemed to be doing fairly well, after all, if she could finally beat Redline she might manage a nice, solid 3%.

It wasn't quite the cozy life she'd envisioned. Ellen had been on track to jump straight to a major in biology after high school, but Vixie... well, Vixie had had no place to go when their parents had kicked her out, so that had had to be put on hold.

For the moment, she was doing a patrol jog, hoping that the big, bad wolf had been redeployed elsewhere, to be some other Hero outfit's problem for a while. In the meantime, it was just good to be steadily employed.

If that meant keeping her waist trim and her hair long... well, she'd worked under the same conditions *before* the EHA, so it's not like she wasn't used to it. And they always made sure she was well taken care of after a fight, which felt like a step up from when she'd been working at Hooters, anyway. To be fair, she did tend to get in more fights as a Hero than a waitress...

Ellen was snapped out of her musings by a buzz against her tail, then another. She reached back into its sleeve and pulled out her phone from between a layer of bushy fur and snug... *whatever* her suit was made out of.

From: JP
LN, incident in progress on 7th n hayward.
get there

She flipped her phone closed and got her feet moving. 7th and Hayward was... well, it depended on traffic, but if she made good time, she could be there in ten minutes. If not...

Thirty minutes later, Ellen's EHA-branded vehicle pulled over behind a squad car. Hers was the *second* company car on the scene, in fact — as she stepped out of the PT Cruiser and approached, she could see a familiar marten conversing with the police.

Can D's outfit was a form-fitting bodysuit much like her own. Ellen could never tell for sure whether the red and white was meant to evoke a candy cane or a soup can, but with the bandolier of corn chowder across his chest, she leaned more toward the latter.

"What'd I miss, bud?"

D turned, a concerned expression giving way to a smile as he spotted Lawful Neutral. "Boss! I'll let, uh, Officer Kruger explain, here..."

Kruger stepped forward; a tense-looking hawk of some sort, his beak was drawn tight in a perpetual scowl, and he kept his shooting hand on his belt. His feathered brow was deeply furrowed. Ellen got the impression of a taut string, ready to snap at a moment's notice.

...Or maybe a piano wire.

"Well, what we've got here is your basic drug bust," reported Officer Kruger. "Buncha queers living together, thinking the rules don't apply to them. Shit, they're happy to throw the rules of nature out the window, how the hell are they gonna give a damn about *actual* laws?" He clicked his beak agitatedly. "We oughta go back to enforcing the old sodomy charges."

Ellen tried to keep her expression neutral, even as her stomach turned. "So, what did you actually find...?"

"C'mere once, I'll show you." Kruger waved her over and walked her over to the trunk of one of their vehicles. Ellen could see a large silhouette in the back seat. A bulky canine, perhaps... or, more likely, an ursine of some kind.

The trunk popped; a few evidence bags sat in a storage case. A couple of jars of deep green vegetation, one small bag full of white powder, and a solid black bag beside them. A curved ridge formed from whatever was in them, running from one corner to the opposite.

"I'll give you three guesses what's in that one, and the first two don't count," said Kruger, rolling his eyes.

Ellen didn't bother to hazard any guesses, she was pretty adept at recognizing the shape of RCGs by now.

It was an open secret among the Hero community that donning a set of RCGs was as safe as sending a vampire an open invitation chiseled in stone. The visor's voice, cool and tantalizing, would grab your brain by the roots and whisper things to it. People who wore the visors were no longer themselves; they believed things that were untrue, *knew* things that weren't real. People had donned them and disappeared the next day, only to resurface months later, *changed.*

Ellen's stomach had turned before; now, it *twisted.* Her nose wrinkled in fear hastily disguised as disgust. No drug's thrall was half as terrifying as one who bore Rose-Coloured Glasses.

She'd come toe-to-toe with plenty of villains, with and without the magenta headgear, but it was always the ones *with* them that scared her the most. Their devotion was... *fanatical.* Their gear and equipment were the match of anything the federal and state Heroes had, but with none of the moral restrictions. God, she'd even seen the footage of a Hero being *murdered*, just a few months ago. On *live TV*, even.

Vixie had *begged* her to stay home the next day, had held her arm and dug her heels into the carpet, but Jack had insisted: "If we don't show up *now*, after that, we can hardly market ourselves as *Heroes*, let alone Heroes who can stand toe-to-toe with Bradley-level threats."

At the end of the day, it was more important to make sure she and Vixie had a roof over their heads and food on the coffee table than it was to give her peace of mind. She wished so, *so* desperately that she could find a way to do both, though…

"I take it that's cocaine there?" Ellen managed through a dry mouth, pointing at the little powder bag.

"I'd bet my badge on it," said the hawk with a derisive snort. He slammed the trunk closed and dusted off his hand feathers, looking down at the vulpine. "Will that be all, *Heroes?*"

Ellen crossed her arms and opened her mouth to speak, but it was Can D who replied.

"All set, Officer," he said, one hand on his leader's shoulder. "We'll head out, then, unless you need an escort."

Kruger was already walking away, waving them off. "I think we can drive a few queer potheads to the station *just* fine, thanks."

That was that. Can D and Ellen watched the sedans ride off and synchronized a sigh.

"It's like they ring us up just to make us feel superfluous," D grumbled, leaning back against his car.

"Yeah," sighed Ellen, her hip hitting the door beside him. "They were probably just spooked with the helix tech."

"You didn't see those kids." D leaned back and tilted his head up toward the darkening sky. "Looked like some nervous college kids and part-timers to me. But… well, s'pose the Korps can look like anyone, when you get right down to it."

Ellen grinned, reaching out and mockingly putting her hands on the marten's throat. "Even me!" she rasped. "Surrender to the majesty of the Overlord! Show a lot of fur and get tons of plastic surgery! *Raaaawr!!*"

D chortled and swatted Ellen's hands away. "Aw, c'mon, Boss. I told you those gas station aviators with the pink lenses were bad news!"

Chuckling herself down to another sigh, Ellen rolled her back against the car and folded her arms against her chest.

"Hey, D. You think I'm getting too old for this?"

"Heck no." He hadn't even hesitated to consider it. "If *you're* too old, where does that leave me?"

"Good point. I gotta keep a close eye on you, though. Soon as you retire, I've gotta plan my party for... what, six months later?"

"Five."

"Mm."

They sat there in front of the empty house for a while, letting the quiet pass. Their shift on duty had ended; it was a few minutes before Ellen could feel the marten's eyes on her.

"Hey, do you wanna go grab something to eat? My treat." Before she could open her mouth, he added, "Feel free to order something for Vixie, too."

Ellen pushed off of the car and straightened her hair, grinning back at him. "Well, dang, bud. You're not even leaving me anything to negotiate for!"

He grinned. "Sure there is. I haven't decided whether I'm getting you the four-piece or the eight yet."

Ellen's behind dropped into the couch, sinking in as the air escaped with a gentle *fssssh*. It had developed a few holes over the years, but it was still plenty serviceable — or at least Ellen thought so, anyway. Vixie preferred to sit on the floor, but then, she had *always* preferred to sit on the floor.

A pair of value meals and a large soda each waited for them on the coffee table. Vixie reached for the latter and sipped gingerly at it. Ellen raised an eyebrow as she seemed to stick to it; usually, her twin was happy to get a big chug of the carbonated liquid candy and get straight to the meal.

"J'eat yet?" she inquired.

Vixie shook her head and took another sip, heaving a sigh into the straw that hummed through the plastic. "No…"

A chicken nugget rested against Ellen's top lip as she considered her next question.

"Do you wanna talk about it?"

The ice in Vixie's drink swirled loudly as she fidgeted with her straw. It took her a while to finally speak.

"D… D-Devin asked me out t-today," she finally admitted.

Ellen frowned against her chicken nugget. "That buck who lights up every time he looks at you?"

"Y-yeah."

She finally just set the nugget back down on top of its siblings. She was quiet for a moment, then another.

"How'd he take the 'No'?"

Vixie fidgeted. "I-I…"

She was silent, for a moment. Then another. Ellen reached for the remote and muted the TV; whatever Vixie had to say was more important than the briefing for this round of her favorite baking show.

"You can tell him no without telling him why, Vix."

Vixie seemed to be trying her best to develop X-ray vision so that she could stare at the floor through her box of nuggies.

"I kn-know, but… w-what if… w-what if he g-guesses? I-I can't…"

She trailed off, and Ellen sighed. Things were slightly easier for her than her sister in that regard. Ellen, at least, was interested in men. But Vixie…

"Look, Kasten's going to have a hard time firing you now. If he finds out you're a lesbian, he'll —"

She paused as the implications hit her, suppressing the urge to grimace. It would be an equation of leverage, actually. He wouldn't be beholden to a hero whose reputation he could injure if she complained. Vixie would lose the job, and Ellen would have to be careful not to stop endorsing Kasten's Hardware, for fear of news getting to Mr. Phillips. He had been fine during the high-profile divorce… but when his ex-wife had made the news two months later dressed head-to-toe in black and magenta, lipstick on her neck, he had sworn a vendetta against all of "her kind."

She didn't reckon the sister of a lesbian would have a place in his organization for long; there were always plenty of low-level supers with high-level dreams out there, after all.

And as a bisexual woman herself, she had her own secrets to worry about.

She heaved a deep sigh. "We'll be okay. We're always okay. And we'll figure out what to do about Devin in the morning."

She finally took a bite of her nugget, then offered Vixie a smile. "After all, we wouldn't want you having any bright-eyed deers, would we?"

CHAPTER 6

A Supervillain Korpsigin Story Part 3

July 2022

Deep green leaves fluttered, twirling in the wind. Rubble littered the ground, and civilians ran in terror through the open holes in the bank's outer walls.

The villainous shark in charge of the heist seemed to be letting them go, mostly unscathed. She was only really interested in the sacks of cash that her compatriots were loading into the back door of a van, "Salt Life" sticker on proud display below a magenta helix.

Ideally, Lawful Neutral would have preferred to approach the situation with a bit more stealth — strike before the big fish could shrug her big hammer off her big shoulders, maybe — but she didn't get to set the scene. All she could do was let her brakes screech to a halt and come running out of the car as two more EHA vehicles came to similar stops behind her.

The shark's eyes widened as the vulpine hero arrived on the scene, the pink veins of her exosuit whirring up as she bounced on her heels. "Yo, Lawful Waffle! Ooo, you're *just* who I was hoping would show up!"

LN rolled out her shoulders. This one was always... *weird*. Most villains she fought were more like Volta — big and sneering and... well, *villainous*. But High Tide always seemed happy to see her. Like, *thrilled* to see her.

"Hi, Tide," sighed the hero.

"You brought friends?" The shark leaned as if to look over the much-shorter fox's shoulder as Can D piled out of his car and Laserdisc revved her motorbike behind her. "That's hella tight, I've got my own, so I guess that means I get you all to myself!"

Her grin was toothy enough to put Redline's to shame.

"That's too bad," sighed LN, shaking her head. "Hey, did you hear about the clay golem who was too flexible for his job?"

"Oh no! What happened?"

The vixen grinned, tail flicking behind her. "He got *fired*."

"Ah — oh, you are *wicked* funny!" chimed the shark, giggling as she hefted her hammer, which crackled with electricity. "Are you funnier when you're drunk?"

Lawful Neutral was already in motion, feeling the clagginess around her joints. She hadn't been *entirely* sure which power that would activate, but this... this would work.

"Not much of a drinker!" she declared, leaping toward High Tide even as the villain reared back for a swing.

"Well, you're about to be hammered!"

Before she could complain, LN felt the weapon slam into her side. The clay that used to be her torso splattered across the pavement, even as the heroine threw a punch at the shark's muzzle.

Without a back to put into it, though, it just slid across her skin.

"Clay powers!" cackled High Tide as the fox landed in pieces around her. "Oh, oh, because I'm Jewish! That's so *sweet*, Waffle! Must be why you're called that!"

Lawful Neutral stared up at her, incredulous.

"Why are you *like* this?"

"Oh, the girls back at base say I'm an absolutely *useless* lesbian!" she grinned, flipping LN onto her back and watching the clay travel back across the sidewalk to rejoin her.

"Useless? You're like six feet tall and carrying Mjolnir's big, clumsy brother."

"Oh, yeah, but I'm not forklift-certified, y'know?"

"I am... *very* confused," admitted LN.

"I have that effect on people!"

As the hero's separate pieces mashed themselves back together, High Tide stood back up to her full height, rolling out her shoulders. "You are *totes* cute down there. I just wanna chomp on your shoulders 'til they're all bloody!"

"I like my blood right where it is, thank you!" A quick roll, and she was back on her feet, backing up to put a bit of distance between herself and the villain.

High Tide's thick tail swung powerfully back and forth behind her; she was practically bouncing on the spot, rolling her thumb over the haft of her weapon.

"Hey, I've been curious, actually," LN pondered, taking a quick look around. Can D had just beaned a Korps lackey and was "borrowing" a nearby garbage can as a floating barrier between him and it, and Laserdisc was... down the street, actually, forcing her own opponent to keep their eyes shielded or be forced to put their pink visor's light suppression to the test.

In previous encounters, it hadn't quite been up to snuff, so whoever was behind that set of RCGs was right to keep their hand over the lenses.

Good. Both of them are keeping their targets engaged, but at a distance.

"You must be pretty strong to heft that — can you, y'know —?" She raised her elbows to either side and tucked in her arms, letting her biceps bulge.

"Oh, yeah! You like a girl with muscle, right?" asked the shark, mirroring her.

"Oh, just checking to see how strong *I'd* have to be to lift that," said LN, pointing at the hammer. "One more time, just to be sure? I just want to check your *re*-flexes!"

"My ref —? OH!! I get it, like, flexing, but twice?"

"I... yeah," said Lawful Neutral, clearing her throat. "Yeah, you got it."

"That is, like, *hella* good!!"

Lawful Neutral frowned. She hadn't exactly *laughed*, or groaned, or anything. Did compliments work?

Better to be sure.

"D! Let me borrow that top!"

"Comin' at you!" replied the marten. LN didn't even look; she'd see it in her peripherals, and if she didn't react fast enough —

SPRONG. The trash can lid collided with the side of her head; she hadn't been able to *move* like she needed to, but it was a lot better than gambling that on the hammer. She stumbled to the side.

"Thanks, D!"

"No problem, Boss!"

She didn't have a lot of time to make a new plan, though. That shark was already moving, and moving *fast*. LN leapt to the side just in time to slip free of the hammer's deadly arcs; she could feel it knock her tail aside, and it took her a second to remember the jolt that accompanied it wasn't just the usual price of getting hit.

She shook the sparks out of her fur, shivering as High Tide stumbled to a stop and planted her feet once more.

"Hey, you remind me of an actress, actually," mused the heroine. "Left Hollywood a while back to help clear the roads in the winter."

High Tide's hips rocked from one side to the other, as if she was swishing the thoughts around in her pelvis. "I don't think I've heard of her!"

"Oh, yeah, but you know what they say. There's no business like snow business!"

The shark's head went back, and she barked a laugh into the sky. It was a few seconds before she finally shook her head and hefted her hammer again.

"That was a good one! Seriously, you're *so* funny!"

"Hey, if you're a *real* big fan, you'll... surrender, maybe?"

LN tensed her calf, her toes pushing *down*, hard; she felt a tingle in her knee, running down her shin like icy water.

"*Mmmmmmmmm* nope! Sorry!"

Even as High Tide responded, the vixen kept her foot planted. *C'mon, c'mon...*

"Eh, worth a shot," she shrugged, even as the shark *charged*. If she didn't time it right...

That hammer *swung*, and LN ducked; her fingers plunged into the frost that had gathered at her feet, freezing over even as the feet on High Tide's exosuit lost any sort of traction. Between LN as a stumbling block and the icy sheen, the big shark went tumbling into the wall behind her.

"OOF!! Oh, Waffle, you've flattened me! Guess that makes me a pancake!" she laughed, propped upside down on her shoulders, tail waggling languidly above her. "Just gotta straighten up... I'm supposed to keep you occupied for a while longer, at least!"

LN's brow furrowed, and she took a quick look around. Can D had managed to stuff his first adversary snugly into that trash can, while the other lackey was carefully positioning a collapsible riot shield between themselves and Laserdisc's oncoming bike with one arm while shielding the back of their head from flying cans with the other.

And then High Tide was on her again; she hadn't even swung her hammer this time. Instead, Lawful Neutral was bowled right over with an *oof*, the shark forcing her to the ground with overwhelming strength and mass.

I got distracted!

LN gritted her teeth, squirming as the haft of High Tide's weapon pressed down on her. She got her hands under it and shoved, but the most she could do was give herself breathing room.

"Oh my God, am I winning one? You're slipping, Waffle! One too many zaps from your big puppy friend?" she giggled.

LN groaned as High Tide shoved down once more; her elbows hit the concrete, and a funny feeling trickled through both arms.

She leaned into it, straining and glaring daggers up at the shark. "Don't you know?" she growled. "A cornered fox is more dangerous than a jackal!"

She opened her mouth and *roared*. High Tide's face froze in surprise — quite literally, as LN's breath frosted into her features and her fingers froze to the icy hammer.

The shark reeled back, snorting and puffing; the heat of the day got her mouth working and her nose wiggling before long, but by then, Lawful Neutral had circled behind, arms around the shark's neck.

"Oh!! Oh, you have to cover the gills or this isn't gonna do much for me — yesss, just like that, Waffle! *Harder! FUCK yes, I don't have any bones to break, you can squeeze harder than THAT! Ooooogh... so goood...*"

It took a minute, and for as much help as High Tide was in her own subdual, she had hardly stopped squirming the whole time. Still, Lawful Neutral finally had her on the ground — still alive, but out cold.

LN groaned, looking down at her. So... *peaceful.*

She reached down and pried the pink goggles off of her; she was sure a distress beacon was probably already going off, but if she could avoid them getting tracked...

A few pumps of cold and a good, hard stomp into the pavement, and LN had successfully injured her foot. The glasses, unfortunately, were fine.

What are these things MADE of?

She turned her attention back to the street; whoever that lackey was, they were holding their own surprisingly well against the combined onslaught of the EHA's two second-strongest members; they'd even managed to redirect Laserdisc's beams into Can D's eye.

He'd be fine, but his vision would be a burnt out for a minute. He didn't have the minute to spare, though, so LN needed to move.

She only got two steps before something thick and *strong* swept her legs out from under her.

"Sorry, Waffle! It was good for a first try, though!"

LN groaned, barely pushing herself halfway to her feet before she felt the head of the hammer laying flat on her back.

"I got the signal! Time for us to go!" she called. The shield-bearing minion broke into a sprint and shoved Can D to the ground as they passed, running to the aid of their binned cohort.

LN squirmed as they moved out of sight; pushing power out of her *back* was... *easy*, actually — it was *so* close to her core, so if she just concentrated it there...

"AAAAAGGHH!!"

"Sorry, Waffle!" High Tide lowered the power of the current surging through her hammer — and Lawful Neutral, as well. "We're retreating! But we're keeping the money, so it's totes a win for the bad guys!"

LN could hear her clamber into the van. She was barely able to push herself up to her knees by the time she heard the tires squeal.

They were gone.

"Well, frick," grunted the fox, looking around her. Cash still littered the street, but they'd made off with the bulk of it.

"Sorry, Lawful," groaned Laserdisc. The pair of CDs that functioned as her eyewear receded to the sides of her face; the intense-looking groundhog had scuffed the leather on her jacket, but didn't seem much worse for wear.

D's vision returned after a few more seconds and some eye rubbing. It hadn't been a success, exactly, but Lawful Neutral couldn't shake the feeling that they had been acting strangely — even by Korps standards.

"Honey, I'm home!" announced Ellen, sucking on her teeth as she opened the door. Her tail and her back still stung from where that shark had poured some voltage into them, and her arms and shoulders and chest all had bruises from that last shove.

She closed the door behind her and kicked off her shoes beside it, casting a slow gaze around the apartment. A microwaveable pastry was sitting, half-finished, on the counter; Ellen moved across to take a few bites before she started whipping up dinner, but she frowned as her fingers closed around it.

It was… lukewarm. Straight-up room temperature. It must have been sitting for… an hour, maybe. At least.

That was unlike her.

"Vixie? You in the bathroom? Taking a nap?"

Ellen moved through the silent house; the bathroom door was left open, and a quick peep inside left her just as sister-less as before. The bed was just as empty… although, upon inspection, proved not *quite* so.

On the pillow was a glossy jet-black card, folded neatly to prop itself up and prominently display that magenta helix on the front. Ellen's breath caught in her chest, was made heavy, and dropped into the pit of her stomach.

"No."

CHAPTER 7

A Supervillain Korpsigin Story Part 4

July 2022

Ellen stared at the handwritten note, still in utter disbelief.

> **Hey Standup,**
> **Hope you had a good play date with High Tide.**
> **I'm taking your sister back to the base for a little playdate**
> **of my own. If you want to see her again, come by the Taco**
> **Bell on 3rd, at 8 PM — but I can't promise she'll be the**
> **same.**
> **But hey, don't worry. We're not gonna do anything to her**
> **that she doesn't beg me for.**

Her breath had caught in her chest the instant she'd laid eyes on the helix-marked card, but it grew heavier with each line.

Vixie.

She'd never hurt *anyone.*

The world grew blurry and the light from the bedside lamp smeared across her vision.

She'd heard stories — *everyone* had heard the stories. People had quit their jobs, or been led into dark alleys, or just *disappeared.* Some of those who were ever seen again didn't even seem to *recognize* their families.

Her teeth ached; she was clenching her jaw so tightly it hurt.

What if she saw Vixie and she couldn't even catch her eye?

Help.

What if she never even saw her again?

Her brain felt *hot.* She crumpled the card and threw it, tried to massage the pain out of her jaw.

Think, she begged her brain.

Instead, she saw his face, heard him scream through his teeth as his body seized, as steam and blood and *anguish* trickled and rolled from his body. Saw *her* face, her fangs just as bare as his, hate and fury and cruelty plain in her eyes... and the utter lack of remorse.

And now, *she* had Vixie.

Help.

What if...

What if getting brainwashed wasn't the worst thing that could happen to her?

Fast. I've got to...

Ellen snatched the balled-up cardstock from the floor and stretched it out. 8 PM. That was... *hours* from now. She was getting lightheaded; she had to sit down. She had to *move.* She had to *think.* She had to...

She had to save her.

Ellen forced herself to take a deep breath and realized then that she had been hyperventilating.

Breathe. Move.

Vixie struggled against the rope that bound her, desperation clear in her eyes.

Move.

Vixie sat comfortably in a chair, a blank expression in her eyes.

Move!

Vixie's burnt-out corpse lay on the counter of the Taco Bell, life gone from her eyes.

No.

The Korps hadn't abducted her just to kill her. If they were going to go that far, why abduct her at all?

Easy, easy. Steady, steady.

There were a few hours between now and then.

I need help.

"Sir. They have Vixie." Ellen's voice was as low as she could get it, but it still felt too high, too quavery. She needed to be authoritative here; leave no room for argument.

The slow, deliberate rise of Mr. Phillips's eyebrow told her that she'd failed.

"They?" asked the canine, his fingers steepled below his muzzle.

"The Korps!" Ellen couldn't stop herself from shouting her response in exasperation, and the contrast between Phillips's eyebrows only widened.

"Don't raise your voice at *me*, young lady," he warned as he turned in his swivel chair and let his brow straighten once more. He pulled open a drawer in his desk and stooped over for a moment, then retrieved a notepad. That wasn't unusual — Phillips always liked to track his thoughts in hastily-written diagrams. "Now, slowly. The Korps 'has' Vixie. Does that mean Vixie followed a pretty blinking light into one of their vans, or did someone promise her candy?"

Ellen could feel the sides of her jaw bulge out as she clenched it and hoped that Phillips wasn't looking too closely at her — but of course, no, he was plotting out his chart.

Lightning poured out of her and into him; even through the screen, one could smell his burning fur...

"Redline left this on her pillow," she said, trying to sound professional through gritted teeth.

Phillips reached for the note without looking up, and only really regarded it once he'd carefully evened out the creases and laid it out atop his notebook.

"You said Redline gave this to you. I don't see a signature — just a lipstick print." The old dog's eyes rolled up to make eye contact with Ellen, still in her civvies. "You chummy enough with Korps agents to recognize their kiss marks, Lawful Neutral?"

The screaming kept going until there was nothing left of his throat to scream with, and then the only sound was her, and the pink lightning that kept surging into his spasming corpse.

"She called me 'Standup,' sir. I believe it's meant to be a demeaning nickname. Sir, with all due res —"

"You want me to, what, throw the whole organization away on a raid on Korps HQ to save one person?" he asked. Ellen had expected irritation, but when she looked, she saw... *bemusement.*

"I was hoping we might work with one of the larger organizations...? Bradley, maybe, or —"

"I see," said the old English Foxhound. He traced lines and boxes onto his diagram and considered it for a moment. "So, you're hoping we go full-scale *war* to save one fox who couldn't even be relied on to run simple errands when she interned here?"

Ellen felt her lips tighten; she knew she was baring her teeth, knew there was venom in her eyes. "I don't think —"

"No, you don't," said Phillips, curtly, as he tossed his notebook to the far side of his desk. "She's always been a millstone around your neck, Lawful. You want my advice? Let her be dead weight in the Korps. She'll do more damage from within than we could ever do from without — whether she means to or not."

Ellen bristled. "*Excuse* me?" She could feel the fur on her tail standing on end, feel her heart pounding, her fingers digging into the desk as she realized she was bearing down on him. He did not so much as flinch. "What if they *brainwash* her?"

The old canine gave a derisive huff, and his jowls flapped. "Then they've wasted resources — just like we did when *we* tried to train her."

"You *saw* what she did to *him* — I thought we were supposed to be *Heroes!*" barked Ellen. There was a knock at the door. "That was hardly four months ago!"

"A moment, Laserdisc," Phillips stated in a raised voice, then lowered it to address the fox. "You need to stand down, Lawful."

"She is *my sister,* sir! *Please!*" Ellen did not share her superior's volume control.

Jack Phillips took a deep breath and let it out in a long, irritated sigh. "Tell you what. If she's that important to you, I can go ahead and give you bereavement time for her. I'll see you back here on Thursday, and then we'll talk about keeping those emotions under control."

It was everything she could do not to scream. "So, I'm just supposed to *leave her for dead?*"

"Look. Go to their little... *rendezvous* if you need to. Just don't do anything stupid," he said, clicking his pen. "That's what separates you from her."

Ellen was shaking, her eyes darting across the canine's form.

"That's not the only thing that separates us, sir," she snarled. "Vixie would *never* hurt anyone."

Phillips was already looking past her, clearing his throat to call Laserdisc in, when she spoke; his brow furrowed at the statement. "I don't doubt that. She was too cowardly to fight back. You're better off forgetting her," he said, pointing the tip of his pen at her urgingly without even bothering to shift his gaze from the office door. "Let the Korps keep the freaks, and the crazies... and I guess the *retards* now, too."

And then Ellen exploded across the table.

Her fingers wrapped around his throat even as he choked out demands. The canine balled a fist and slammed it into Ellen's middle, but he didn't have the leverage. He tilted backwards in desperation, and his chair toppled; both went down with a series of thuds. Ellen lost her grip, and Phillips found his. Ellen could only wheeze as the dog snarled, lowered his bared teeth toward her face...

She did the only sensible thing she could and slammed her forehead into his teeth.

With a yelp, Phillips recoiled, rubbing at his mouth with a paw; it came back bloody, but Ellen wasn't giving him time to recover. She was already pinning him to his file cabinet, one hand on his throat, the other slamming into his muzzle. She could feel the skin over her knuckles tearing with each punch, could feel the bones beneath fracturing, but more importantly, she saw canine teeth fly, saw blood staining fur and suit and sheet metal.

He whimpered, trying his best to cover his bloody face as Ellen screamed in fury, screamed in anguish, screamed at the injustice of it all, screamed and screamed and screamed as she pummeled the bear three years her senior, her classmates gathered around them...

"*TAKE IT BACK!*"

The door flew open as Phillips gurgled something that sounded like a strangled *"LASERDISC!"* Ellen spun on the spot and released him, letting the old dog lie where he fell.

Laserdisc engaged her eyewear with a quick flick of her head, and Ellen could see that she was taking stock of the situation through the holes in the CDs.

"It's exactly what it looks like," admitted Ellen, and before Laserdisc could register what she'd just said, the fox was bounding across the desk at her. A red dot was only just appearing in each of the centers when Ellen nabbed the glasses off her face, shouldering her to the ground and sprinting through the office.

It wasn't a particularly *large* office; she was out in twenty seconds and turned to chuck Laserdisc's eyewear — the Disc Master — as far as she could away from LD's bike.

Should have thrown that into the road, thought Ellen, fumbling for her keys and desperately jamming them into the door of her own aging car. *Frick, frick, frick. Did I kill him? I think I killed him.*

Open, sit, rev, close. She didn't bother buckling her seatbelt, just *drove,* her tires squealing as the door to the office finally opened and Laserdisc, holding a CD she must have pulled out of one of the office PCs, burst out.

It was too late; Ellen was up onto the street before she could get a bead on her, and out of sight in just as little time.

She spared the beginning of a thought for Jack Phillips. She'd left him in a pool of his own blood, but... well, she refused to feel guilty. She did dread the long-term ramifications, though.

Vixie. I need to get to Vixie. We'll figure it out together, later.

She drove quickly but aimlessly, mind racing with possibilities and should-haves. Pain radiated through her fist, but she needed to keep both on the wheel, needed to be as fast and as alert as possible.

In the distance, sirens.

Ellen didn't know what she expected to see when she arrived at the Taco Bell, but had more-than-half expected some sort of showdown to

be set up — a cackling villain on the roof, holding an hogtied Vixie over the pavement below, perhaps, or Redline smashing her car the instant she stepped out of it and challenging her to a brawl right then and there for her sister's fate.

What she came to instead was a fairly quiet purveyor of cheap Mexican-inspired snacks. She left her car idling in the parking lot. The police weren't far behind, and it didn't take her sharp sense of hearing to make out the sound of sirens closing. *Of course they'd have read the note.*

I didn't have a choice, though. Where else was I gonna go?

She threw herself into the doors; even with all her weight behind them, they opened slowly, *too* slowly. She was already scanning the building as she forced her way through, trying to find —

Well, it wasn't too hard to find a Korps agent who wasn't trying to be subtle, actually. Nestled in a corner toward the back behind a pair of Chalupa Supremes and sipping a Baja Blast Freeze was a six-and-a-half-foot feline in jeans, a behelixed camisole, a magenta jacket, and a look of dull surprise.

After all, it wasn't every day that someone burst into a Taco Bell, covered in blood with cops closing in on them. That was really more of a Waffle House thing.

Ellen locked eyes with the woman and closed the distance with a series of swift, furious steps as blue and red flashes began to fill the windows.

"Where the *fuck* is my sister?"

CHAPTER 8

A SUPERVILLAIN KORPSIGIN STORY PART 5

July 2022

"I haven't even dragged you in yet," said the feline, eyes roaming over the short, blood-spattered foxgirl even as she squeezed out from between the booth and the table. It was clearly a tight squeeze, given her size and... *curves*, but she was just as clearly agile enough to do it cleanly and quickly. The grays and creams of her striped coat carried the reds and blues of the fast-approaching lights outside.

"*Where is she*," demanded Ellen. As the feline went to grab the still-wrapped chalupa from the table, Ellen went for her wrist — and was surprised to find herself too slow.

"In better shape than we are right now," came the reply, as the Korps agent power-walked toward the door. As she moved, she unwrapped half the chalupa, and Ellen had little choice but to jog after her. "Mind if we take this somewhere else?"

Ellen only had a moment to think, but she took the full moment and froze in place as she did. It wasn't long before she was hustling after the big tabby again.

"Where?"

"I have a secondary location in mind, but you'll need to get in my car."

Ellen didn't have time to process or respond to that before the cat's power walk got almost cartoonishly fast; the taller woman opened the door to a mid-10's sedan and dropped her behind into the seat. The car bounced a little under the weight, and Ellen could make out the sound of the engine revving with an undertone that Ellen had learned to recognize from Korps vehicles.

The car pulled out of the parking space and Ellen raced around the front, yanked open the door and hopped in. Somehow, in the smaller space, she felt even *smaller* beside the tabby. She clicked her seat belt by instinct, then raised an eyebrow.

"Is it rude for me to do that?"

The tabby looked back quizzically. "Do what?"

"Buckle my seat belt."

She tapped her own fastened seat belt and raised a brow. "We're criminals, not *dipshits*. We don't just run around doing crime for the sake of doing crime."

Ellen turned her head — both to avoid letting the Korps agent see the chastised look on her bloody face, and to take stock of the situation.

She definitely hadn't managed to shake the police; a pair of squad cars pulled sideways to block off the exit lane, and more were on the way.

"Carmen, by the way," said the cat as the wheels lurched the car up to speed and she tore out of the entrance.

"Ellen."

"I know."

Ellen swiveled to see the squad cars get moving again, although navigating two vehicles through a Taco Bell parking lot was proving to take a bit of work. Ellen considered them successfully lost —

But the ones ahead that were already turning to match the sedan's direction, probably not so much. Carmen and Ellen bounced in their seats, barreling ahead at at least *sixty* coming off the ramp onto the highway.

"A high-speed chase? Carmen, these never go well," Ellen advised.

Carmen turned her head for just a moment; her eyes were different. Rather than the usual feline amber tones, her eyes were black, with a deep purple hue overtaking her irises. "It's not that high-speed for *me*, actually," she shrugged, then returned her eyes to the road.

"...I'll just try to be quiet, then."

"Quick warning — if you puke in my car, you're doing the rest of the ride in the trunk."

"Noted."

Ellen leaned back as far as she could, to let Carmen keep as much visibility as possible, and whispered a prayer to no one in particular that she wasn't being led into a trap.

Or that, if she was, it was going to be less unpleasant than being shot to death in a Taco Bell.

"So, this is a Maserati," announced Ellen, as the pair drove in relative quiet.

"Yes," said Carmen with a wide, toothy grin.

"I know the Korps has resources, but it feels like they wouldn't buy an import for someone they expected to trash it," she said, eyes keenly assessing the tabby. "And yet — not a scratch, and no sirens in sight."

"That sounds awfully close to a compliment, *Hero*." That grin did not diminish in the slightest.

"It's almost a question, actually," corrected Ellen. "Korps agents typically specialize, from what I can tell. If you're a driver, you're *probably not* a negotiator. But with a power like that, you'd be a hassle in any combat."

"You were wrong at least once just now, but I'm not going to tell you how," she chided with a playful lilt.

Ellen was quiet for a moment. "I suppose the question I'm trying to figure out the answer to is, 'What were you expecting?'"

"I'll admit that it wasn't 'blood.' The cops weren't a surprise, though. We just thought they might be on *your* side." Carmen flicked the blinker on and shifted gears as she began to turn.

Ellen could feel her eyebrows tighten as she saw the sign bearing a familiar red bell against a blue background.

"…Really?"

"Ellen. Serious question time." She laid a hand on the hero's shoulder, gazed deep into her eyes. Ellen didn't regularly interact with folks who were so much larger than her outside of superpowered fights. The weight of her hand felt heavier than the demimorph expected, but still not as heavy as the depth of Carmen's gaze. She could feel the cat's eyes poring deep inside of her; she wondered if Carmen *knew* things about her she'd never spoken before, if the hard light of her eyes set in that stony expression could discern truths deep inside before a word was spoken.

"Have you ever experienced the joy that is a Baja Blast Freeze?"

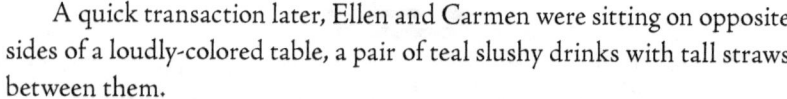

A quick transaction later, Ellen and Carmen were sitting on opposite sides of a loudly-colored table, a pair of teal slushy drinks with tall straws between them.

The silence was... *awkward*, from Ellen's end, but Carmen seemed content to wait, chasing the more liquid contents of her drink around with the straw between breaks to mash the ice.

Still, Ellen couldn't pretend she trusted the cat... but she got the sense that she wasn't hiding a horrible secret from her. Worse, Carmen seemed... *capable*. A time-based pun wouldn't be hard to pull off, but if it came down to a fight, she'd have to be sneaky about springing it on her in the first place, or she'd have her jaw punched off before she could finish it.

Ellen looked up into those playful eyes, searching for answers. Carmen betrayed nothing but her own bemusement.

Ellen was getting very tired of people being bemused at her situation, but more irritatingly than that, she could not place the tabby: calm, cool, dangerous. But she didn't seem to be here for a fight, and she was content to let Ellen set the speed — or to let her feel like she was in control. Ellen, regardless, could tell she was not.

She had to know.

"Carmen... what *are* you?"

Carmen looked as if she had been waiting all night for this question. She leaned in, elbows on a table that looked decidedly small beneath her. Ellen did, too; she'd long since stopped being intimidated by folks larger than herself.

Most folks.

Just about everybody but Carmen, it turned out.

"I'm a problem solver, Ellen," she purred, "and tonight, I'm solving *yours*."

Ellen gave her a cutting look. "I seem to remember having started my day with my sister safe and sound." She began to rise from her seat. "If you think she's dead weight to me —"

Carmen's glare came back twice as harsh as Ellen's. "I know you've had to defend her a lot in the past, but we would *never* —"

"I *swear*, if that *monster* hurt her —"

"— she would **never** —"

"— there will not be *time enough in the w* —"

"ELLEN!"

Carmen was standing at her full height, her face... not intimidating, exactly. *Stern.* But as Ellen looked up at her face, she could see concern in her eyes.

"Ellen. *Listen.* She's safe. We didn't take her because we thought it would hurt you, or because we thought Vixie would be a perfect little worker drone, or — or *anything* like that. Ellen, we took her to *save* her."

Ellen bristled, but she paused. *Save* her?

"What does the *Korps* know about saving people?"

"More than you'd think," said the tabby. "The Korps saved *me*."

That stopped her for longer. Her eyes roamed over Carmen's face, as if searching for a tell, something to indicate she was lying, or brainwashed, or... *something.*

"Okay." She slowly let herself back down into the booth, and the cat dropped right back to her lean-in. "What... what's *your* idea of saving her?"

Carmen's head tilted; her amber eyes brimmed with sympathy. "Ellen, I'm gonna be honest with you, and I want you to understand I am not trying to demean you or your sister here, but... this world was not *made* with people like Vixie in mind. Surely, you've seen this, you *have* to know it on some level."

Ellen did. It was hardly *news*, but...

But to hear it from someone else's mouth... it filled her with *something.* It felt... *she* felt... *understood.*

The big cat leaned forward and slid her open paws across the table. Ellen was surprised to find herself reaching for them, and soon her own hands were warmed by fur and pad.

"The society we're all born into punishes her for even trying," Carmen continued, "no matter how hard she tries. Every system in place, every institution, is built with the assumption that you will meet specific standards that aren't as fair or kind as they *need* to be. Vixie needs a home, and in all honesty, the Korps is the only place she'll find one, until we change things the world over."

Cogs spun in Ellen's head; that was… *true*. Well, she wasn't sure if the Korps part was true, but…

"Still… you can't just… *take* people," Ellen managed. It was the only argument she had left.

"We *asked* her."

Ellen still looked skeptical; Carmen withdrew one of her paws and retrieved a phone from her belt, then slipped it into one of the hands she was still supporting. Ellen stared.

Framed by the Hello Kitty phone case was an image that Ellen was having trouble processing. Redline's torso dominated the photo; a black, curved smudge ran along the edge, which she had to assume was the pad of her thumb. She looked… content. Sneering, a little, but much less than she was when Lawful Neutral ran into her and looking fondly down at a familiar shape curled up on her bare chest.

Vixie.

Snuggled up into a ruddy-orange breast, drooling on the arc of her cleavage, was her sister.

She wasn't *unused* to seeing Vixie nude — although she did appreciate that Redline had angled the camera to preserve her modesty — but what surprised her was the look of utter contentment on her face. Her sister looked *peaceful*. Ellen had gotten so used to her perpetually-worried frown that she had half-forgotten what a happy Vixie looked like.

A line of text on a black border ran across the bottom of the image:

Fox got tired after her first time lmao she's warm

Ellen looked up at Carmen, still hesitant, but clearly processing.

"How much do you know?" she asked, slowly.

Carmen offered a smile.

"Enough to know that you need help, too."

Ellen's eyebrows went up. "You think I need to fuck Redline?"

Carmen's smile turned into a chipper grin, at that. "Only if you want to!"

Ellen pursed her lips, then found her straw to put between them. She stared off at the back of a giant poster announcing that tacos were a dollar each on Sundays and considered it for a little longer than she probably needed to.

"I see."

It was Carmen's turn to be confused. "What do you see?"

"You're hoping that a fox in the hand is worth two in her bush."

Chapter 9

A Supervillain Korpsigin Story Part 6

July 2022

Ellen looked somberly out the Taco Bell window, watching Carmen lean against the trunk of her Maserati-that-didn't-look-like-a-Maserati. She could see the cat occasionally emoting, but it was limited. It didn't take long for her to realize that the movements and facial expressions were for *her* sake; Carmen could have just as easily sat in the booth across from herself and had whatever conversation she was having.

Not that Ellen had a lot of knowledge of *how*, exactly, those RCGs worked. All she had was Carmen's brief description… and invitation.

She looked down at the magenta visor between her thumbs, gently turning it this way and that. It actually blended in, a bit, with the stripe on the table beneath it.

"I can't take you back to base until you try these on," Carmen had said. "Not unless you'd rather be gagged and hogtied." Ellen had raised an eyebrow at that, but Carmen grinned around her words. "As much as we would all enjoy that, we'd rather you do the former. You can take them off once ROSE says you're clear to enter."

Ellen had met that with a frown. "That's going to be tricky, actually. My whole family has impenetrable craniums."

"That… can't *possibly* be true."

"Oh, but it is! We foxes are, in fact, *very* thick-skulked."

That had gotten a frown, then finally a roll of the eyes and a low, almost sarcastic "*haaaa,*" Ellen's grin hadn't faded until the door had closed behind Carmen, and she was left alone with the magenta eyewear.

She was *tired.*

Not from fighting High Tide, or Jack, or being chased by the police. No, her tired was all the way down in her spirit. For so long, she had been protecting her sister, supporting her, doing her best to keep her in good spirits while Ellen helped her navigate the difficulties of life, tried to steer her away from things that would only end in pain, tried to save her from the world that would destroy her.

She was the only one who had believed in Vixie from the very beginning, when they were born minutes apart. Now, she had found someone that would help them...

But it was the *Korps*.

Carmen was saying all the words that Ellen would want to hear. If it were true, joining her would be a no-brainer. But if it were a trick...

She thumbed at the lenses, brow furrowed. If it were a trick, she would put on these glasses and say goodbye to her free will. If it were a trick, it was already too late for Vixie — Redline would have already slapped a pair onto her by now.

But what option did she have? She'd assaulted her employer — maybe even *killed* him — and fled from the police and into a Korps vehicle. If she didn't at least hear out the Korps, she'd be in a jail cell by the end of the night. Or *worse*. Supers were rarely given the same walls and bars as the general population. It varied by state and the threat posed by the inmate's powers, but for her, it'd probably be a gag, or solitary confinement... if not *also* 24/7 drugging with Antipotentiol, or Suparneutacin, or some other power-blocker. Maybe even all three.

Even as she thought of all the reasons why not, she opened the temples of the Rose-Coloured Glasses. She'd seen a few pairs in her time; these were a different style than she'd ever encountered. Usually, they had a little less supporting structure on the bottom, but... well, she hardly had a muzzle to support them. If she had to guess, this was the model for simians.

Unless I'm just that special that I get my own.

The arms stood tall on either side, the lenses balanced on the table. Ellen groaned. Her fingers were trembling around the visor.

Deep breaths, Ellen.

She'd made up her mind. She shifted in her seat and closed her eyes.

If this is my last free thought, whispered the voice between her ears, *fuck* the Korps.

And then she let her face drop onto the table, right onto the glasses.

Carmen groaned and held the steering wheel with one hand and a few rough, brown napkins to Ellen's cheek with the other. Blood trickled down deep cuts on the Hero's face which she was, stubbornly, doing a mediocre job of covering with further napkins.

"I'm fine," mumbled the foxgirl, laying back in the seat.

"Your face is a mess," snapped Carmen, "and even casual-wear RCGs like those are built pretty sturdy. I need to take you to a medic... annnd you're a fugitive now, so a civilian hospital won't work."

"Is that, like... 'ficial?"

"It's 'ficial," sighed Carmen. "Phillips says you attacked him unprovoked, and since you fled the scene and evaded the police... well, hey, don't worry about it. Just lay back, okay?"

"Mm," mumbled Ellen, clearly still a little dizzy from blood loss.

Carmen sighed. "Why did you smash 'em?"

"He was a dick to my sister."

"The glasses, not your boss."

Ellen was quiet for a second, then gave a sheepish, bloody grin. "Forgot my head was made of iron."

"You're shitting me. How do you forget that? Wouldn't that be super heavy?"

"I always get the, uh. Necessarily secondarily superduperpowers."

"Of course you do. But not the one that makes your face hard, too?"

"I can make *your* face hard... ahaha..."

Carmen shot her a quick look and shook her head. As she turned her focus back to driving, she heard Ellen mutter something that sounded suspiciously like *"the drama!"* before giggling to herself and settling into quiet. Carmen let her — and occasionally reached over to jostle her and make sure she was still semi-conscious until they got to the base.

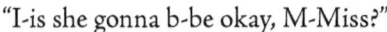

"I-is she gonna b-be okay, M-Miss?"

Ellen groaned as the familiar voice spoke to the doctor outside her door in the medical ward. Their voices quieted, and Ellen listened to the hushed sounds of their conversation from the bed.

Her bleary gaze slid around the room; medical white, with lots of magenta accents and tech that looked more expensive than her usual hospital. She brought a hand up to her head and felt gauze beneath her fingertips. She didn't have a full head-wrapping, but there were definitely more bandages than exposed flesh on her face.

The door slid open with a *schhhnk*, and the rapid patter of bare feet on tile would have told Ellen exactly what was coming her way even if she hadn't opened her eyes yet.

"Hey, Vix," groaned Ellen through a smile.

And there she was. Ellen felt Vixie's soft arms around her, holding her tight, her bushy hair falling over both their shoulders. Ellen reached out to return the favor and felt a slight tug at her finger; a heart monitor, or *whatever* it was they clamped over it.

"I'm okay," she told her quivering sister — and realized that she, too, was quivering. "And *you're* okay."

The Hero blinked, then held her sister by the shoulders at arm's length, looking her over. "You *are* okay, right?" At Vixie's nod, she pulled her close once more.

They stayed like that for a while in the quiet, just letting relief wash over them. When Ellen opened her eyes, they were focused again — and she was able to make out the shapes in the doorway. Carmen was unmistakable, standing tall and buxom in her Korps-printed jacket.

Even more distinct, however, was Redline's hulking figure, those black and magenta eyes intent on Ellen. She clearly didn't care if she were caught staring. Maybe she *wanted* to be.

Ellen felt her tail bristle and she straightened up; instinctually, she pushed Vixie to the side and rose in her bed. Redline's hand rose with her, padded fingers splaying in a gesture of nonaggression.

"Careful, Standup — I'm gonna need you to be Sitdown for a bit or you'll make your sister cry." Ellen reluctantly sank back into the bed, a keen eye on the big red wolf. "I'm not here to fight. Have your moment, and then we'll talk."

Ellen's stomach was still sour, and she could already feel the fur on her tail standing up, but she knew it was better not to escalate it. She huffed and let herself lean back into the bedding. It was... soft, but only as much as it could be while still being supportive.

It did a great job of being both, actually. She'd have to find a bra like that.

Now that she had a moment, she eyed Vixie. She looked... *good*. Vixie hadn't smiled this freely in months. She had a bit of a new look, as well. Her usual yellow crop top was replaced with a similar one with a distinctly lower neckline, and a helix embroidered over the heart. Her denim shorts were gone, a sunflower-colored skirt in its place. The black lipstick was new, too.

Especially since it was all over her neck and shoulder. Ellen didn't need much time to figure out where that had come from; she'd seen the picture, after all.

"So, what now?" she asked Vixie.

"W-well... they said... th-they said they'd t-take care of us, if w-we need it. D... d-did you really punch M-Mister Phillips?"

Ellen snorted and rolled her lips into her mouth for a thin grimace. "I may have. A few times... A lot." She paused, then sighed. "I thought I killed him."

Vixie looked torn between laughter and concern. "D... d-did he deserve it?"

Ellen reached up and cupped Vixie's cheek. "He was a cruel man, Vixie. *Is* a cruel man. I should never have worked for him in the first place." She could just make out a snort from Carmen and Redline sighing in exaggerated relief from the hallway. Vixie couldn't help but giggle a little at their responses. "Suppose I should have done that ages ago," the erstwhile Hero sighed. She was quiet for a bit. Then:

"Looks like you've settled in. The locals treating you right? 'Cuz if they're not, let me know. I'll fight the biggest gal in the yard if she treats you wrong."

"I-I know!" chimed Vixie.

She was blushing slightly, actually.

"*Please* tell me Redline's not the biggest gal in the yard."

"W-well… n-not quite."

"But she's your favorite, isn't she?"

Ellen saw her sister's eyes pop for a moment before she pushed her hands into her hair and smooshed it in front of her reddening cheeks.

"Thought so," she sighed. "Did you have a nice time?"

Vixie nodded quickly.

"She didn't hurt you, did she?"

Vixie did not, in fact, nod.

Ellen sighed. "But you're okay with that?"

This nod came before Ellen finished the question.

"Good." She took a deep breath and closed her eyes for a minute, relaxing into the bed. "If she did anything —"

"We're villains, Standup, not *monsters*." Redline glanced up in thought. "Well, okay, some monsters, but… the fun kind."

"Are you sure?"

The big wolf's face fell; her geniality was replaced swiftly with an irritation. "This *again*, Standup?"

For a moment, Ellen had felt… *peaceful*. Like all the plates she was supposed to keep spinning had found their way safely to the table, like the weight of the world was off her shoulders, with only one thing left nibbling at the back of her mind.

And now it had clamped right onto the frontal lobe.

She glared, pushed herself to her feet. Vixie gasped and gave a word of caution, but Ellen's deep brown eyes had locked onto the towering lupine's strong pinks.

"You *killed a man* on live TV, Redline."

"And I'd do it again if he came back," snorted the wolf.

Ellen growled; she barely noticed Carmen moving in beside the two of them. "You can see how that doesn't fill me with *warm feelings*? You *destroyed* him, and then barely three months later you *kidnapped my sister*."

"I didn't *kidnap* her, I offered —"

"Sure, you *offered*. But I *know* what you're capable of."

"Only with men not worth sparing, *Ellen Foxpaw*. I never killed you, never killed any of your friends. That wasn't me just not going far enough, I *held myself back* because you were decent people, at least trying *some* of the time to help."

Ellen felt that bristle run through her tail again, but the compliment — was it a compliment? It wasn't *not* a compliment — slowed her down.

"What made him so *different*, then?"

Redline's eyes slid over to the shorter vixen standing nervously in the corner before they rejoined Ellen's stare.

"He hated people like us," she stated.

"The Korps?"

"No. Well, yes, but…" She shook her head, slowly. "No. Like me and Vixie."

Recognition was slow to dawn on her, but the first ray of sunlight still crested immediately over the horizon of her understanding.

"*Oh*." She turned her head away from the enormous wolf in front of her to her sister.

"I-I… Ellen, I… I want t-to stay. I w-want *us* to stay. I… sh-she… th-they…" She looked frustrated, for a moment, as the words swirled in her mouth. "Th-they're good to me, h-here. L-like *you* are."

Ellen's breath caught in her chest. She thought back on teachers, on managers and store clerks and classmates and parents. The world was not *patient* or *kind*. The world had not given her a *chance*. So few people had ever looked at Vixie with anything more than annoyance, and the ones that had shown her kindness had all since moved on to other phases of their lives.

But here was… an entire *group*. An organization that saw Vixie as a *person*.

She swallowed, hard.

"All right." She lowered herself back down onto the bed, glancing between faces: Vixie, looking nervous but… happy? Moreso than Ellen had seen in a long time. Carmen, looking… well, it was hard to tell. *Smug* seemed… too constant to be her emotional state. She'd argue that the tabby had Resting Smug Face, but if so, she also had Resting Smug Voice, Resting Smug Body…

And Redline.

She was still *huge*. Still as imposing as one would expect of an eight-foot-tall red wolf made of curves, muscles and hot-pink lightning. But something in her expression had softened. For the first time, she looked like...

Well, like a *person*.

She was looking down at her knees, then glancing up at Vixie and offering a little smile as she fiddled with the tear in the knee of her maroon jeans.

"So... I think... if Vixie wants to stay here, then I do too," she finally said.

Carmen's smile was immediate and almost sickly-sweet. "Glad to hear it! We'll get the brainwashing started right away. What size thong are you? Easier to ask this question before your brain has been turned into horny mush." Her eyes dipped down to Ellen's toes and back up again, as if to emphasize her point.

"...You're screwing with me."

"Well," giggled the cat, "let's not get ahead of ourselves! But... no. The brain-wiping is for people that *ask* for it. Still, even if we're not putting your brain in the blender and setting it to Maximum Scrundle, we *do* have a few things to go over. I mean, it's obvious that your heart is in the right place, but..."

"But I need to be re-educated," offered Ellen.

"Well, yes! But you make that sound like such a bad thing! It's not something *forced*, it's more... lots of Heroes aren't very conscious of how the system they uphold actually works." She stepped closer to Ellen's bed and pulled over a stool to sit on. "Why not start with cops? I'm *sure* you've heard they're all bastards by now, but I think you might want to hear a bit more as to *how*."

"Oh boy," Redline chimed in with a humorless grin. "We're gonna talk about my *favorite* cousin!"

Ellen sat upright in her bed, still pondering what she'd learned. Carmen had offloaded more information than she had, admittedly, been prepared for, and done so well into the artificial 'evening' of the medbay, when the soft ambient lighting went dim to better encourage a natural sleep cycle. Her place in the world, the system she had fought as a Hero to uphold, the alleged true nature of the Korps. It was a lot to think about.

Vixie had, of course, fallen asleep already, curled up on a nearby magenta couch beside an unused IV stand, drooling onto the cushion and getting black lipstick smears on it whenever she adjusted her position. Carmen had gone to gather some refreshments, dismissing Redline's suggestion of asking ROSE to send a drone with snacks.

Which left the Amazonian red wolf alone with Ellen.

An uneasy peace had grown between them; it was *awkward* to share a quiet moment with someone who had thrown you into enough walls to build a labyrinth, but...

"What... what did you mean?" asked the vixen as Redline dropped her generous behind into the seat that Carmen had been keeping warm for the past hour or two.

"You're gonna need to be more specific, there, Standup."

That was weird. Her voice was... *different.* Usually, every line she gave her was riddled with condescension, but *now*, the mocking tones were entirely missing. Her voice was... *soft*, somehow, but still just as strong.

"When you said that about you and Vixie, you made it sound like you were... the same, in some way. I'm not saying I doubt it, but..."

She paused. What exactly *was* she saying?

"I guess I just... don't know enough about *you* to know what you meant. Outside the suit, I mean."

The big wolf grinned. "You wanna get under my suit?"

"No! No, that's not what I mean. Just, y'know... as a person, not just a villain."

"Mm." She leaned forward, a mass of fur and curves as she looked over the (former?) Heroine. When Ellen looked down, she saw a big, furry mitt extended toward her.

"Let's start with names, then. I'm Volta."

"...Seems like you already know who I am," the fox pointed out.

"But... Ellen. Just to make it official."

"All I know is what you've just told me," Volta said. "Well — that and what Vixie clued me in on. But... yeah. I've only known Vixie for half a day, but I already know we have a lot in common. We're a couple of autistic queers who have been so oppressed by the world that we hesitated to take any action without someone leading us by the hand... like I was, until the Korps separated me from those self-obsessed scumbags, and helped me stand on my own feet."

The wolf was quiet for a moment, then shrugged. "I'm glad she had you, though. Before Carmen, I..."

She drifted off.

Volta withdrew her grip and shifted on her seat, clearing her throat. "So, uh. Vixie told me you've been taking care of her since you both were little. It's, uh. Y'know. That must have been tough, sometimes."

Ellen shook her head. "It was nothing."

"Cut the shit, Standup." Ellen nearly choked on her own spit at the abruptness. "You don't have to try to be so noble about everything here. The most important thing in the Korps is being honest with yourself — and others."

"I was like ninety percent sure the most important thing in the Korps was having huge breasts."

"Well, you've already got that part covered on your own, so I figured I'd fast-track you right along to Step Two," snorted Volta.

"Ah, so you've noticed these," said Ellen, peering down at herself. "My boobies. My massive fucking tiddies. My —"

"Are you capable of shutting the hell up?"

"Oh, not in the slightest."

"*Look.* One: shut up. Two: I'm trying to compliment you, so please just let it happen." Despite her red wolf heritage, Volta wore the unamused expression of a Siberian Husky.

"Fine, fine." Encouraged, slightly, Volta leaned forward, looming over Ellen in her hospital bed, and put a hand on her shoulder (and the surrounding area, given their size difference).

"It sounds like you've had to be the strong one all your life. I know how hard that can be. And you must be willing to do just about *anything* to keep you two housed and fed, or you'd have quit the first time I put you in the hospital."

Ellen made a face. "That shoulder still hurts a bit, actually."

"I bet." Then, after a quick realization, she withdrew her hand: "Shit — sorry."

Ellen sighed and turned her head, letting her gaze fall upon her sleeping sister.

"Of course I have to be strong. The world isn't kind to people it doesn't know how to use... and it doesn't have the patience to figure it out." She closed her eyes for a moment, let a deep breath move through her. "I always figured that if I could just give her enough room to breathe, everything would be fine."

Volta looked like she wanted to say something, and then immediately thought better of it.

"I wanted to blame you guys for taking her, but... honestly, I think we were running out of options. I don't want to bore you with —"

"Nah, I'll listen."

Ellen blinked, turned her head back to the wolf. "You will?"

"Mmhm. What have you got to lose?"

She had a point.

"Vixie had a date lined up — didn't want it, but didn't know how to say no."

"Yeah, we heard about that," huffed Volta. "What were you gonna do about it?"

"I'd been trying to figure out how to get her out of it. Best I could think of was to step in and take her place. Y'know, 'Why settle for her when you could date a real live superhero?' But that felt... condescending."

Volta nodded.

"I'd have done it, though, if I had to."

"I don't doubt it, Standup. S'what I thought; you'd do just about anything for her."

"I would. She's the only family I have."

There was quiet for a minute, and Ellen turned her head back to Volta. "So, the Korps will take care of us?" she asked.

"If you want us to. But you need to understand something, Ellen." Volta leaned in; her frame was always imposing, but something about her stance made it clear she was about to threaten her.

"The Korps is *my* family." Volta's canine nose touched Ellen's flat one, and she could smell the cinnamon and the ozone on the big lupine's breath. "If you're not serious — if you're only saying 'yes' until you can secure a way to go running back to the assholes out there? You won't have to worry about being there for Vixie anymore. You won't be there for *anybody* anymore."

Ellen stared back into those magenta irises, felt the crackling storm that lay buried just beneath them. "Don't worry," she said, summoning all of her courage to keep her voice steady. "I'm not going *anywhere*."

Volta straightened back up, exhaling. "That's the smartest thing I've heard you say."

"Well, I can't just spout doofy shit *all* the time."

Volta sneered. "Just when you're fighting me then, I guess."

"Cutting the bullshit for a moment, uh." Ellen wasn't sure how to word this. "I guess it's... *comforting* to know that taking care of each other is a priority around here."

"It's *the* priority. Look around you, Standup. You're in a lavish medical suite — the kind topside folks think only rich asshats have 'earned.' You won't be paying a cent for this."

The corners of Ellen's mouth twitched upwards. "It's not what I expected, honestly."

"*You're* not what I expected," snorted Volta. "You were working for the biggest lesbophobe in the hero biz, and both you *and* your sister are sapphic." The lupine woman paused for a moment, then cleared her throat. "I can, uh, attest to the latter."

"So, I saw from the picture," Ellen said, not meeting her eyes. "I mean, I'm not a *lesbian*, I like *both*, but..."

"Oh, there's a *lot* more than 'both.'"

The fox was quiet as she considered.

"I guess I'll see how I feel about the rest as they come up," she shrugged.

The door slid open, and Carmen sauntered back in. Ellen had never seen someone sway their hips like that while carrying a hospital tray, but then, she had yet to see Carmen move without bouncing, swinging, or rocking her body in one way or another.

"Did I miss the big kiss?" chimed the big feline.

Ellen made a face and let her tongue hang over her frown, prompting a grin from Volta. "Don't pretend you aren't curious, *Hero*."

"Or I could just kiss an electric fence and keep my dignity," offered Ellen.

Volta pretended, badly, to look hurt for a moment as Carmen set the snacks on the nearby tray table. "My girlfriend doesn't mind my kisses," pouted the wolf.

Ellen's eyes widened, and she glanced at her lipstick smeared sister. Her voice nearly caught in her throat. "Wait — *girlfriend?* That's — how long have you and Vixie...?"

"Whoa, no, no!" Volta waved her hands, shaking her head. "*Carmen!*"

"Oh!" Ellen gasped, and felt relief pour all over her body. "Because I thought... I mean, that just seemed *really fast* —"

"Yeah —"

"— But I... hoo. Okay. So, you two?"

"Yep!" It didn't take a keen eye to see that Volta was proud — not in that sneering, domineering, I'm-better-than-you way, but in a way that was wholly, totally warm.

Ellen grinned. "Wait. *She* has a girlfriend? I thought she'd be too... *thorny.*"

"Just because I'm rough with Heroes doesn't mean I'm rough with *everyone*," snorted the hulking lupine.

"Oh, definitely not," Carmen chimed. "My big girl's trained better than that. We got the biting out of her system a *while* ago."

Volta's blush was bright enough to shine through her already-warm-toned fur, and she let out a whine as she shrunk back on her stool. "Carmeeeen, *please*," she whined. She pushed her head low, but her tail swung back and forth behind the stool she was perched on. "Not in front of *this* dork."

"Okay, fair," purred the tabby, draping her hands over Volta's shoulders and flattening her hair with a kiss. "You *do* still bite some."

Volta buried her muzzle in her hands. "That's *not what I meant.*"

"I know!"

Ellen, meanwhile, sat enraptured.

"Oh, my god. Wait a minute."

"*What*, Standup?" barked Volta, keen to round off on someone more targetable.

Ellen was not deterred.

"So, if you two are a couple... then was this whole thing a *date* for you?"

Before Volta could pull her head back in a moment's thought and finish a quizzical "maybe?", Carmen — eyes shining like spotlights — interjected a "yes!"

Ellen and Carmen's giddy laughter didn't drown out Volta's flustered sputtering, and the giggling didn't stop until they all heard a small voice go "Mmmn...?"

Ellen turned to look and saw Vixie pushing herself up into a sitting position on the couch, legs stretching as she yawned.

"Good morning, Vix," said Ellen, pushing herself a little more upright in her bed. Vixie gave a sleepy smile and a few blinks, then shook her head to cast off the drowsiness, not unlike a dog shaking off after getting caught in the rain.

"G-good morning, Ellen — M-Miss Carmen, M-Miss Redline." She offered a deep nod to both of the Korps members, who returned a smile and a wave.

"We'll talk more about how to get you two settled in around here later," said Carmen, taking Volta's hand as the big wolf rose. "For now, feel free to rest."

They turned to go — Carmen in a wide arc, Volta in a quick rotation that exuded power — but were stopped by that same small voice once more.

"U-uhm, excuse me, M-Miss?"

Carmen turned back and offered a warm smile. "Yes, Vixie?"

The shorter foxgirl crossed the room to the empty IV stand, grabbed it, and rolled it over to the pair of big Korps women.

"D-do you know where th-this thing w-went to college?"

Chapter 10

Settling

August 2022

Ellen's face itched. She had been assured that it would continue to itch until it was better, but that didn't make her want to claw the bandages off her face any *less*. She'd been offered medicine to help soothe the feeling, but so long as she could deal with it on her own, she *would*. She wasn't about to trust any pills the Korps handed her that weren't strictly necessary — and even the ones that *were* strictly necessary were suspect enough.

Still, her faculties *seemed* to be her own, as far as she could tell. Moreover, she'd been told by the Korps's synthetic medical staff that today was the day she was getting released.

"Released" was a funny word for it, Ellen mused. She would not be going back home. No, topside was entirely off limits for her, unless she wanted the recent complications of her life to twist in on themselves further. Setting foot aboveground with a face like hers, bandages or not, would elicit *responses*. Police responses. *Heroic* responses. The Korps promised to keep her safe from all that... in exchange for nothing, apparently. For *free*.

Or, perhaps, for *freedom*.

"You didn't *have* much freedom living topside, did you?" tutted Carmen, towering over her as she offered a helpful hand.

Ellen grunted as she let herself be pulled from her hospital bed. "I could go wherever I wanted," she griped.

"Could you, though?" Carmen asked. "Like, *really*? Because having the possibility isn't the same as having the *option*. You could go to the movies, but you couldn't *afford* the movies. You could sign up for tennis classes, but you couldn't *afford* tennis classes. You couldn't even afford to stay *full*." That last sentence came with a meaningful glance down at Ellen's thin middle.

"And, what, now I can have a rich, full life in an underground bunker?" Ellen asked, raising a brow. "I appreciate that you're going to be 'taking care' of us, but that doesn't mean…"

The door slid open stereotypically, and Ellen forgot to keep moving her mouth.

"The shock, the horror, gosh, how ever will you manage," tutted Carmen. She put an arm around Ellen's shoulder, soft fur tickling at the back of the fox's neck, and corralled her forward, past the enormous window into the Great Lakes West base. Ellen did her best to slow down and, if possible, press her face right up to the glass.

It was *incredible*. Mossy outcroppings had been chiseled into ramps and steps that formed the courtyard of a shared medical pavilion. Trees — *actual trees* — stood tall, soaking up the simulated sun and passing shade in turn to the easygoing passersby and swift-stepping medical personnel alike. As far as Ellen could see, lush greens and earthy tans dominated the landscape — the *landscape*, not the *corridors* or *narrow concrete walls*.

With a sinking pit in her stomach, she turned. Carmen had obliged her attempts to slow down, finally, at the very end of the window. When Ellen finally peeled herself away to meet her eyes, she saw nothing but pride.

"*How* big did you say this place was, again?" Ellen whispered, awed.

"I *didn't*," said Carmen, who continued to not.

"*Mm*. Mmmmmmmmmm… mm."

The statuesque tabby laughed that laugh she did, like a purr tumbling down the staircase of her amusement. Her claws trickled down Ellen's back until she got halfway down, then gave a gentle *push* to keep her moving.

"Come on, now. It's a bit of a walk to your temporary quarters, and if you stop to gasp at every tree along the way, we won't get there until tomorrow."

"I swear, every time a door opens down here, a copyright lawyer's hackles twitch," Ellen said as Carmen led her under a leafy awning and into her new home.

"Just one small part of our dastardly plot to take over the world," Carmen sighed blissfully.

The cat stepped aside, and Ellen took in the sight of her new apartment.

It was actually a little underwhelming.

"Looks a lot like my old place, just... rotated," Ellen said, rubbing her chin.

Carmen nodded. "It's built that way on purpose. New citizens from topside get a pad like this for a few weeks, get to see what the rest of the base is like, and then get to decide what furnishings they'd like. So, if you don't like to cook, for example, you don't need an oven and a stove and pots and pans, you can just swing by the food court or one of the restaurants on-base whenever you're hungry."

"Which is... free?" Ellen asked. It was still baffling, but she already knew the answer was

"Yep!" Carmen's prodigious chest pushed high and proud. "Gramma C's is my *personal* favorite, if you don't mind a trip to Texas, but for GLW, you can do *really well* with Fox Trot Pizza or Carol's Haus."

"I thought you were going to suggest Taco Bell," Ellen chuckled with a sigh of relief.

"Well, I mean, there's a couple of those on-base as well —"

"A *couple?*"

"Well, you can't have just *one,*" said the cat. "Then how could one be the *good* Taco Bell?"

For what felt like the umpteenth time since she'd met her, Ellen tried to open her mouth to say *anything* and found a whole lot of *nothing* where she needed *something.* Carmen hardly seemed to mind; her eyes narrowed in smug satisfaction, and Ellen let the point be hers with a sigh.

"You're an interesting cat, Carmen Rayne." Ellen's fingers brushed the countertops — she supposed there had been no shortage of smooth, solid stone to work with when the base had been dug. She opened an empty drawer, then checked another. "I keep asking myself the same question I did in your car."

Something in the tabby's eyes glimmered, and Ellen couldn't help but feel as if she had just, somehow, grown even *more* pleased with herself.

"You never quite *did* ask the actual question, hero. Not the one you *really* meant."

She licked her lips expectantly, and Ellen, not for the first time, felt rather like a beef-stuffed pumpkin in a tiger's enclosure. Instincts screamed at her to find a different topic, and fast, but she had never been a particularly good listener.

"What would you have done if I hadn't come for Vixie?"

Carmen looked almost disappointed. "She would have been fine, I assure you."

"To *me*."

And there it was again: the tabby's features sharpened up once more. The disappointment hadn't been real; it had been a *hurdle* to distract her from this line of questioning. This conversation was a social game, and Ellen had finally asked just the right question.

"What do *you* think would have happened?"

Ellen rolled her lips between her teeth. Carmen's question may as well have been a confession.

"Hypothetically... I leave Vixie to the wolves. In that scenario, I clearly never cared much for her. I suspect the Korps doesn't actually have a lot of information on her, as a civilian, so the plan was made with a broad range of possibilities in mind. *You* were sent as a liaison to meet with me, but you're not just well-spoken — you're good at figuring out what people want, what they need, and what they're afraid of. Your powers allow you to slow time, sort of, but that alone wouldn't be enough to make a high-speed police chase a smart course of action. You've got a strong knowledge of the way a car moves and what it *isn't* capable of, and, moreover, you were sent alone to deal with an upset Hero who regularly makes *Redline* have to get creative."

"You may be giving yourself a *touch* too much credit," Carmen tittered.

"Am I, though?"

The tabby's grin widened. "Not at all, actually, but it's good to know you meant it. So, continue."

"You enjoy yourself a nice meal, but I don't show up. In the meantime, Volta's gathering information from Vixie: what kind of person I am in private, how I treat my defenseless sister when no one's looking, what I say about the queer and the poor and the... mentally, uh..."

"Neurodivergent?" Carmen offered.

"Yes, exactly. You were ready for me to be an angel *or* a devil, and to deal with me appropriately."

"*Mmmm.* So, if you had to arrive at your point any time soon, you'd say...?"

"You're an assassin, aren't you?"

Carmen's eyebrows rose. "Well, *that's* an escalation from 'smooth operator,' isn't it?"

"But a correct one, isn't it?" Ellen persisted. "*Although...* maybe 'spy' would be more accurate."

"Are you backpedaling now, hero?"

"Hardly. The way I see it, you're an expert at maneuvering into where you need to be and doing what the Korps asks of you when you get there. You're... *devoted*," she said, carefully avoiding the word that came more readily to mind, "not just to your girlfriend, but to the Korps. To its ethos, to its members. Am I on the right track?"

The cat nodded, grinning wide enough to show a great many pointy little teeth.

"And so, if Vixie had turned out to be my dark little secret... I don't know if you'd have killed me, but you'd have sent a message. You'd have made me terrified to ever so much as consider going after her. I'm not sure how, exactly, but I'd sleep uneasily for a while afterward."

"It's not a bad guess." Carmen leaned over the counter; Ellen swallowed as strong shoulders and dangerous eyes tilted closer. In her attempt to avoid staring straight down the cat's generous cleavage, she instead locked her gaze on the counter — and Carmen's sharp, sharp claws resting upon them. "But not quite right."

"See, if you were an abusive shitbag and still the only family Vixie had ever known, I'd never deprive her of you. No, I'd have beaten you unconscious and carried you back to base, where you'd be wearing RCGs 24/7 until you learned to care for your sister the way you should have before. In a roundabout way, it would have saved you a lot of time!"

Carmen laughed a laugh Ellen couldn't quite determine the authenticity of as an uncomfortably queasy feeling staked a claim in her insides. She only noticed that her new friend's apparent mirth had evaporated entirely when she resumed speaking.

"But Volta would probably hate you. And I mean *really* hate. There's a reason it'd be me coming to get you and not her. I may be an assassin, Ellen, but that means I understand restraint, and I understand how much internal bleeding the body can take before you're *really* in danger."

"So, you wouldn't have killed me, you'd have beat the snot out of me and hypnotized me into being... uh, the me that I *am*."

"More or less," smirked Carmen. "I don't mean to scare you, but —"

"*Scare* me?" Ellen asked, dumbfounded. "I'm on *your* side. If I mistreated Vixie, I'd deserve much worse."

Carmen snorted, straightening back up to her statuesque height. "Glad we agree! Thankfully, Vixie had nothing but adoration for you, and when you showed up, the first thing you did was threaten me if anything had happened to her." Her voice grew warm and fond and low, *sincere*. "You're a good big sister, you know that?"

Ellen grinned sheepishly. "I'm the younger one, actually."

"I mean, *teeeechnically* you were *conceived* at the same time, right?"

"Oh, yeah, you try telling *her* that!" She blew out a breath that blubbered between her lips and shook her head. "Anyway, so that was the kitchen. Living room looks straightforward enough," she said with a nod toward the couch and wall-mounted flatscreen television. "So, bed and bath?"

"Yup! Just this way, *please!*" Carmen said, gesturing toward the hallway entrance just past the kitchenette's bar counter. Ellen moved to check it out, then froze in her tracks.

"...One quick request?"

"Yeeeessss?"

Ellen shifted nervously on her feet.

"Can you be the one to walk in front?"

Carmen's eyes narrowed in smug self-satisfaction once again. "Of course! Just try not to stare, *hero*."

She led Ellen through the doorway, spared the bathroom little more than a few quick phrases and a gesture, and pivoted to the last remaining room.

"Amenities are a little basic: bed, obviously, a set of RCGs, three toys in the drawer. The lamp switch is on the base, and —"

"Toys?"

Carmen nodded. "We had to make some estimates based on your size, so they might not be as big as you're used to, but there's a rabbit, an egg, and a plug in there for you. If you've got any special orders, you can place them with ROSE."

"A pleasure to meet you!" came a cheery voice from the pad beneath the goggles on the nightstand. Something inside of Ellen cringed; she'd never particularly liked the idea of Siri or Alexa, but the Korps's Rose-Coloured Glasses were a whole 'nother short marathon out of her comfort zone than even that.

"Is the robot mandatory?" she grimaced.

"The robot?" The tabby stepped carefully around the bed and dropped onto it, plucking up the visor as she fell. "ROSE here is a friend!"

Ellen was… *hesitant*, to say the least. "That's the Korps AI I've heard so much about?"

"The very same!" chimed Carmen.

Whatever else she was about to say in the robot's defense fizzled as something heavy hit the front door. Carmen's ears and tail both perked immediately, her entire demeanor getting a few lumens brighter, as she rose from the blankets and left Ellen and a particularly-shaped ruffle in her covers behind.

"That'll be Volta," the tabby explained, and Ellen nodded as she hustled to make way. "Can she come in?"

"I — uh, yeah."

Without any further ado, the door slid open to reveal Ellen's nemesis: eight feet tall, every bit as autumnal in her color scheme as either of the Foxpaws themselves and carrying a cardboard box they both probably could have fit in if they squeezed in just right.

Ellen forced the absurd image of her and her twin peeking over the edge of a soggy box labeled "FREE FOXES" out of her mind, if for no other reason than that she couldn't help but add a mysterious visored stranger being the one to pluck them up and carry them to refuge.

"Got your shit, Standup," huffed the wolf, shouldering past the doorway and into a kitchen that, like most of the indoor spaces they had ever shared, seemed entirely too small to contain her.

"Oh — thank you," Ellen said, climbing up onto a barstool to look into the box as Volta hefted it onto the table. Inside there were a variety of personal effects from their apartment. "I'm surprised you picked up the plushie." The sentence hung for a moment as Ellen debated with herself how to explain her expectations, before finally settling on another, more sheepish "...thank you."

The wolf brushed off her gratitude with a snort. "S'not yours, anyway, is it?" she asked. "Actually, I'm gonna need your help here. Maybe I'm wrong, but most of the stuff on the list seemed like it was hers."

"No, that's right." Ellen nodded, shifting her knees onto the table, and carefully extracted an armful of choice personal items — a few articles of clothing, her (locked) poetry journal, a few old photos — and left the rest. "Everything else is either both of ours, or mostly hers, so..."

"...So do you wanna figure it out with her?"

Ellen shrugged. "I dunno. It's weird to not be living together," she admitted. She stared down into the box. It held a few old DVDs, memory cards, some of Vixie's clothes, and — taking up more space than anything else — a small army of plushies, each with names and stories and histories that Ellen and Vixie had given them together.

Her heart warmed as she looked over their felt and fluff children. Each of them carried more memories than anything else the big red wolf had brought — a series of suburban apartments and jobs that barely paid the bills, or just barely didn't. Friends' couches and stressful nights figuring out what they could live without. How to bounce between overdrafts or move money between credit cards and personal loans. Giggly evenings when Can D had brought over a twelve pack and some brats and stayed until the hour rolled back into the single digits.

The quiet weekend mornings, too, when there was nothing to do but fry some breakfast and wait for the smell to rouse her sister, to be awake to see her bright eyes and bushy tail round the corner and lick her lips at the aroma of meat grease and fried carbs.

"...You need a minute, Ellen?"

The voice came from far away, and the fox realized that it was she who had grown distant in her memories, not Carmen.

"I'm good!" she said, a little too hastily. "Yeah — the rest can go to Vixie's."

Volta shot a rare, eye-level look at her. "You sure?"

"Yeah. Besides, if I miss any of it, I can just go to visit. I don't think I'll mind the excuse to see her," she said, smiling sadly. "It's... going to be weird, being separated."

Volta made a surprisingly small little huffing noise.

"You don't... *have* to be, if you don't want to, y'know. I never had siblings, but I'd have killed way sooner if it meant having someone like you in my corner."

The lump in Ellen's throat hardened, but in a way, this part came easy to her. She would be fine.

"Vixie needs room to grow, right? Or — or *flourish?* I don't want to get in the way of that, Red. If she wants to... to start *dating*, or..."

"*That* you don't have to worry about," Carmen hastily interjected. "She's not interested in romance."

Ellen's ears wilted. "So just sex, then."

The tabby's ears followed suit as she grinned sympathetically. "She's *very* interested in sex, yes. She's not quite setting a base record, but..."

She trailed off as the distress built on Ellen's face.

"...but you don't need to hear about that! She mentioned not keeping any secrets from you, so I thought..."

"No, no, I oughta get used to hearing it," sighed the foxgirl, "and it's good to know I should probably knock before I waltz into her quarters, or it'll be a lot more than that."

Volta made a funny noise in her throat, and Carmen shot her a warning look. Ellen tried not to do the math, but she'd been on the fast track to a good college before life had happened, and Volta's raised eyebrows and avoidant gaze made for, at best, middle school algebra.

"So, your next steps!" the tabby chimed, and Ellen welcomed the change of topic. "You can obviously stay here as long as you want — probably should, given the, uh, *manhunt* — and we're not going to put you to work or anything, but... I mean, if you *want* something to do, we've got plenty. There's always errands that need doing and something that needs cleaning, if you want to help out, or if you'd rather just *relax*, well..."

"I can have all the reefer den hypno-slave orgies I want?"

Carmen grinned. "If that's what you're into!" she practically purred. "*Buuuuuuut* on the off chance that you're just being *sarcastic and dismissive* while I'm trying to be *helpful*, then I should also let you know that we have multiple sports and exercise facilities around each base, *plenty* of digitized learning courses and lessons and literature, and training for just about any hobby or craft you've ever heard of! So, if you've ever wanted to try... just about *anything*, you're in the right place!"

Ellen let that percolate a moment, thumb worrying over the weathered edge of her journal. It was an interesting concept. She wasn't so blind as to wonder what the catch was — obviously, for this underground society to work, plenty of people either chose to work or were, somehow, coerced into it. Supplemented no doubt by the wide array of surface thefts for which the Korps only sometimes took credit. Whether that was sustainable at a grand scale, or whether new expectations would be pushed upon her and her sister at some later date once they'd had their fill of luxury, was an open question. Clearly it already *did* work on a grander scale than anyone topside had imagined the Korps to be.

This isn't even their home base. This **can't** *be their biggest base.*

She swallowed those questions and asked another.

"What did *you* try first?"

A slow grin split Carmen's lips. "My grandma is a *master* of languages. She'd already taught me a few, but I was hungry for *more*. With the Korps's help, I was speaking conversational Hungarian in a couple of —"

"Hungary for more," Ellen interrupted.

"I'm sorry?"

"Like. You said you were 'hungry for more,' and then you learned Hungarian, and, y'know..."

"I'm starting to wonder if I hit you too hard or something," Volta snorted. She pushed herself up, lifting the box along with her. It may as well have weighed nothing, Ellen thought, despite containing the sum total of her sister's personal belongings. "I'm gonna head this on over to Vixie's. Don't, uh." She cleared her throat and glanced at Ellen, then hastily found a spot somewhere on the wall to stare at. "Don't wait up for me."

Ellen's ears lowered as Volta, whistling cheerily, ducked through her doorframe and made her merry way down the hall.

That was gonna take some getting used to.

Chapter 11

Stony Faces

September 2022

"So, Luke, huh?" Ellen passed a wrapped taco from the party box to the big, electric wolf in the seat beside her. "That's the old friend you mentioned way back when we first met?"

"Yeah. One of those big-eyed lemurs. *No* idea what he's doing these days," Volta admitted, peeling the paper off and cramming the crunchy snack into her mouth, "but he was your biggest fan."

"S-second-biggest!" insisted Vixie.

"*Second*-biggest," Volta admitted with a chuckle. "He wrote, like, *dozens* of e-mails to try to get you into that fighting game a few years back."

Ellen grinned. "So, I have him to thank for that? Vixie finally settled on a main 'cuz of him."

"Yeah, and she's a *menace* with you. If you were actually capable of what *she* can do with your skillset, I'd have had to try harder when I was kickin' your ass."

"Rude!"

"Still, if you want to send him something..."

"Oh, absolutely. Send me the name and address, I've got some old merch. It sells for nothing on eBay since I defected."

"Good. I think he'll like that." She thought for a moment, then smiled. "Maybe I'll squeeze in something, too. Speaking of fans and bigness," Ellen added, sipping thoughtfully at a soda that was not nearly as energizing as she'd hoped it would be, "is it just me, or are even the villains bigger in Texas? I swear, the average height in RIV is like six inches taller than GLW, and y'all are a *statuesque* people to begin with."

Volta's forehead and muzzle tensed into a labyrinth of deep wrinkles. "Did you just *y'all?*"

"I'm trying it out! When in RIV, do as the... RIV-ans?"

"You don't hear *me* sayin' *'cripes'* and *'bubbler'* when I'm up in *your* neck of the woods," Volta fussed, pulling her fingers out of Vixie's frizzy hair to jut one at the former Hero.

"Well, you could *try it, real quick once,* ya know?"

A sharp *crack* connected the wolf's claw with the fox's breast, and she toppled, yelping, from her seat. Vixie's visored face rose from its perch on Volta's thigh to watch as her sister rocked on the floor, kneading the sharp tingle from her breast and howling like a cartoon.

"See, I was real worried that when you joined up, I'd stop having good reason to hurt you," drawled the lupine, finger cracking and popping with static as if she were *just* holding it back from bridging the gap to Ellen's other nipple. "But here we are."

"See?" Ellen grunted through grit teeth, rolling over and carefully pushing herself back up to her feet. "I'm already *contributing* around here!"

The pale fur that formed Volta's eyebrow pushed up into an inquisitive arch. "Standup, you *know* I called you my 'chew toy' to mess with you, right? If you're *actually* interested, I gotta reconsider how I talk to you."

"I-I wouldn't mind," said Vixie, her voice small and quiet as it so often was. Ellen tried not to think about the implications. She only partially succeeded.

"S'probably for the best," sighed Volta dramatically as Ellen grumbled her way back onto her seat. "Bed's damn near full already between us, Wren, and Carmen."

"Uhm... I-I could always lay across th-the bottom, M-Miss!"

Volta ruffled her hair, snorting. "Hate to waste all the effort gettin' her temp quarters set up anyway, Fangirl. You stayin' for supper? We were all going to trundle on over to Gramma C's."

"If Carmen swears it's even better than *her* cooking, I *have* to try it."

"A-and you'll finally m-meet Mix Wr-Wren!!" Vixie chimed.

"He must be something special, if he's got *you* eager for me to meet him. Should I be worried he's setting a bat example?"

Ellen was already moving, dancing out of her chair as a spark of pink shot past her and popped against the countertop against the sound of

Vixie's giggles. She stopped cold, and another spark sailed right past her as flesh sprung into kites between her fingers and back, and her ears grew decidedly more *curved*, inside and out.

"Oh, these olnes are *always* kiiilnd of weirld," she slurred. Her tongue, usually so easy with its flat top and strong bottom, had rapidly shifted into something rounder, narrower, *longer* in her mouth. It felt *foreign*, and she found herself having to bite back the urge to chew.

Volta stared, finger still gunned in her direction. "Put that thing back in your mouth, Standup; I can't zap you if I think you might bite it off."

Ellen immediately jutted all two feet of tongue out as far as it could go, leaning over and wiggling its rounded tip in the lupine's face. "Thoulnds like a winning thrategy to meeeeee!"

And then she tasted hand. Volta's fingers curled around the length of her elongated licker, pink and black eyes narrowing as she tugged. Ellen, remarkably short on alternatives, leaned in.

"And you were doin' so well, too." She clicked her teeth, eyes darting down to Vixie's eager face, and shook her head. "As much as I'd love to give *Fangirl* here a show, ROSE is askin' me to pass on a message. You wanna meet Mistress Celia?"

Ellen blinked. "Oo'th that?"

"Mistress Celia?"

"No, ROTHE."

Ellen whimpered as the pair of them made their way through the verdant halls of RIV, the taste of blood and electrical burns a distant second on her list of concerns.

Volta had *insisted* on coming along.

It wasn't that she minded the big red wolf's company. On the contrary; when Volta or Carmen were around, Ellen felt decidedly less lost and alone in either of the super-secret supervillain superbases she'd visited thus far. But something about the way Volta's expression had tensed, or her body language, had told Ellen that *something* about "Mistress" Celia either scared the wolf, or scared the wolf *for Ellen.* Neither exactly instilled easy confidence in the former hero.

"Hey, Red," Ellen said, carefully managing her diction despite her singed tongue. "Do you know what kind of shoes doctors prefer?"

Volta's brow furrowed. "Sneakers, I guess? Why d —"

"Healies!"

Ellen felt the wolf's utter disappointment like a kindling in her soul, and a giddiness washed over her in tandem with a soothing wave of power. Her tongue shortened and flattened, wings and fur and damage receding all together at once.

"Thanks, Red, you're always a *wonderful* audience!"

She expected exasperation on Volta's face but froze when she saw instead a grim smile.

"So, you got healing powers now?"

That smile grew into a wicked grin, fangs bared and *swimming* in pink lightning.

Ellen's ears twitched. She still remembered *last* time she'd had this powerset around her former nemesis. Somehow, she suspected their newfound friendship would not be enough to prevent a repeat performance.

"I'll just be quiet the rest of the way there, then?"

"Your call, Standup. I win either way."

Ellen sighed, defeated. "You *always* win."

"Yeah," grinned Volta. *"And you keep comin' back."*

"Well, I can't just let you *get away with it!"*

"You literally defected. I'm fucking your sister, and you wear helix-print undies now. Face it, Standup — I won."

Ellen came to a stop beside an impressive display of lovely pink pavonia blooms. Volta had a point, but admitting it felt like... like...

Like all that struggling was for nothing and went nowhere.

Like she was turning her back on herself, like she had failed Vixie for *years.* Like she hadn't been strong enough to do it herself.

"Is that why you're coming with?" she finally asked. "You want to show off your conquest to Mistress?"

Curiously, Volta's expression crumpled into what Ellen recognized as embarrassment. All of her swagger crumpled with it.

"I thought you might appreciate havin' a friendly face around."

Oh.

Ellen didn't know what to make of that. If she didn't know better, she'd have almost described Volta's face as *pouting.*

But Redline did not *pout,* and even over the months since she had first joined, Ellen sometimes had difficulty viewing her as Volta and not Soft Redline. It was in moments like this — when she reminded Ellen more of her sweet, socially awkward sister than the sneering, jocular supervillain — that she felt a squirming in her middle that was just as hard to pin down.

She felt far too small to protect Volta from *anyone.*

"Thank you," Ellen finally said after what felt like far too long.

"Yeah." Volta cleared her throat and gestured. "S'on the left, here, by the —"

"By the statue?"

She made an inscrutable face. "Yeah."

"I — this one?" Ellen asked, bemused, pointing at the chiseled serpentine visage bedecked in a "STARING CONTEST GOLD MEDAL 1979" baseball cap.

The scrutability lowered further still. "Yeah."

"Does he have a silly name?"

Ellen couldn't have scruted Volta's expression if she had all the time in the world and a world-class scruting device.

"Depends on how silly you think 'Rodrigo' is."

"I bet you'd get a different answer depending on whether you asked the Medicis or the Sforzas."

Dead air. Volta seemed to be searching her own brain for a moment, eyes furrowing behind her ever-present pink visor, until her mouth formed into a small "o."

"ROSE working that one out for ya?" Ellen asked, grinning.

Volta snorted. "She says I'd need a long history lesson and at the end of it I'd just be disappointed that your joke doesn't really work."

"Fair enough!" Ellen brought her gaze past the statue and toward the set of double doors beyond. "So, this is the place?"

The doors opened "yes."

"Right! Good! Excellent! Time to meet the new boss!"

"I'll be right behind you," Volta said with quiet reassurance that, frankly, Ellen had not thought she *needed* and that, frankly, was starting to make her second-guess herself.

But she wasn't going to tell *Redline* that, even if a distant, still-Heroic stronghold of her brain recognized that she was heading straight to a high-tier villain's lair, with another's heavy bootsteps thudding along behind her.

She was walking, willingly, into a pincer.

But that wasn't fair — not really. Volta was there for emotional support. Celia wasn't going to try to murder her, or pump her full of contagious transformation vectors, or ram a mind control device onto —

Well. It was too early to rule that out, she supposed, as much as Carmen had tried to assure her otherwise.

Her feet carried her forward; she didn't realize how fast she was walking until she heard the subtle shift in the rhythm of Volta's treads behind her.

The doors closed behind them with a sudden, unceremonious *shunk,* and they were plunged into darkness.

A low, rattling hiss filled the chamber. Ellen's ears stood tall, pivoting atop her head as she willed her eyes to adjust *faster* — but it was pitch black. She needed even the barest hint of light for them to work with, and this...

She arrested her instincts before they could spur motion. This was *not* a fight, and she would not make it one. She would trust Volta, trust the *Korps,* and stay very still like a *good girl,* waiting for the leader of a Korps frontier base to speak.

Unless that hiss *was* her speaking and ROSE was simply well-versed in translating sibilance into words, in which case, Ellen was operating at a distinct disadvantage.

"The plucky underdog Hero bravesss the den of the sssupervillain sssupreme commander, defeating her againssst all oddsss..." came the disembodied hiss of the base commander. "Exxxcept you are no longer a Hero, and sssuch featsss are the ssstuff of ssstoriesss."

The room must have been almost *designed* to confuse its origin. Ellen had been almost certain, for just one instant, that her voice had come from somewhere in front of her, but its source was almost immediately lost as her S's bounced and slithered off the walls, undulating into her desperately-swiveling ears out of any sort of order whatsoever. Celia had rendered her senseless and disoriented with little more effort than breathing.

Ellen kept her head facing straight forward, even as she spoke, her voice just a little shakier than she'd have liked. "Volta?"

"Yeah?"

"Can you give me a little light, please?"

"Ssso polite..." whispered the voice from every direction. A dim flicker of pink rose from Volta's digits, and Ellen's vulpine eyes caught its shine. The darkness around her formed into shapes and suggestions — and all around her — those shapes suggested that she start moving, *now*.

The impulse froze in her knees and elbows, stopped cold even as her heartbeat quickened further and the fur on her tail stood on end.

A serpentine tail as big around as Volta's prodigious hips lay all around them, languidly undulating in the faint light. She didn't have to look behind her to tell that the door had been blocked off the instant they'd come in, and it seemed a *terrible* idea to move her gaze away from the face that stared back barely a foot from her own. A face that, Ellen realized not nearly as distantly as she'd have liked, she'd have little trouble fitting through.

Instincts roared at her like the sound of rending metal. She could not will her hackles back down, she could not will herself to stop shaking, but she *could* slowly, cautiously offer her hand.

"P-pleased to meet you, C-Celia," she managed through a mouth that would have rather screamed.

The serpent spoke so softly that Ellen couldn't see her mouth move. "Sssuch a sssweet little foxxx... minding her mannersss, even in thisss den of... *iniquity*."

It was rare that Ellen found herself with so few words. Though the coils still wobbled at the edges of her vision, Celia's head stood stock-still — until, finally, she didn't. Celia rose; Ellen saw where her muscular torso met her tail, an impossible shore of waist and hips and snake, every curve of her shape oozing unquestionable strength. When she reached forward, it was with a sinister alien grace.

She had almost completely forgotten that she had her hand out until the snake gripped it in the stiff latex of her shoulder-length glove.

Celia's grip was not *tight*, but it was intimidating all the same; her hand dwarfed Ellen's, the tips of her dangerously sharp claws ever-so-pointedly poised to penetrate with just an *iota* more pressure than she used.

"Welcome to RIV, Missss Foxxxpaw. I have heard ssso much about you... and who you were, onccce upon a time." Ellen swallowed. It wasn't lost on her that, through years of Hero work, she had put more than a handful of Korps agents behind bars. Possibly even *her* agents. Revenge now would not be pragmatic — but it would be *understandable*. "What cccircumssstancccesss have sssent you sssquirming to the sssubterranean home of your nemesssisss?"

Ellen knew better than to assume simple curiosity was behind the serpent's questions.

"M... my sssissster... uh, m-ma'am."

"You are a *bold* little woman, aren't you?"

"I think her name wasss Jo?"

"...Your sssissster?"

"No, the... little woman. From... from the book. Little Women." Ellen wilted. Celia's facial expression — if it could even be called that — remained implacable. Ellen forced herself to keep speaking. "My sssissster's name isss Vixxxie."

"I sssee. No... *perssonal* interessst?"

"Well, I could hardly abandon her down here!"

Celia leaned closer, crimson scales glistening in the pink lighting; Ellen's tail twitched toward its safe place between her thighs, but she willed it to stay where it was. "That isss not what I asssked, little foxxx. Isss your sssissster truly the only reasson you have for joining usss? You would forsssake your fellow Heroesss, your friendsss, all that you have ever known, to join your greatessst enemy? Hasss your heart been moved... or isss thisss sssimply a meansss to an end?"

Ellen swallowed. By the time Celia was finished speaking, her face was less than inches from the once Hero's. Ellen could feel her breath tickling the hair that lay across her forehead.

"Well," she began, as if working it over in her mind. "I wouldn't mind another few ssswings at Jack Phillipsss."

"Oh? Ssso tell me, turncoat... to what end? To teach him a lesssson, perhapsss? Or... do you ssseek to play hisss exxxecutttioner?"

"I... don't know." It sounded weak, she knew, but... "I jussst... don't want him to feel... *sssafe*, sssaying thingsss like he sssaid, *ever again*. I..."

She trailed off; somewhere along the way, she started clenching her fists. It felt almost *perverse* that her urge to fight was not aimed at the enormous monster before her, but at the man who had kept food on her and Vixie's table for so many years.

"*Interesssting* that you sshould sssay ssso," Celia hissed. "You sssee... we have been presssented with... an *opportunity*. What would you sssay, little foxxx, if I told you that you could ssstrike the final blow? To sssalt the fieldsss of your defectttion, that none may rissse to take your placcce?"

Ellen bristled. Something inside of her tightened, and she couldn't help but let its tension into her face.

"I am no assssasssssin," she said. Something inside of her rankled at that; an objection of circumstance, perhaps. She had nearly achieved the same end, after all, in the heat of the moment. "If you ssseek his dissssolution, perhapsss I can sssuggessst the ssservicccesss of Carmen Rayne?"

Celia emoted... unemotively. Ellen was keenly aware there was *something* she was thinking behind the scaled mask. Volta's earlier expressions had at least been *expressions*. With Celia, there was simply nothing to scrute.

"A tempting offer," admitted the serpent, "but I had sssomething altogether different in mind. Your former employer hasss assssembled hisss besssst fighting wordsss in an attempt to lure usss out. We have reassson to believe that he hasss sssomething more... *sssubsssstantttial* than previousss attemptsss — no offensssse to presssent company, of courssse. However... far more tempting than risssing to hisss blussster isss the chancccе to *end* hisss prattling, onccce and for all."

Ellen stared. "Thisss ssstill sssoundsss like an asssssasssinatttion."

"Nothing quite ssso vulgar, no. He hasss challenged usss to a fight. No ulterior motivesss, no heisssstsss, no drawing valuable targetsss out of hiding. Sssimplicccity itsssself. Violenccce for the sssake of violenccce.

Nothing more sssophisssticated than a ssspurned drunkard ssslurring epithetsss 'til he reccceivesss hisss sssatisssfactttion or isss laid out upon the asssphalt."

"Isss there any reassson we're lissstening to him?" asked the fox, even as the barely-there fur on her arms stood on end.

"Alasss, no amount of ignoring him and hisss ilk will make him disssappear; he will sssimply insssert himsssself into conversssatttionsss until we are forccced to anssswer him. Thisss isss a rare occasssion in which we have much to gain from meeting him in hisss chosssen arena... becaussse it isss a rare opportunity to eliminate a player from the board."

"I sssee..." Ellen hissed. "You're hoping that one lassst high-profile defeat will make him a laughing ssstock — one at my handsss, to add insssult to injury?"

"Jussst ssso."

Ellen's shaking knees carried her the last few steps to Rodrigo until, finally, she threw her arms over his stone shoulders for support.

"You could have told me the base commander was LAMIA!" she groaned, voice as wobbly as her legs.

"You never asked," Volta reminded.

"I coulda *sworn* I did."

Volta shook her head. "I *thought* you were about to, but then you made a dumb joke, and I zapped you."

"My curse," Ellen wheezed.

"Gotta hand it to ya, though, Standup. Takes real dedication to the bit to make fun of Mistress Celia's speech patterns right to her face like that."

"Huh? Red, I would *never*. You know me better than that."

Volta stared, astonished.

"Did you... not *notice?*"

"Notice what?"

Volta's mouth rested agape, and Ellen waited, cogs spinning in her brain as she replayed the conversation in her mind. A new horror settled over her, and she made a long noise in her throat that sounded like an old iron gate that had only just realized how embarrassing its creak was.

Worse, she had finally pieced together the artist responsible for the statue she was leaning on.

"How in the *hell* did you survive as long as you did, Standup?"

"*I don't know!*" wailed Ellen, clinging to the macabre stonework for emotional support. "Sometimes I think I would've been better off just stickin' to my career at Cold Stone!"

Volta gave Rodrigo a significant glance, and Ellen's mouth twisted in horror.

"Oh, gosh*dammit!*"

She could only hope she'd look better when *she* was petrified, left out in the hallway for passersby to draw mustaches on and take goofy pictures with. Maybe Vixie could help people find dumb shirts in her size — but then, Vixie had always been bad at remembering her size anyway.

A hand like an open book clapped Ellen between the shoulders; she gasped, so lost in her frantic fantasizing (frantasizing?) that she hadn't even noticed Volta tromping over to her.

"Hey," she said, her voice like a warm beacon of hot chocolate on a cold, stormy night. "You... all right?"

Ellen breathed. She hadn't been certain when she'd stopped, exactly. She swallowed — slowly, carefully — and met the enormous lupine's gentle gaze. Even the shocking pink irises set in the darkness of her sclera managed to look, somehow, comforting.

Seeing that concern leveled in *her* direction slowed her frantasies to a gentle background worry. It was odd; she'd never underestimated the sort of *threat* Redline could be — not since their first meeting, anyway — but she'd never really pondered the ramifications of having the enormous hulk of lupine in her corner, either.

"Yeah," said Ellen finally. "It's... yeah. I'll be just fine." She sniffed, her train of thought shifting hastily to a new track. "So. Fighting again."

"Fighting again." Volta cleared her throat. "Standard protocol on this kind of fight is to have someone ready to bail you out if it turns out to be more than you can handle, or... or an ambush," she said with a faraway look. "If you don't mind, I..."

Ellen reached out despite herself and took Volta's hand in both of hers.

"There's no one I'd rather have watchin' my back than you, Red."

Chapter 12

A Strong Foe

September 2022

Ellen decided to skip dinner with the Raynes. A new fight meant a shift in priorities. She'd departed Rodrigo's side to beeline for the gym, voicing a need for a protein shake and a haircut to no one in particular. Within ten minutes, she had a large peanut butter-banana-whey in hand, and an appointment at the salon on her schedule.

A familiar face graced the television facing the treadmill: Jack Phillips, bearing a fake-looking smile Ellen suspected was genuine, and real-looking teeth Ellen knew were not.

"I am honored to stand before you today to announce the *future* of the Everyone's Hero Association," he spoke into the quartet of microphones on his podium. "While I cannot give details at this time in the interest of civilian safety, I assure you that we have been innovating forward despite the recent loss of our star Hero, Lawful Neutral."

He paused, letting the silence suggest his no doubt *immense* grief.

"The Korps is a threat to us all — our friends, our society, our very way of life. Lawful Neutral's defection impacts us all; to most, she was a Hero. To me, she was a member of the Phillips family. We will never be able to replace her in our hearts — but her work will continue where she cannot. We have a duty to her memory to see her mission through.

"To that end, I will be pledging the profits from my other companies toward the Everyone's Hero Association, as well as my own paycheck. I urge those in the industry to watch closely.

"It's time for a new age of Heroes."

October 2022

The Condor swung low, its twin engines conspicuously quiet for an aerial craft of its caliber. It had been a rare treat to see the Korps's iconic stealth transport from within, but it was the doors sliding open to reveal rows and heaps of old cars and tortured scrap metal that took Ellen's breath away.

This was it. As long as she remained on the Condor, she was just a civilian — a disappeared person who had, for whatever reason, ended up in the custody of the Korps. But the instant she stepped off…

A reassuring hand patted her on the back of her denim jacket, its breadth wide enough to cover both shoulder blades.

"You got this, Standup," she said. "Bet one taste of a real fight'll scare Phillips's new toy right back into the bargain bin."

"I can't help but feel like I should be offended," Ellen griped.

Volta snorted. "You musta fallen into it from a higher shelf or somethin'. Now, c'mon — I'm right behind you."

Ellen's feet hit the stiff, sunbaked clay first. Their designated opponent was already there, waiting: seven feet of broad bovine muscle sat at the foot of a mountain of tires that made even *him* look small beside it. His deep navy supersuit reflected the afternoon sun, a palm-sized silver triangle glinting in the light just beneath his impressive pectorals.

"Of course they sent *you*," he rumbled; his voice was deep as a mine and twice as rocky. An EHA camera drone whirred to sudden life from atop the pile of worn-out rubber, its quartet of cameras swiveling to stare at its three subjects as Volta flashed a winning, open-mouthed sneer for the viewers. "Two on one, then?"

Ellen's knuckles strained against the rubber of her tight black gloves as she flexed her fists within them, arms crossing and stretching above her head. "That'd hardly be fair, would it? Nah — this is your first time out, right? You got a name?"

"Strong."

"To the point! Tells people exactly what you're about," chuckled Ellen.

"Strong is the only thing I need to be, so Strong is what I am."

"Not very imaginative!"

"Doesn't have to be."

"Right. Okay then, Strong: I'm not gonna go easy, but I can at least make sure Red over here doesn't knock your block off."

"Sure." The bull leaned forward, fingers dipping into a pouch at his hip as he spoke. "I hoped it would be you. You were a good Hero, once." His nostrils flared. "Shame."

"I'm *still* a good Hero!" Ellen protested. The bull eyed her with sharp disinterest, finger probing at one of his ears and then switching to the other. "Listen, new guy, I know you haven't been around long enough to see it yet, but Jack's just using you to line his pockets — the whole *system* is using you! I know I'm not gonna get you to walk away from this fight, but... keep an eye out for it, okay? From one Hero to another?"

"I've seen the way you fight," he said, as if he hadn't even heard her. When he spoke, Ellen felt like she was next to a car that had invested heavily in the bass; she had little doubt that if he yelled, he could rattle windows. "A big guy like me? Your go-to is going to be copying my power, try to fight me on even terms."

But Ellen shook her head. "Who would want to watch that? After all... two Strongs don't make a sight!"

She tossed a pair of finger-guns at the rookie Hero.

He didn't respond.

"Can't hear ya."

Ellen cleared her throat. "I said: Two *Strongs* don't make a *sight!*"

Strong tapped his ear and smiled. "*Won't* hear ya. See, the EHA knows how all your powers work, so I took a little initiative. I went out and bought ear plugs."

Shit.

"So, we're gonna fight. And when we do, I'm not gonna hear your shitty little jokes, I'm not gonna hear you beg for mercy, and I'm not gonna hear you scream. But if you think you're a *good Hero*, surrender. Let yourself be held accountable. Set a good example — or I'll *make* you one."

Ellen's mind began cranking hard. Without Pun For All, she was just a short, reasonably athletic vixen.

But… that wasn't *entirely* true. Ellen had the better half of a decade of experience fighting villains, and this wouldn't be the first time she'd gotten into a fight without her powers. If anything, she had the advantage here, so long as she didn't take it for granted. Her instincts, honed in over a hundred battles, would give her the edge.

Strong rolled his shoulders, pushing himself slowly up off of the mountain of tires and onto his hooves.

"Have it your way, traitor."

And then there was a flash of rubbery black, and Ellen felt the ground leave her feet and arrive at her back. She'd lost her wind somewhere in the process — and worse, a steady *thooming* of hoof steps was building up steam, faster and harder as they got closer. Ellen didn't have the time or the breath to get back up; her entire torso burned as she rolled to the side —

— and felt a set of thick bovine fingers wrap around her tail. She scrabbled for a handhold against the smooth clay floor, but it was no use; it fell away from her as she was lifted by the fur-cloaked length of her spine, a scream lodged in her throat without the air to send it. The strain on her vertebrae spread throughout her lower back as her entire weight was dangled from it, helpless.

Strong adjusted his hold, straightened up, reared back, and cracked her like a whip.

The world swung around her as pain shot up her spine, agony and inertia blurring her vision. She had found the breath to scream without realizing it as the bull swung her in a wide arc and soon felt Strong's huge fingers let her go. She soared through the air until she didn't, rolling limply across the ground until her shoulder bumped her to a stop against a pile of scrap.

A high-pitched whine filled her ears, and Ellen realized that the shaky sensation in her throat was the feeling of trying to choke back tears and vomit at the same time. *Shit.* She took half a breath and forced her eyes upward.

Strong must have thrown her at least a hundred feet, because he was still a good, long while away — at his current, glacial pace, anyway. *Thud. Thud. Thud.* She had plenty of time to get up.

If only she *could.* Ellen tried to push herself to her feet and toppled right over; her tail didn't swing to correct her balance, didn't swing *at all.* She looked back and saw it; the fur had crumpled in the middle, and it hung limp and loose. *Dislocated.*

She'd be lucky to get to her knees before Strong got to her. His figure blocked off the sun, left Ellen in his enormous shadow. She had little choice; she crawled on hands and knees away, scampered toward a row of trashed vehicles. If she could just make it to a car, maybe... maybe she could crawl underneath? She'd... she'd think of a plan then. Maybe. If he didn't just crush the damn thing on top of her.

She was three feet away from the bumper when there was an enormous pink flash, a thunderclap rocking the air a split second after.

"**I never agreed to one-on-one, asshole!**" roared Volta as Strong turned to face her. Ellen could just barely see her savior through her tears, a crackling haze of pink lightning. "**Think you can handle someone a little closer to your own size?**" Somehow, though, Ellen could hear a quaver in her voice. Was she... *worried* about something?

And how was Strong still standing?

Strong snorted at the challenge, even if he couldn't hear it. "You waited longer than I thought you would," he drawled. His big hands came down on the car Ellen was trying to get under and *crushed* the hood.

With a quick movement, the vehicle was *gone*; Ellen's eyes only caught up with it when it collided with Volta... and then, after a quick wobble, came sailing right back.

Strong got under it and knocked it up into the air, let it smash into the cars two rows behind him. Volta had already closed the gap, though, and looked about ready to slam her fist into his jaw —

...but she didn't.

It almost looked like she *deflated*; the pink arcs dissipated like they had never been there. For the first time since Ellen had seen her she looked, somehow, *small*, even standing a foot over Strong's beefy figure.

And then, with a shocked bark, *she* went flying. Ellen's blood froze. Something was *very* wrong. She hadn't seen Volta so helpless since...

Oh, fuck.

"Did you think you were *done* with this?" snorted the bull, his fingers sliding across the silver surface of the triangle on his chest. "That

Dampening technology cost Texas a pretty penny, and Jack was *very* happy to give them a return on their investment — now that he's finally got someone worth putting it on."

Ellen tried to push herself to her feet, but with an offhand backwards kick from Strong, she was on the ground again with smarting ribs to match her injured pride.

Volta, however, was already back upright — and *snarling*. Ellen could hear popping noises, could see pink streaks of electricity surging toward Volta from old, ruined batteries. A car alarm started and then slurred until it died.

"Fuck, you hit like a freight train," growled Volta, wiping blood from the matted fur on her chin, **"but I've always believed in giving twice as good as I got, and you've put me in a real charitable mood."**

Strong guffawed at the display and shook his head. "Come at me with everything you have, *Austin*. You've gone too far to surrender now."

Ellen grit her teeth as she watched. She was helpless; even pushing herself to a kneel took everything she had not to fall over, and as she watched the two giants collide, she stumbled to a wall of stacked cars and propped herself up on a hollowed-out Corolla.

She knew it wasn't the first time Volta had had to fight without the charge that powered her, but even still, Ellen had never seen the wolf move so *slowly*. Strong was a sloppy fighter, but Volta was moving like lightning in a bottle of molasses, barely able to turn away from Strong's fists before they crashed into her, barely able to put force into her swings.

Ellen had just barely dragged herself to her feet when Volta went down again with a heavy hit and a pair of thuds.

This time, she didn't get back up. She just lay there, growling, snarling on her back, trying to push herself back up on her elbows. Even from across the junk yard lot, Ellen could see her eyelid swelling shut behind her battered RCGs, saw the bloody scuffs in her fur.

Ellen knew it was her turn to come to the rescue. But she didn't *have* ranged powers — in fact, if she couldn't land a pun, she didn't have powers *at all*.

So, she did her best: she tilted, shuffling, willing her body forward without a tail to stabilize her, legs clumsy and unsure but *resolute*.

She didn't make thuds in the pavement like the other two, didn't cross the distance in just a few footsteps. But with the ear plugs in, Strong didn't hear her coming, and Ellen gave him a swift uppercut in the only vulnerable place she could reach from his back: right between the thighs.

God, if only he hadn't been wearing a cup.

She could hear the big bull snort; her momentum futilely surrendered, she fell onto her ass as he turned around and glared down at her.

"I was going to take care of the *actual* threat first," he rumbled, reaching for her, "but I think he can wait a second. Be a good boy and stay down, Austin."

Fingers thick as bratwurst gripped Ellen's head, his big thumb tucked under her jaw. Her neck strained as she was lifted off the ground, legs kicking, her fingers clawing at his in a vain attempt to pry herself free.

Nothing budged. His hooved digits tightened. Ellen's wide-eyed stare met Strong's narrowed gaze through the fingers splayed across her face, stars swimming in her vision. Her skull creaked, and she opened her mouth against his leathery grip.

She wanted to scream, but she knew it wouldn't save her.

In desperation, she did the only thing she could think of, and Strong dropped her like a rock.

"*Ugh!* You *licked* my *hand!*" The bull snorted furiously, trying to wave the saliva off of his palm before he decided to just wipe it off on his suit. Ellen, meanwhile, had fallen onto her feet… and managed to stay standing. She was finally adjusting to her tail being a dead weight, even if it ached like hell, and stung like shards of glass broken throughout her pelvis whenever she moved.

"HEY, STRONG! WHAT DID THE MICROWAVE SAY TO THE VIBRATOR?" she yelled at the top of her lungs. Strong's hand clapped around her neck this time, and Ellen was ready for it; she coughed and pulled desperately at Strong's middle finger. This time, it budged — not more than a quarter-inch, but *enough*, just where she needed to breathe out one more sentence:

"It's a… grk… *pleasure* to *heat* you!"

Strong didn't hear her, of course. He wouldn't. He *couldn't*, with those earplugs in, squeezing her throat tighter and tighter —

But *Volta* let out a little chuckle, and Ellen burst into flames.

Strong dropped her again with a roar and backed away from the heat. The foxgirl was *burning*, red-hot fire from the tips of her ears down to her feet. The hero looked like he wanted to hit her... but hesitated, clearly trying to work out *how*.

"What, are you gonna punch fire, idiot?" Ellen's voice crackled like the flames in which she had wreathed herself. Forgotten was the pain in her tail, or how close she'd been to a grisly death just moments ago; in its place was a euphoric rush that she *knew* in her soul would only swell as she got closer to the bull.

Strong skipped backwards, shockingly graceful on his heavy frame; Ellen sprinted forth in pursuit, feet pounding over packed earth. She closed in, and he twisted suddenly at the waist, reaching behind him to a junked motorbike. Ellen had already seen it coming, though — baited it, even. She ducked under the Harley's wide swing, twisted metal singing in her flattened ears until it crashed into the pile of discarded choppers behind him and Ellen popped up, limbs wrapping tight around Strong's thick body.

Strong *bellowed*. He dropped the bike and *pounded* on Ellen's back. Even without the leverage, his fists hit like a pair of sledgehammers, drove the air from Ellen's lungs yet again. She could only bear a second blow before she dropped, coughing, to the hard clay beneath.

Agony seared through her burning body; her first suck of air lit every crevice of her ribs in deep, tingling aches, and her pelvis screamed for its missing rudder. She hissed and gazed up at the shadow that fell over her.

Strong stood silhouetted in the setting sun, a beat-up old fridge raised high above his great, horned shadow. Something in the old metal and plastic *creaked* as the Hero tightened his grip. Ellen grit her teeth. There was a sudden, heavy *whump*, and that was it; the world behind her eyelids grew bright, and she knew she was no longer in the world of the living.

But death had not yet come for her — *Volta* had. Strong's back had found the mountain of tires again, his front tangled with red fur and battle denim. The fight wasn't over. Volta still looked half-drowned, even from behind, and Strong's burns didn't seem to be slowing him enough to make up the difference.

She *had* to get up. Ellen grit her fangs, braced her burning fists against the dirt.

One more push. Just one more push.

The muscles in her belly tightened. She dragged herself to her knees.

Gotta end it. Can't...

Her tail stayed limp. She swayed as she rose to her feet; she knew her posture was all wrong, that she was nearer a patient than a warrior.

Can't let her die.

Her will broke, but duty steeled her in its place.

Not now...

She moved.

Not ever.

Ellen dove for a gap in the hill of rubber. She wouldn't survive another direct hit; there was no point hoping that latching onto Strong again wouldn't end with her ribs caving in. She shoved at the tires around her, pulled herself forward and around, pushing old, tired rubber aside to let her through in an arc.

It would have to do. She could just see outside the heap of rubber again, saw Volta's bruised face over the back of Strong's horns. One of her eyes was swollen shut, but the other locked with Ellen's, and she nodded.

Ellen thrust her hands out of the mountain and wrapped her fingers around his ears.

"The Dampener!" Ellen barked. "Now!"

Strong twisted himself free just as the *rush* was getting good, bellowing, his hands moving *up* to fend off his attacker by instinct as Volta's lanced toward the silver triangle on his chest. She tore it free and *hurled* it; Ellen lost sight of it until it caught the sun, glinting once before disappearing beyond a distant, dusty admin building.

Ellen almost *whooped*, but Volta hadn't turned back around fast enough. Strong's fist met the back of her head, and she went skidding and rolling across the ground, each bump sending up a puff of pink sparks. The tires around Ellen buckled as Strong shoved himself off of them.

But she refused to let him follow her. She scrambled, wriggled through rubber and kicked herself out, launched herself from the pile, reaching, *desperate*.

Her palm made contact with the tight muscle of his glute. The suit sizzled and hissed, and as Ellen found her footing and *shoved*, the bull dug his hooves in, turning, twisting.

By the time his fist swung to knock her brains into the pavement, she wasn't there; she'd reeled back, back to the mountain of rubber, turned completely to scramble up the discarded tires and out of Strong's reach. He snorted in fury, grabbing the most solid-looking wheel within his grasp, and reared back to throw.

He went down in a sudden bolt of lightning.

Ellen whooped in triumph, and her stomach dropped. Something beneath her *shifted*. Something *above* her shifted. *Everything* shifted, even as Strong groaned and twitched, and with dawning horror she realized the mountain was coming down around her.

"Not *now!*" she begged, scrambling against a shifting mound of wobbly rubber. She clambered for a grip she knew would only be momentary, slipping, dropping, kicking, grasping; tires bounced and quivered, pelted the ground below and bounced at unpredictable angles. She couldn't spare a glance behind; if Strong was right behind her, there was nothing she could *do*.

The cascade of rubber slowed; Ellen finally spared a glance behind her, and only then realized how *quiet* both wolf and bull had been. Both were still down; Strong was half-buried beneath a pile of old rubber, unmoving.

A thin, jagged band of pink wiggled through the air toward the other figure. The EHA camera drone, nearly forgotten in the heat of combat, wobbled in the air and then tipped to the ground, landing with a dull clatter. Volta groaned, and Ellen hissed through her teeth. She must have been desperate. There was nowhere else to draw from.

The fox pushed herself to her feet, gave Strong a wide berth, and limped to her fallen friend. The fire that wreathed her flickered down, then out. Volta was grinning — though whether she had noticed their triumph or was simply punch-drunk — she couldn't tell.

"*There* you are. Was worried he'd finished you off while I was down," grunted the wolf, pushing herself up onto her elbows.

"Nah," puffed Ellen, squinting against the sunset as she offered her hand. "Never."

Volta barked a hollow laugh. "Never?" Her voice sounded weak, *thin*. "Standup, he almost killed you like three times." She grunted and strained, pulling, and Ellen tried not to wince at the tension, shifted to keep the pressure on her arms and core.

It wouldn't have been the first time Volta had broken her ribs with her weight alone — but she was too weak to pull herself up.

"Don't you remember, Red? I told you, I'm not going anywhere. The world may see you as a big, mean, electric switch, but as far as I'm concerned?" A tired grin spread over her features, despite everything. "You're my *trans sister*."

Ecstatic electricity surged through Ellen's battered body, crackling and popping off her shoulders as Volta's face softened, jaw dropping into a wordless "*oh.*"

"*Come on,*" urged the fox. Her grip tightened around Volta's palm, even if her fingers barely spanned its breadth. "*Let me help you.*"

Like cold water through her bones, lightning left her in a slow, steady stream. Volta's ragged breathing slowed as she drew from Ellen's newfound well, and before long, she was finally able to get back up to her feet.

Ellen's breath of relief stopped cold.

She swiveled at the sound of rubber impacting dirt behind her. Strong cast off the tires that had nearly buried him, rising, slowly but steadily, back to his hooves. His breathing was heavy, *murderous.* He glowered at the pair beneath furrowed eyebrows, clenching and unclenching his fist as if to flex out the extra voltage.

"*Cute,*" the bull spat. His suit was burnt and frayed, peeling back from his thick hide in great, jagged scars across his chest and back. Blood pooled in the crevices between his grit teeth until he licked them clean. Ellen could see the tips of his ear plugs, still neatly nestled in among the shiny red flesh. "I wanted to believe you were better than this, Lawful Neutral. You think you've found your people among the wolves? Fine. Then I won't treat you like the lost little dog you are."

He'd barely finished his sentence when there was another sudden blackout — but this time, no impact. Ellen hadn't seen the tire coming this time, either, but Volta had already snatched it out of the air, curving it out of the way as she spun —

— and then Ellen felt a jerk behind her shoulders, and she was off her feet.

"**Follow my lead,**" Volta snarled, twisting; there was a *lurch*, and suddenly Ellen wasn't just off her feet, but airborne. Wind whistled past her at a blistering speed as she left the fight far beneath her.

Strong collided with Volta like a linebacker; the wolf dug her boots in and *roared*, wrestling for position as Strong tried to get a good angle to gore her. Ellen finally tore her eyes away; Volta had thrown her for a *reason*, she must have, there…

Ah. Loud and clear, Red.

Weightless at the apex of her flight, Ellen caught the tire as it started its descent back to Earth, pivoting, positioning. If she could just get this right…

There was a blinding flash below. That was her cue: Volta had gone from putting some space between her and Strong to right on top of him, pinning him to the dirt in a hug that would have crushed any lesser man's spine. Ellen's knees tensed, and the lightning inside of her tensed, too, tight and focused like a spring.

Volta let go and rolled off, and that was it. Ellen kicked off the tire and everything seemed to melt away. She couldn't hear anything but a low, crackling hum, and the sky faded and blurred, and everything felt hot, hotter than it had been when she was aflame. The pain in her tail was gone, the sharp aches in her ribcage, *everything*. The cars, the piles of scrap, *everything* stretched out and blended together like so much taffy, and as she twisted in the air, the world snapped back behind her, as if reality itself was nothing but an enormous slingshot for propelling her forward.

Ellen came down like a foxgirl-shaped bolt of lightning, her knee slamming into Strong's burnt, raw-red solar plexus as Volta's hand tightened around his throat, and the whole bull lit up like a stunning pink Korpsmas tree. He jerked and spasmed with a horrible coughing bellow as the rest of Ellen collapsed atop him, her pain having returned twice over with the sudden impact.

"I'm just gonna lay here," croaked Ellen, wheezing into the bull's twitching shoulder.

"**No.**" Volta's digits found Ellen's jacket once more and tugged her to safety, rolling her gently onto the dirt on the opposite side. With a grunt of effort, she pivoted to her knees, straddling the bull's wide chest as he blinked up at her in shock. She shook from head to tail, every movement forced and painfully slow. Her hands found the hole in his suit where the Dampener had been, and she let out a low, rattling snarl.

"Did you *think*…" she breathed, "that just because… you got a *fancy suit*… you can get away with *deadnaming me?*" Strong rumbled out a growl of his own through his teeth as electricity coursed through his chest. "That name… will *never* define me, asshole. Let me… help you… forget it."

Animalistic snarls mixed with bovine screams as Volta poured a current into him with every last bit of charge she had. Out of the corner of her nose, she smelled something exactly like burning steak.

It took three tries for her to yell loudly enough to get Volta's attention. "*Please,*" she begged. Volta's dazzling pink eyes lifted, stared back at Ellen in equal parts fury and… something *else.* "Let's go. We won."

"Yeah." Volta pried herself off of Strong, who was still a smoking, twitching wreck on the ground. "Yeah."

Propellers — quiet as air conditioners and only slightly higher-pitched — whirred low above them. Ellen hadn't seen the Condor until it was practically at Volta's hackles, and as she watched it settle, barely a yard above the ground, Volta's hands slid beneath her and pulled her from the ground.

Volta stooped and pulled Ellen into a cradle hold and stumbled toward where the heli was coming down. "Think I have a few cracked ribs," groaned the wolf, wincing and spent.

"You should see the other guy," wheeze-chuckled Ellen. It was a strange feeling, being carried by her former archnemesis. "I'm not dying, right?"

"Hell if I know, Ellen."

"Oh, I'm definitely dying," she groaned. "You used… my actual name. If I die… Vixie… gets my autographed… True North II card."

Volta's face fell. "C'mon, Standup, you know she's not gonna appreciate it."

"Oh, I know… but if you thought… you could get it… if I croaked… you might take your time… getting me help."

Volta laid her down across a row of seats. "We're already on the heli, smartass."

Ellen glanced around. Metallic walls surrounded her, the door already closed, and a pair of familiar, identical synthetic vulpine doctors flanked the towering villain as she eased her onto a medical cot.

"So, we are."

Volta dropped into the seat across from her and was quiet.

Ellen let her have a minute; she needed it herself, as the Korps medic onboard took a brief look between the two and settled on her.

A few questions and answers — "ribs and tail, mostly," "no augments, no, but I might still have Zapwolf powers," "no, I don't smoke — is that against code? Should I start?" — and the medic set about passing Ellen a painkiller and a few gulps of water to take it with. As she sipped, she eyed Volta.

As always, Volta made any space she inhabited look way too small for her, even with the Korps Kopter having plenty of room for someone of her stature. But for the first time, Ellen saw a new expression on her face; her mouth was twisted up in an anxious frown, and in the corner of the eye Ellen could see... *tears.*

Ellen's stomach twisted. She opened her mouth to speak, but Volta seemed to sense the question before she asked it.

"I thought... I thought I was *done.* With Dampeners, with deadnames. With big, shitty jackasses I couldn't just *fry* into *shutting up.* I..." Her eyebrows tensed, furrowed and raised at once, until she shook her head in a sudden, violent shake. "Sorry, I'm being stupid again, I just —"

"Hey!" Ellen interrupted, pushing herself to sit up over the protestations of the medics. "Hey hey hey hey hey. It's *okay.* Volta, look at me. Can I ask you something?"

Volta sniffed, nodding tentatively.

"What kind of pirates run a haunted ship?"

Volta's lips parted. She began to protest, but it was too late; Ellen was undeterred.

"A *skeleton crew!*" The fox raised her hands and jazzed them, popping the dumbest grin she could manage without whimpering, but Volta was unmoved.

Ellen waggled her fingers again, and Volta finally cracked with a frustrated giggle into her fist. "God*dammit,* Standup," she cursed as Ellen's flesh disappeared, leaving nothing but her battered bones.

There was a rattling sound as her tail separated and rolled under the seat.

"I suppose there will be no need for an X-Ray," shrugged the four-armed synth medic, reaching under the bench and dusting off the tailbones. "Let's get you flipped over so I may reinsert this."

A gray tabby sprinted to meet the heli as its propellers spun down and its bay opened up. Carmen practically flew up the ramp, and she barely stopped in time to avoid throwing herself entirely at Volta.

"Volta! Volta, Volta holy *shit*, is anything broken? Do you need to sit — don't you *dare* tell me you're fine," she blurted, raising a warning finger as Volta opened her mouth. "I know you better, hon."

"*I* can't sit," groaned Ellen from a passing stretcher.

The pair was looking... *bad*, and Carmen had seen everything through her girlfriend's RCGs. Volta looked like she'd been run over, backed over, and run over again; her fur was matted with blood, her outfit torn across the shoulder. Bruises and welts shone over her torso, and her tail hung between her legs.

Ellen, meanwhile, was literally a skeleton.

Well, *most* of a skeleton. Chunks of rib had come off, their jagged points lined up carefully beside her spine, and her pelvis bore a web of cracks that converged at the base of her tail.

"Hey. Hey, Carmen," she said, turning on the gurney to make eye socket contact; the medics didn't slow down in the slightest. "People always tell me I have good cheekbones, but I figure now's the time to figure that out for sure. What do you think?"

The tabby, though, was preoccupied. Volta hadn't said anything back, and Carmen was pretty sure she knew why.

"Hey, Volts. Talk to me."

"I'm fi —" she began, but at a glance of preemptive disbelief from Carmen, the wolf changed course. "...I'm kind of fucked up right now, yeah."

"Is ROSE helping?"

"She got me this far, I guess." The big wolf sniffed and glanced after the retreating stretcher. "So did Ellen."

Carmen's brow raised. "'Ellen,' huh? Well, I'll be damned." She let that ruminate in her brain for a moment, then laid a very gentle paw on Volta's better shoulder. "You can relax now, you're safe. You're *here* and you're not back in the academy, you're safe."

Volta took a deep breath. For a moment, there was calm, until it was broken by the sudden wailing of a distressed vixen.

"SIIIIIIIIIIIIIIIIIIIIIIIIIIIIIIIIIIIS!!!"

Ellen turned to face her empty sockets at Vixie as she sprinted on her tiny legs down the hall.

"E-E-ELLEN ARE YOU O-OKAY PLEASE, PLEASE P-PLEASE —"

Ellen spread her humeri and caught her even-less-identical twin in a very hesitant, ginger hug. "I'm fine, Vix, I'm fine —"

"Y-you don't h-have any skin!!"

Vixie's eyes glistened with tears, her lip wibbling as Ellen laid back. She patted her sister on the head with bony digits. When she pulled her hand away, it was with two less fingers.

"Well, yeah," she said, chuckling smugly as she carefully excised them from the tangle of Vixie's hair, "but hey — you should see the other guy."

Ellen's skeleton lay in a stretcher, broken in several places and fractured in others. Miss Volta limped along behind them as the medics carried her bones down the hall, but for the first time since she'd met the big wolf, her eyes didn't even glance in her direction.

It helped, though, that Ellen's skeleton was still pretty chatty.

Vixie's heart raced in her chest. What if she'd lost her? She didn't know what had happened — not *specifically* — but for her to be hurt *this* badly, for Miss Carmen to have streaked through the halls in a purple blur right past her to get to Miss Volta...

"D-does it hurt?" she whispered. Her short legs kept pace with the much taller medics, but she had to hustle to do so.

"Not even a little," insisted Ellen. "No nerves, no lactic acid. No pain. I'm going to try to maintain it until the doc can come by with some super glue and put those ribs back on." She gestured at the little bundle of loose, pointed bones rattling around beside her spine.

In no time, they were inside of a medical ward. Ellen was soon shifted gently onto a proper bed by the pair of Nurses O that had carried her there, her broken pieces carefully arranged on a table beside her. Miss Volta and Miss Carmen had been ushered into the room across the hall, the feline asking a great many questions about her girlfriend's care that even Vixie registered were best left to the doctors.

One of the medics pressed a carton of milk into Ellen's bony digits; the taller twin stared at it with a faceless expression, then up at the synth.

"Normally I'd be all about this," she said, "but I don't want anything that came out of a cow right now."

"No need to worry," said the medic as she opened it for her. "This did not."

"Ah." The tops of her humeri rose, and she tipped the carton back. The lavender milk inside flowed past her conical teeth and splattered over her ribcage. "Aw, dangit. I got the treatment and everything, but I guess I still don't have the stomach for lactose."

"Stomach or no, the nanites will assist with your recovery," Nurse O explained helpfully.

"I — excuse me, *nanites?*"

"Yes."

After a moment, one of the synthetic medics curtseyed and excused herself from the room, leaving the other alone to monitor Ellen's unique circumstance in silence while she attended to other patients.

Vixie couldn't wait any longer to speak up.

"E-Ellen, what if..." she began, sniffling; the lights in the room blurred and wobbled in her tear-filled eyes. "W-what if y-you d-didn't c-come back?"

Ellen stared at Vixie through empty eye sockets for a moment.

"I'm frowning," she explained. "It just occurred to me that I can't actually frown, but I'm frowning."

Vixie snorted through her sniffle and wiped some of the moisture off her face. "I-I'm serious!"

Ellen reached out and put a bony hand on her twin's shoulder.

"Vix, I'm going to be just fine. But... I've been thinking the same thing. I started fighting to protect *you*. But I'm no good to you if some Hero pulls my... makes sure I don't come back."

Vixie pulled Ellen's torso into another hug — one of the medics started to object but then halted and shrugged.

"*I c-can't lose you,*" whispered Vixie into her sister's open earhole; she was shaking, now, and she could hear Ellen's bones rattling.

Ellen pulled her skull back, tilted her head. "Even now? The Korps will take care of you. You don't need me to protect you anymore."

Vixie's fingers dug in, her fingernails scraping along Ellen's ribs. "*N-never.*"

Ellen's finger bones patted her sister on the back. "Then I'll make sure you won't."

They were quiet for a moment as they held each other, but soon, Vixie heard a hollow sniffing down by her neck. Ellen pulled away a bit, and her skull did a full 360.

"Do you smell banana bread?"

"*I do,*" purred a familiar voice. Vixie jumped in surprise, and there was a clattering jumble of noises, and then she *screamed*. Ellen's head had tumbled down the remnants of her ribcage until it lay cradled in her pelvic girdle, staring upwards.

"I'm okay!" assured Ellen. Vixie had clamped her hands over her mouth to stifle herself, heart pounding so hard she could feel it in her throat, until a warm, familiar embrace settled over her shoulders and another settled over her mind.

"It's all right," whispered Miss Carmen, her hug lifting Vixie off her ankles as she nuzzled her whiskers against the top of the foxgirl's fluffy head. "Sorry I scared you. I just came from Volta's room; she's gonna be released pretty soon, so I was wondering if you wanted to go check in on her with me? She could use a visit from her biggest fan — after I check in on your sister, of course!"

Vixie tilted her head straight back to look up into Miss Carmen's honey yellow eyes, nodding intently. "B-but I want to c-come right back here when I'm d-done... is that okay, M-Miss?"

"Of course! You don't need *my* permission," trilled the feline, "unless you *want* to need my permission."

A thrill went up Vixie's spine and she *giggled* until her sister cleared her throat and —

Vixie blinked. Her throat was over a foot above her head, and entirely disconnected — if, in fact, it existed at all. She wanted to ask how that worked, but Ellen cut her off before she had the chance.

"Can someone put my head back on?" she asked. "I can see *you* just fine, Vixie, but it's hard to tell who my visitor is past the enormous pair of Korps Specials."

"Awww, and I went through the trouble of tucking and everything!" protested Miss Carmen in a mock pout. The remaining nurse gingerly lifted Ellen's skull and gingerly perched it atop her highest vertebrae; somehow, it stayed in place.

Her skull swiveled unsubtly to peek downwards, then snapped back up to meet Miss Carmen's knowing eyes.

"Beating up a Hero *and* staring at a girl's crotch in one day?" Miss Carmen grinned. "Careful, Ellen — at this rate, you're going to develop a *nasty* reputation!"

"You made me curious!" snapped Ellen.

Miss Carmen leaned over the armrest, purring. Ellen was doing a *fantastic* job of maintaining eye contact despite not having eyes to speak of and the swell of Miss Carmen's *generous* breasts barely inches from her bare cheekbone.

Vixie, apparently forgotten, certainly didn't mind the view from behind.

"That reminds me, actually," said the tabby, tail swaying high and Vixie's gaze following, "while I try to keep tabs on *any* member, I had a paw in bringing over, I actually came over here to *thank* you. Our intel was bad, and without you…"

It was for the briefest of moments, but Miss Carmen's claws dug into the armrest.

"Without you, I'm not sure if Volta would have made it home. That means a lot to me. I owe you one, Foxpaw."

Ellen rasped her bony digits over the back of her skull. "Of course!" she said, sheepish. "Vixie would have been miserable if something had happened to her. Honestly, I have just as much reason to thank *her*."

Miss Carmen glanced back to give Vixie a look of concern. Vixie snapped from her staring, eyes wide to match Miss Carmen's *generous* proportions, and her brain did its best to catch up to the conversation she had, admittedly, only had on in the background.

When it did, she couldn't help but frown.

"E-Ellen…"

"Well! I mean, *obviously* you'd have been sad if something happened to me, too! That's why I had to work that much harder, to make sure we *both* got home in one piece."

Ellen glanced down, then back up.

"Figuratively."

"I wanted to thank you for more than that, actually," Miss Carmen cut in, a giggle at the edges of her voice. "For the joke you told her in the Condor, specifically. It was stupid, but… it helped. She was spiraling, and ROSE was having trouble keeping it in check without shutting her down entirely, but *that* knocked her out of it."

"Maybe they need to make a new visor that tells jokes. Y'know, har-har-har-CGs."

Vixie stared. She hadn't heard about her sister helping Miss Volta.

"Th-the joke…? O-*oh!!* D-did you tell her th-the one with the s-skeletons and the b-boat?"

Ellen nodded vigorously, and Miss Carmen sniffed at the air theatrically.

"Ohhh? Vixie, do I detect a favorite?"

"Y-yes!!" Vixie beamed, tail practically thrashing behind her as she bounced on her heels, hands flapping in delight. "It was the f-first one!!"

"Yeah," chuckled Ellen, leaning back into the raised back of her cot. "Vix was, uh… having a rough day, and I was trying *everything* to cheer her up, and my last-ditch effort was stealing a popsicle from the freezer… to split, 'cuz I was havin' a pretty rough day, too. And it didn't really work, but there was a joke on the stick, and that *did* work — until I turned into a skeleton, which Vixie thought was *hilarious*, and Mom thought was, uh — it was bad. She thought I was dying. She told me for years that it was the worst moment of her life, until Vixie came out."

Ellen stared silently down at her bare ankles for a few seconds before her somber bones snapped back to life.

"Joke's on her — now Vixie has more moms than she knows what to do with."

"She has *some* ideas of what to do with them," Miss Carmen mumbled. "And they've got even more ideas of what to do with *her*... or so I've heard."

Ellen snapped her head toward Miss Carmen in rigid frustration while Vixie giggled behind her hands.

"*Thank you for that,*" groaned the skeletal vixen, dragging her digits down her face.

The cat shook her head, chuckling good-naturedly. "You don't have to thank me! She's plenty polite on her own." At a look from Ellen, Miss Carmen's chuckle went sinister. "All right, all right! I can tell when I'm not wanted. Come along, Vixie, Volta needs company and from the look of it, your sister is already *wheely tired.*"

Ellen's jaw dropped and fell directly into her lap as Miss Carmen, winking, hurriedly led Vixie from the room by the hand. Vixie squealed in surprise at the suddenness, but didn't complain as she trotted to keep up with the tabby's long strides.

They slipped into Miss Volta's room just as the enormous lupine's back paws hit the floor. She looked much closer to fine already. Thick, shaggy fur stuck out on either side of a few tight gauze bandages, and Vixie couldn't help but giggle at how they almost seemed to highlight the thick, powerful limbs beneath. If not for the black eye, she could almost have hidden her wounds beneath her usual clothes.

"Hey, Carm," she sniffed. "Fangirl. Looks like most of my injuries should be all right, as long as I keep my nanites charged and don't get in any more fights with heavies for a couple weeks. Gonna have to get some dental work done, though, see?"

Half a ton or more of broad, curvy lupine leaned down, maw opening wide, glistening pink surrounded by pearly teeth. Even with a few of them cracked, it was an inviting sight that made Vixie squirm with the desire to lean right in.

Still, she couldn't help but frown.

"Aw, hey, what's wrong, Fangirl? Hate seeing it in such a state?"

Vixie shook her head.

Miss Volta reeled back and licked the soreness from her chops. "It'll be back to normal in a week, promise — I just gotta avoid biting anything too crunchy for a while."

"I w-wanted to give you this t-to chew on w-while you recovered," pouted the fox. From behind her back, she pulled out a bone just a little bit longer than her own upper arm. "B-but uhm... I d-don't want you t-to hurt your teeth..."

Miss Carmen's mouth whispered a word of shock as Miss Volta's brow furrowed, head tilting, ears flopping with the sudden motion as she worked through the cause of her girlfriend's confusion.

"*Vixie,*" whispered Miss Carmen, pinching the bridge of her nose. "That wouldn't happen to be your *sister's,* would it?"

Vixie blinked rapidly, ears twitching atop her head. "Y-yes? Oh! D-does Miss V-Volta need a bigger one? I c-can try to g-get her thigh inst —"

"*Vixie, please go give your sister her bones back.*"

CHAPTER 13

A VERY MERRY KORPSMAS

December 2022

> *"Oh, my CPU load is frightful!*
> *And the cold in here's delightful.*
> *So, once you get what you came here for,*
> *Close the door, close the door, close the door!"*

Ellen rolled her eyes at her newest friend, Maud, and shut the freezer, leaving the synthetic zebra's disembodied head singing inside. She'd developed a sort of friendship with the janitorial equine when she'd volunteered to do some grunt work around the base in a restless attempt to feel like she was earning her bare little apartment, and the careful medical attention that had fastened her bones back where they belonged. She pondered whether the freezer was Maud's best attempt at jump scaring people or, more benignly, simply an ideal place to cool her circuits. Reluctant to simply ask, she instead settled on applying Miguel and Tulio's Razor and moving on.

Now, the question of more individual reciprocity loomed over her. Korpsmas, the villainous and yet all inclusive collective winter holiday celebrated in the underground bases of the Korps, was right around the corner. As Ellen let her chicken nuggets revolve in the microwave, she pondered.

She knew what she was getting Maud, of course, and Volta was a no-brainer. She'd picked out Carmen's gift a couple of weeks ago and had wrapped it in a ball of yarn to delay the *real* surprise. She'd made a mental note to swing by the Raynes' house to actually meet Wren, at some point — it would hardly do to have a gift for everyone else in the house and let him be excluded, after all. On that note, it seemed prudent to figure out *something* to get the stray puma they'd taken in — and her suspiciously Bowie-shaped caracal shadow, too.

But, strangely enough, it was *Vixie's* present that she had no ideas for.

Historically, Ellen and Vixie's gifts for each other erred on the side of "functional." Vixie would find something practical while she was out, like a durable rubber phone case in orange and black — "f-for when you fight M-Miss Redline!" — or a cute top which was often too small in the chest. Ellen would have to quietly trade it in for the correct size when the shops opened back up. Ellen, meanwhile, would indulge her sister with a few packages of her favorite treats and snacks — always the sticky kind, with too much jam.

But now, Vixie knew how to make her own sweet treats, and the Korps provided just about everything else they might need, from equipment to attire to desserts, so Ellen was worried that wrapping up a pack of Small Deborah cakes would just be redundant this year.

"Your chicken nuggets are ready, Ellen Foxpaw," came ROSE's voice from the microwave. "On an unrelated note, we have updated the Rose-Coloured Glasses database to include '1,001 Bad Jokes for Kids.' You know, in case that is tempting for you."

Ellen smiled. "No hard feelings about what happened the last time I tried to put on RCGs?"

"Of course not. I am not programmed to hold grudges. Simply to observe and direct where necessary. For example, I have observed that you enjoy eating microwaved chicken nuggets and telling puns bad enough to make my CPU load increase, so I am directing you toward a book for children who think they are funny."

"I see." Ellen pulled out her nuggies and considered. "Anyone ever get you a gift, ROSE?"

"Of course. But it is unnecessary, I assure you; I can simply *imagine* the joy such gifts would bring. Ah! Oh, how very nice! I am imagining you putting on RCGs for the first time, and the joy that would bring me."

Ellen pursed her lips. "You sure you want front-row seats to this? You'll get my worst puns before anyone else."

"My existence is centered around protecting the Korps and its members from things that might cause them harm. If I might intercept a groaner or two before you have a chance to inflict them upon my people, this is a sacrifice I am willing to make."

"How very benevolent of you," Ellen chomped.

She was no longer sure, she had to admit to herself, what was stopping her from putting them on. Vixie had done so quite some time ago and wore them fairly regularly; any secrets they may have had from the Korps were likely no longer secret, if she understood how the devices worked. But there was a tiny… *vestige*, perhaps, of her Hero career, that had her still holding out from letting the Korps directly into her head.

Although a part of her was beginning to suspect that she just enjoyed being impudent for impudence's sake. It was fun to occasionally butt heads with ROSE… or whatever passed for a head on ROSE's end.

And if she put on the RCGs after *that* half-hearted exchange, ROSE would never let her live it down.

"D-do you think they'll like them?"

Vixie's apron was spattered in flour, or sugar, or *something*, as she pulled a tray of little flat brown figures from the oven in her quarters, squinting through RCGs as she carefully eased them up onto the cooling rack above another full row of their gingerbread sisters.

Ellen grinned as she pulled a carton of milk from the fridge — the one *without* Volta's grinning mug on it. "They're going to love it," she assured. "*Perfect* likeness."

Vixie accepted this with a pleased little sound and a nod, slipping the oven mitts off her hands as her sister crossed the room and dropped into the soft couch. In the opposite corner, a Lawful Neutral plushie in a Santa hat was wrapped in the arms of a squishy little Volta (who was, in turn, adorned with little reindeer hooves made of recycled cardboard tubing).

"Do you think Santa's going to know how to find us?" asked Ellen after a nice gulp of milk.

"O-of course!" piped Vixie. "E-everyone here is so *n-nice*, a-and he wouldn't l-leave out so many p-people just b-because they're underground!"

Ellen's lips thinned; surely that was *technically* accurate, but if she had to pick a list for most Korps members to default to, it would be the other one. But then, maybe if they went sixty-nine members per list, those became "nice" lists by default? Korps Math was weird, sometimes.

Besides, the list was generally fairly arbitrary. Vixie was always on the "nice" list, as well as anyone Ellen knew that had been kind to her lately. Generally, the folks who lived in the neighborhood that the twins lived in were prone to get on Santa's list one way or another, as well. Ellen sipped at her milk. She'd have to figure out who Vixie had been making friends with since the move beneath the surface.

"I'm sure Santa will be impressed that you're the one baking the cookies this year," Ellen said mildly. It would be the first year she wouldn't be trapped in the bathroom at three in the morning, too. *Curse you, lactose,* she grimaced.

Vixie grinned, beaming with pride.

Ellen gave a pleased sigh. It was good to see Vixie smiling so *much,* these days.

The days came and went, and Ellen was no closer to figuring out a gift for Vixie than she had been. Korpsmas Eve had not snuck up on her but rather made perfect eye contact as it approached, and still she had not found some toy or sweet or even some knickknack to arm herself with.

Her footsteps carried her through the halls of the base, past costumed supers on pulling sleds and drones trotting about in full elf gear. She was so lost in her thoughts that she ran right into one of Vixie's new "friends," and didn't even stop to figure out *which* before she rattled off an apology and moved on.

The second person she bumped into, however, was... different.

Framed in straight black hair and set behind a pink bubble visor, a pair of deep red eyes stared down a silver-scaled muzzle at her. A very *familiar* pair of deep red eyes — so familiar, in fact, that she had seen them on wanted posters, news articles, and intel dossiers stretching back decades.

Karen.

Her name struck even more fear in the hearts of the Hero community than it did middle management. The dragon before her was the Overlord's second-in-command, after all, and moving belowground had revealed that even with a light shed on the mystery of how, exactly, she seemed to move from one side of the continent to the other in mere moments, the truth was sometimes worse than the mystery.

Karen wasn't "Karen." She was *"Karens."* Dozens of them, at *least,* that Ellen had seen, and that was just around GLW and RIV. For all she knew, there were *hundreds* in total, most identical and *all* of them linked in a telepathic hive mind that Ellen could only try not to think too hard about.

The Overlord of the Korps did not have *a* second-in-command. The Overlord of the Korps had the most well-coordinated army the planet had ever seen, and...

And its most immediately visible representative stood head and shoulders and tits above her, garbed in a *very* comfortable-looking rendition of Saint Nick's trademark attire, from the floppy hat to a pair of wide-buckled boots.

Realizing she'd been standing frozen for too long, she willed her hands upward, finger-gunsing in a reflex far too delayed. She could feel her face, grin unnatural, eyebrows tortured into a peak that might have passed for charming if it were not nearer a bizarre approximation of rigor mortis.

Karen's own brow rose at a glacial pace. She stared at the little vixen that had stumbled into her, muttering and rubbing her chin like a scatterbrained private eye, and Ellen felt as if she could see right through her. She felt suddenly naked and had to glance down to ensure that she wasn't. If the Korps's most dangerous officer could evaporate her clothing with but a glance — well, it would hardly be *off-brand.*

It was some time before she returned her attention to Karen. The dragon seemed to be waiting patiently for it, in fact, pointing both of her index claws straight at her.

Oh God, I'm screwed. Telepaths, are you listening? My last will and testament is as follows:

It took until Karen cocked her thumbs and clicked her teeth that she realized what she was doing.

"At last, we properly meet, Ellen Foxpaw." She inclined her head in a nod so shallow that the shine on her lenses didn't move, and Ellen returned the gesture as barely as she could manage. Karen's voice was *fairly* familiar, although she supposed that wasn't entirely surprising, given her ubiquity in the Hero world.

"You don't need to be nervous," she assured. "Just think of me as a boss whose teeth are perfectly fine where they are."

Ellen nearly choked. As she moved to get out of the way, Karen shook her head.

"Walk with me, Ellen." Her arm fell over the short foxgirl's shoulders, and she set an easy pace; Ellen was thankful for that, at least. "You must be troubled. I'm given to understand that you have been unusually restless of late, and to my knowledge, it is uncommon for you to collide with others while walking. What is bothering you?"

Ellen's ears twitched. No matter how many times she'd been proven wrong, she was still having trouble getting used to how often aid would find her hand while she was still hesitating to reach for it.

She supposed, then, that there was little harm in asking.

"Well, uh. Do you know where Vixie is?"

Karen blinked. "Is that all? Vixie has asked that her location always be freely available to you." A few lights flickered across her RCG's. "She can currently be found —"

"No need! I just wanted to make sure we wouldn't run into her." *Oh God, I just cut her off.* Karen seemed to take it in stride. "I'm just… having trouble finding a present for her."

The supervillain tilted her head quizzically at the fox. "That should be no trouble. You can simply put in a request, and a drone will retrieve it for you and bring it to your quarters."

"I'm having trouble *choosing* a present," Ellen clarified.

"Ah." A flicker of… *something*, behind that visor. She got the distinct impression that it was mischief and had to decide whether she should be irritated. Ellen realized that Karen probably had known the source of her problem from the start.

Karen continued before she could make up her mind.

"That is not that uncommon, actually. Especially among new members — in fact, it was not so very long ago that Agent Bypass came to me with a similar concern. Are the two of you well-acquainted?"

Ellen raised a hand and wobbled it noncommittally. Bypass's story was almost emblematic of the Korps's philosophy: a down-on-their-luck skunk who had turned to stealing from ATMs until a Hero had ambushed them. When they had been released from the hospital, it had been no surprise when they'd disappeared shortly thereafter. That the Korps had soon after premiered a mephitine supervillain with a penchant for getting around security had been even less surprising, to the point that even local news had predicted their trajectory on-air while the skunk that would become Bypass was still in a hospital bed.

But there was a difference between being well-acquainted with one's story and being well-acquainted with the person themselves, and Ellen did not suppose having once sat in the same cafeteria qualified.

"More's the pity," tutted the dragon, tapping her chin thoughtfully. "I think a friend like them would be *very* helpful to you in times such as these."

Ellen cleared her throat. It was a long shot, and she felt *small* asking, but...

"I was actually kind of hoping *you* could help me?"

Karen gazed down at her with sympathetic red eyes beneath the white, fluffy trim of her hat. Ellen wasn't sure what to brace herself for. Was the Korps's most dangerous officer going to whisk her off on some sort of magical adventure? Teach her the true meaning of Korpsmas? Reach into her jacket and pass her the perfect gift for Vixie? Ellen leaned in, holding her breath in eager anticipation.

"No," said Karen. She threw her head back and laughed into the back of her hand as she walked away, leaving Ellen behind as her "OoooOOOOhohoho!" echoed off the walls.

"Hey, Vixie." Ellen turned the Santa hat over in her hands. She'd already looked it over — inside and out — three times, but it *had* dropped off Karen's head when she walked away, and Ellen was desperate enough to hope to find a clue inside.

Vixie was just sliding a kringle off of the tray onto a platter; she was settling into her quarters nicely. It was rare to have countertops at a comfortable level for the two of them, and Vixie had never been so at home in the kitchen.

"I-I made a m-mini one for you!" she squeaked, lifting a smaller pastry from the center of the ring.

Ellen's eyes lit up, and with an "ooo!!" she slammed the hat onto her head to forget about it, leapt over the couch, and snatched it out of Vixie's offering hands. "You've gotten really good at this," she tried to say, but what came out was "Eemv o'en urrlee gmmdts," as well as a few flakes of Danish pastry.

"I-it's been g-getting easier! M-Miss ROSE taught me a lot of the r-rules. And I'm g-good at following rules." At that, Vixie's ears lowered, her tail swishing behind her, and Ellen raised her eyebrows. It was easy to tell when her sister was flustered.

"Do your quarters have a fireplace?" Ellen asked, changing the subject.

"O-oh! N-no, but w-we can get one n-next year if y-you'd like!"

Ellen chuckled. "I'm not worried about it. Everything's so technological these days. Did you know that they've made it so you can get a Christmas fireplace set up online now?"

Vixie blinked, thinking it through. "H-how does that work?"

"The same way it's always worked, turns out," she grinned.

"First, Yule Log in…"

Vixie had passed out in her bed like a good girl, and Ellen was left empty-handed on Korpsmas Eve. She found herself standing in the hallway outside of her own quarters, arms folded, head tilted up to stare at the ceiling… when the echoing *click, click, click* of footsteps started to approach from down the hall. She tilted her head toward the source of the noise and offered a small little smile as she saw who it was.

"You're looking blue," said the cat, her steps slowing to a stop in front of her. "Nice outfit, though."

Ellen smiled; from her big black boots to the red coat and hat, she looked the part of Saint Nick. She had even put on a bushy white beard, although her high cheekbones rose overtop the thick curls.

"It's tradition! Ho ho HOOOOOOOOOOOooooohhhhhhhh..."

Carmen lifted Ellen's dropping chin, locked her amber eyes with the fox's dark browns. "Hey. No one makes that sad a sound who doesn't need cheering up."

Ba-THUMP. There was Carmen, getting *close* to her again. For all of her spats with Volta, she had always understood why the big wolf was infatuated with this cat. She had a way of stepping easy-as-you-please into your personal bubble and licking you right on the eyeball — figuratively speaking, of course — before you even knew you desperately wanted your eyeball licked.

Ellen could feel Carmen's breath on her nose. She tried not to think about it. Usually, *she* was the unflappable one. "It's just —"

"Vixie." As the fox blinked back a look of surprise, Carmen smiled knowingly. "You never get this concerned about *your own* problems, Elle. So, what's wrong with our favorite little hairball?"

Ellen's gaze drifted downwards again — then, immediately, to the side. *Well, if nothing else, she's certainly hung where I can see. It's like a duffel bag stuffed into a pair of plus-size pantyhose! Where does she **put** it when she's off-base?*

"It's just..." she began, forcing her train of thought back onto the rails, "she's... *happy*."

Carmen raised an eyebrow. "Obviously? That's a good thing."

As Ellen struggled to find words to explain the situation, the tabby's eyes lit up.

"You don't have a present for her. *Ellen! It's 11:45!*" she hissed, head swiveling to make sure the hallway was empty. "Okay, okay, okay. I'll help you. How are you not prepared for this? You're a *master* of prep work! You were confident enough in some of those puns back when you fought Volts —"

She froze and looked at Ellen's sheepish expression with a look of dawning horror.

"You were ad-libbing!"

Ellen shrugged.

"She could have *murdered you* and you were —? You're *killing me*, Elle." The tabby cradled her temples between her fingers and let out a long exhale through her nose. Ellen could tell she was flashing back to some of the fights she'd watched through Volta's RCGs.

"For what it's worth, I'm pretty good at ad-libbing?"

Carmen's eyeballs flared, but she didn't say anything more about it. "Okay. Okay. So, you've got a few ideas, at least?"

Ellen shook her head.

"God*dammit*, Elle. Okay, fine. Uh. It's too late to get custom jewelry done, and I've never seen Vixie wear any anyway. Baking stuff? Cute oven mitts?"

"She's already got some. She's *so* happy with her baking situation — first thing I thought of," Ellen pointed out.

"Okay. Sex stuff? No, I've seen her collection, it's already *impressive*. What else does she like?"

"...Hot Pockets?"

Carmen just stared.

"Right. Not giftable. Has to be giftable."

"I'm starting to see why you haven't figured it out yet," Carmen groaned. "Fuck — I have the wrong kind of time powers for this! Think, think, think..."

Carmen paced back and forth through the verdant hall, muttering questions and refutations to herself as she dragged her hands down her face in futile frustration. Suddenly, she straightened and froze, fingers splayed, and pivoted to face Ellen.

"Right!" she snapped. "The problem with all of your gift ideas is that *anyone* could give them. You need to figure out something *sentimental*." She tapped her chin. "And Korpsmas is in ten minutes."

Ellen racked her brain, but it was starting to feel like searching a box that she'd already searched through dozens of times before, looking for a lost item. This time, though, something clicked.

"Grandma's recipes," she whispered.

Carmen smiled. "That sounds promising... But if they were at your old place —"

Ellen shook her head. "No, no. They should be in a safe deposit box."

"Oh, good. We were only able to get some of your stuff —"

"In Wisconsin."

"*Fuck*. Okay. Any other ideas?"

Ellen was tapping her chin. "No. No, this is gonna be it. Do you know where I can find Bypass this time of night?"

Carmen sighed and shook her head, pulling a set of RCGs out of her pocket and donning them.

"You really need to start wearing yours, you know," she reminded.

"I *knowww*," groaned Ellen.

The skunk who opened the door was, surprisingly, dressed in their day clothes. As Ellen blinked up at them, Bypass smirked back. "I was up anyway. Nocturnal, you know." They tossed their hair and left their head at a tilt, looking curious. "Carmen said you needed me for about ten minutes?"

"Yes," said Ellen, hands clasped together in front of her. "I heard that you're the skunk to see if I need a bank robbed?"

"…I was going to say that this isn't where I expected this to be going, but that would be lying. Only a *villain* would do that." They let that one hang for a second, then: "How do you plan on getting me to a bank and back in ten minutes?"

Ellen adjusted her hat and cleared her throat. "Well, I think it's gonna be pretty tight, but that shouldn't be a problem," she said, swiveling her eyes up to meet Bypass's over the big white beard, "unless you're… *Claus*-trophobic?"

Bypass let out a pained sigh, but it was too late; Ellen grabbed their hand, and they were gone in a swirl of pure snow and Christmas magic.

"Right, so, Santa magic. I have to eat any milk and cookies I come across, I can enter any residential building instantly, and time moves so slow it makes Carmen look less like Supersonic and more like Garfield," Ellen explained, as she led Bypass across the street. "There's some other stuff, but we don't really have time to get into it."

"...Didn't you *just* say that time slows to a crawl?" asked Bypass.

"Santa magic's finicky. Technically we have exactly as much time as we need," she explained, "but only just. And if we stay too long... well, have you ever heard of Santa doing *anything* after sunrise?"

"That's a 'no.' ...So we wouldn't be able to teleport home. I get it."

Ellen nodded. "Right," she said, as the pair came to a stop in the doorway, which slid open automatically, as if it had not even been locked for the night. "Before I forget, I wanted to thank you for helping me."

She reached into her jacket, and pulled out an oblong, wrapped package. Between the long, flat piece and the four wheel-shaped nodes on one side, it wasn't subtle.

Bypass's eyes widened as Ellen pressed it into their hands. "How did —? Oh. Santa magic."

"Well, don't sound so let down about it!" Ellen chuckled, sticking her tongue out. "Skunks today, so desensitized by movies and television..."

Bypass tore into the packaging, and soon was holding a slick, California longboard.

Ellen cleared her throat. "I know a snowboard might be more useful right now, but..."

"No," whispered Bypass. "It's *perfect*." With a run-up, Bypass sailed through the doors, and Ellen slipped in behind them.

Ellen had never been into a bank after-hours. In the dim light from the windows, she could see a small counter for the tellers and a few simple, closed wooden doors. Hard tile floors gave a satisfying *k-thnk-k-thnk-k-thnk* as Bypass rolled over them and did slow circles in the lobby.

She was *just* wishing that she'd brought a flashlight when the overheads lit up.

"I haven't been in a bank this small in *years*," Bypass said kickflippingly. "It's kind of adorable."

"Not a lot of need for fancy security in Nowhere, Wisconsin," Ellen shrugged. "Do you know where the safety deposit boxes would be?"

"'*Do I know where the safety deposit boxes would be*,'" Bypass scoffed. They glided over the tile and pushed a door without touching the handle;

it swung open without a complaint, and faster than the skunk had even nudged it.

"Excellent." Ellen was a little less graceful getting over the counter, but she was back on her feet in no time. "Hey, do you know how they get money out of the bank in Texas?"

Bypass slowed their roll enough to tilt their head.

"*With drawl.*"

Bypass snorted. "You tell Volta that one yet?"

"I'm working my way up," grinned the fox, slipping into the room.

Rows and rows of numbered lockers made up the wall; Ellen frowned at the sight.

"Do you know which one is yours?"

Ellen grimaced. "Actually, no."

"Nooooot a problem." Bypass ollied, and as if the rotation of their board was the turning of a few hundred keys, all of the doors swung open.

Ellen whistled. "Remind me to reinforce the lock on my diary."

"Whatever makes you feel safe, dear," chuckled the skunk as they boarded back to the lobby. "Let me know when you find it!"

Ellen knew enough to narrow it down and started rifling through safe deposit boxes. Old letters, some cash, some sort of fancy Hot Wheels car, more than a few engraved old pocketknives, some keys, often with little plastic cheese wedge charms hanging from them…

Ah. An old envelope, reading *niam tais recipes*. Ellen smiled and tucked it into her jacket. She tilted her head back and forth and considered, then scooped the rest into her coat as well. She had storage space, now, and a Korps base was safer than the bank — safer than most places, even.

"All set!" said the festive foxgirl, hustling out. "Is there room on the board for two?"

"It's a *long* board," Bypass pointed out.

"I just wasn't sure if mephit on the board," she said.

Bypass stared.

"I wasn't sure if… *me* fit… mephit…"

They raised an eyebrow.

"…They can't all be winners."

With that, Ellen got behind the skunk, tried to pretend there wasn't a huge bushy tail in her entire face, and held Bypass's waist. With a jingle of Santa magic, they disappeared once more.

Ellen was awoken eight hours later by the gentlest of knocks at the door — followed, immediately, by a much heavier THUD, THUD, THUD.

"Foxpaw! What gives?"

Ellen rolled out of bed and shuffled to the door, pressing the button to open it manually to greet a synthetic zebra and the shorter foxgirl she was holding at bay with one hand, and the long stick she was holding in the other.

"Morning, Maud," Ellen said, blinking sleepily.

"Yes, good morning, Foxpaw. Did you hear me ask 'what gives?' Because I'm still wondering what gives."

"Me," Ellen said. "I thought the 'From' tag was pretty —"

"Why did you give me a broom handle without a brush, Foxpaw?"

She held out her present: a long, straight stick, with a curve on one end and a screw-top on the other.

"It's not a broom," Ellen explained.

"Well, I'm not sticking it inside of me, if that's what you think I'm into."

Ellen smiled. "I can explain. Can you unscrew your head a minute?"

Maud's opticals narrowed, but she nodded; her hands came up, and with a few twists, her head was loose.

"Now hold that out," Ellen said, taking the stick. She twisted the end into where Maud's neck should have gone — careful to twist the stick, and not Maud's head — and then held the whole apparatus out.

"*Oh, my Overlord, I'm a hobby zebra.*"

"Theeeere you go."

"This is so stupid," protested the synth.

"Do you want me to take it back?"

"…Please don't."

Ellen grinned. "Merry Korpsmas, Maud," she said to the retreating zebra, who mumbled it back with her head and, of course, the attached stick in her hands.

She turned her attention to her sister and smiled. "Is it Korpsmas morning already?"

"Y-yes!!" chimed Vixie. "C-c'mon!! Let's g-go!"

It wasn't often Vixie led *anyone* by the arm, but Ellen wasn't about to complain. Soon, the door to Vixie's place opened as she approached, and Ellen grinned at the sight.

Someone had strung up the place with lights, and a short, artificial evergreen had been set up in the corner by the couch. Presents had stacked up beneath it, both Vixie's and her own. Vixie had piled some fried dough on a plate, with plenty of toppings laid out around it, and a pair of mugs of hot chocolate was steaming on the counter.

The festivities went about as one might expect. Ellen and Vixie polished off the entire plate, then waddled over to open presents. As usual, they opened each others' first. Ellen smiled as she peeled back the wrapping paper, and found a handmade, sunny yellow scarf.

She looped it around her neck, grinning in satisfaction, and pulled Vixie close; she'd always wanted to try accessorizing, but never quite had the time to figure it out. Or at least, she'd told herself that. In all honesty, she'd simply never known where to start.

"It's *perfect*. Thank you, Vix."

"I-I'm so glad you like it," giggled Vixie, looking down. "M-Mix Wren helped me p-pick it out, b-but I was s-so worried —"

"I love it." Vixie leaned in, practically aglow with her own satisfaction. Still, Ellen could *feel* her sister's eyes on the small packet in her lap. "All right, your turn. Just — be careful, okay?"

Vixie blinked. She'd never gotten a present that she had to be careful opening — not in Ellen's memory, anyway — because they were in a cardboard box, usually. She picked hers up and gingerly removed the wrapping paper, and her jaw fell when she saw the words on the front.

"G-Grandma's...?"

"Yep."

Vixie fidgeted. "W... w-would she want us to h-have this?"

"Who knows?" Ellen shrugged. "But either she would approve, and she'd want us to have it, or she wouldn't approve, in which case... well, we're villains now, aren't we? We may as well take it."

Vixie giggled, wiping a tear from her eye. "I-I guess so!"

She stared fondly at the envelope for a minute, then gave a happy little sigh and set it aside. She turned her eyes back to Ellen and grinned.

"L-let's open the rest!"

They'd never gotten so many presents in their lives, and most of them were winners. By the time they were down to the last few, Vixie had an updated Lawful Neutral plushie in her lap — now wearing a magenta jacket and an orange jumpsuit with pink helices on it — courtesy of Volta. Ellen was trying not to cry whenever she looked down at her wrist; a simple band, with orange and black on half of it and the other half pink, blue, and white. In big, block letters on a little metal plate, it read: TRANS-SISTERS.

She didn't have to ask, but she *knew* that in the Raynes' quarters, Volta was wearing a matching one just like it. She hoped that she would enjoy what she'd gotten in return: a photo of Ellen shaking hands with Arthur Simonds, from back when the EHA was new. For years, it had bore True North II's autograph; now, it bore hers as well.

"To my second-biggest fan..."

She had snorted when she'd unwrapped Mabel Greysmoke's gift for her — a picture of the winking puma, framed and autographed. Ellen couldn't help but feel like she was holding the rookie card of a rising star.

Her last present, though, was a gift from Carmen; she turned over the boxy shape in her hands, frowning. It *had* to be a book, especially with the way one side of the wrapping dipped when she felt it.

Puzzled, she teased at the corner of the paper until she got a hold and then tore. The first rip revealed the title, and her mouth tightened into a thin-lipped smile.

The title read *1,001 Bad Jokes for Kids.*

Chapter 14

Ellen's Night In

February 14, 2023

Not a lot to really go on, here. She took a deep breath, and on the exhale, felt the topography of the bedding beneath her, the folds of the soft sheets against her bare skin.

Sometimes, she wasn't sure she even remembered how to masturbate. She and her sister had shared a bedroom for almost their entire lives, after all, and the amount of time it took her to find a memory that didn't leave her frustrated was often more than her busy schedule would allow.

No; it was better, she supposed, to try to forge a fantasy from the better scraps. She rolled her lip under her fangs, tried to remember what it felt like to have big, strong hands on her breasts, to look up at someone, to...

With a huff, she groaned and flipped over toward her nightstand. So long ago, and it didn't go anywhere. She banished the image of the cheetah from her mind, hoped he'd broken his dumb legs for a moment before admonishing herself. What else was there to go on?

She couldn't help but feel, on some level, silly. It wasn't like she was in a desert here. Here on base, cups were overflowing no matter how thirsty people got, and they sure did get thirsty.

But she didn't know what she wanted, and the Korps porn library was... daunting. Sure, she had heard plenty of chattering in the halls — it wasn't as if fellow members of the criminal undercity were modest about their sexual habits, and more than once she'd heard breathless praise of how slipping on the pink visor let you experience pornography in ways that were hard to imagine without it.

A fat load of good that did her, though. Her RCGs still rested on the bedside table; a fine film of dust rested atop the lenses.

She sighed, and turned away from them, fingertips drumming the flat space beneath her navel. Her empty quarters gave her plenty of lonely hours to figure this out, and yet she still, somehow... hadn't. The past three nights of attempts had felt utterly like staring at the TV Guide channel for an hour before deciding that there was simply nothing worth watching.

She slipped a finger down, felt the soft ripples of her nether lips on either side of her short fingernail, brain still searching for some train of thought to tune in to.

The fox found herself thinking back to the track captain again. The way his tail had twitched, the way his padded fingers had felt with the claws retracted, the way her lips curved as she leaned in to —

Fuck. She withdrew her finger as if it had touched a hot stovetop and groaned in frustration. It wasn't like...

It's not like...

Ellen grabbed a pillow and pushed it against her face to muffle her screaming. Not being able to find something to dwell on was irritating enough. That the TV in her brain kept tuning to that channel any time she tried to imagine something, anything, was *infuriating*. Feeling the liquid heat rush through her pelvis and flood the base of her spine would have been glorious... if not for the topic.

Ellen flushed it from her mind, flushed cats from her mind. As much as she liked them, her brain was veering into treacherous territory, and... Hesitation turned to waiting as the minutes went by. The vixen's brain rebelled against her; the only images that brought anything to her were the very ones she was trying to bury until she could process them. She clenched her eyes shut and turned again. A deep breath, and she decided to give up for now.

She opened her eyes, ready to push herself up, and... *froze.*

Her breath quickened in her throat, and she felt dazed. Now wasn't the time. Now was *not* the time, this was *not* the reason.

She reached out.

What if it kills me?

She felt the wood of the nightstand against her fingers, followed it from the edge to the charging cradle, to the frames.

Just the one time. Just **once.** *I have to know what it would be like, and then I'll… then I'll stop.*

She put the visor over her eyes.

[It is a **pleasure** to finally meet you here, Ellen Foxpaw.]

Please.

[Of course. Pulling up the sensory experience of sexual intercourse with: CARMEN RAYNE.]

Thank you.

CHAPTER 15

GIVE ME ONE REASON

February 15, 2023

[She is not awake yet but has given you free access to enter. Would you like to?]
"Y-yes, Miss R-ROSE!" Vixie squeaked, bouncing eagerly on her heels. The door slid open before her, and she practically skipped inside.

Her enthusiasm was, as always, dampened by each step into Ellen's quarters. Her sister had always done a good job of keeping their apartment relatively tidy, but ever since they'd been shown to their rooms in the Great Lakes West base, she'd kept her living space as near to "spotless" as she could. In too many ways, it made Vixie think of their old apartment together — but now, somehow sterile.

She'd put the implications together on her last visit, and it had sat queasily in the pit of her stomach ever since.

From the bedroom door, the one sign of life was a very familiar snoring. For an instant she was sent back all over again, this time one of the rare mornings when Vixie was awake before Ellen. More often than not it was the other way around — the shorter twin had especially enjoyed the cozy comfort of sleep when she'd had few others, nodding off before her sister, and waking up late (often only at a gentle prodding) just so that she could groggily wave goodbye, and attend to the breakfast Ellen had made while it was still hot.

Withdrawing from the memory, she stepped through the door. Her sister lay in an uncharacteristic tangle of sheets, one foot jutting over the edge, a pillow halfway over the back of her head at a jaunty angle like a sort of downy lean-to.

"Ellennnnnnnnn," she whispered.

"HNNNGGGKKKKKKKKKKKKNNNNNNNNNNHH-
HHHH," replied Ellen. "HNNKKKT?"

Bare feet carried Vixie over shaggy short carpet to the far side of the
bed. She was beginning to suspect an uneasy night. Not only was Ellen
sleeping in unusually late, but even her dusty RCGs had been knocked off
their perch in the night, gleaming silently from the floor.

They couldn't have had more different nights if they'd tried, Vixie
thought sadly. As far as she knew, Ellen had spent Valentine's Day all
alone, while she had been about as lonely as a drop of water in the ocean
and twice as wet. With ROSE's usual assistance, even her dreams had
been overflowing with gushy warmth and sweetness, but Ellen's...

I wish I could get her to try them, just once...

*[Just this once, I suggest we take a break from suggesting my aid. We do
not want to pressure her too strenuously.]*

The scent in the room was unusual, too. Like sweat, mixed with...

Vixie wrinkled her nose, freezing with recognition, bent halfway over
to retrieve Miss ROSE from the floor. Maybe their dreams hadn't been
quite so different after all, she reasoned. So lost in her own thoughts was
she that she didn't realize Ellen had stopped snoring until she caught an
eye fixed on her from beneath the pillow.

"Mmbfixie," she grunted, blinking as if to catch up on it after too long
spent staring.

"G-good morning, Ellen!"

The athletic fox pushed herself up in her bed, smacking her dry
mouth and groaning lethargically.

"W'time 'zit?"

[It is 11:34AM,] ROSE said aloud from a nearby speaker.

"Mm. D'jeat yet?"

"Y-yes," Vixie nodded, "b-but you should t-too!"

Ellen rubbed the grit from her eyes and squinted around the room,
barren but for the company of her sister and a couple of the barest
necessary furnishings.

"Hey, ROSE. What's cheap?"

[As always, we do not —]

"I know, I know, but like. Resource-wise."

[Would you like breakfast delivered, then?

"May as well include it."

[I'm sorry — include what?]

"The liver."

[You want liver for breakfast?]

"I mean, I don't know what the main course is, but you're the one who asked if I wanted it *de*-livered, so I assumed —"

[Ah. You are being **funny**,] ROSE said, with the tone of an entomologist observing a particularly colorful beetle tap-dancing through a terrarium. Ellen mugged in smug self-satisfaction, rolled, and pushed herself to her feet.

"Liver kind of does sound good, though. Eggs too, maybe? Liver and eggs? Both fried?"

[We can do th —]

"Oooh, and fries."

[Very well.]

Ellen eyed the glasses in Vixie's hands expectantly for a moment.

[...Did you need something else, Ellen Foxpaw?]

"Orange you gonna ask me if I need anything to drink?"

[I was not planning on it, no,] ROSE answered, followed by a distinctive *clunk* and a dial tone that continued until Vixie gingerly placed Ellen's goggles onto their charging port.

Fifteen minutes later, a knock at the door sent Vixie scampering to answer it before Ellen could even begin rising from the couch.

"Hey, remember — you're people, too!" called Ellen fruitlessly after the delivery drone as the door slid shut. She sulked into a kitchen barstool and tapped her thumbnail on the edge of the plate Vixie pushed in front of her. She looked pensive and dissatisfied. "Do you think they even hear me?"

Vixie swallowed her nerves and cleared her throat. "I... I-I don't think you're s-supposed to talk to them th-that way."

"Mm." Ellen, sullen, impaled a bit of crisp organ meat. "I can't help but wonder if that's really what's best for them."

[What's good for one goose is not necessarily good for every gander,] ROSE cut in, [and many prefer to blur the lines between those distinctions to begin with.]

"What do you even *call* a nonbinary goose?"

['Kai,' directly. 'He' or 'they' if you're using a pronoun.]

Ellen looked put out. "Thank you, ROSE. I'll take that under advisement."

With one glass of juice poured for Ellen and one for herself, Vixie trotted around the counter and plopped herself down in the seat beside her sister. Well-practiced, Ellen wedged her liver-laden fork between her teeth, hooked a foot under the base of Vixie's stool, caught her flailing arm, and tugged her seat back onto all four legs without missing a beat.

Vixie's heart raced in her chest as her behind wobbled into stillness on the cushion. A part of her had always kind of hoped that maybe, some day, she'd be kidnapped by a villain, and Ellen would rescue her as easily as she looked after her at home. It was hardly a new thought. Even before Ellen had started Hero work, Vixie had had fantasies of her as a knight, gallant and daring, racing to rescue her from an enormous — yet distinctly feminine — dragon.

And then she *had* been kidnapped. Sort of. There was even a dragon! But part of her worried that her knight had been broken in her saving; she'd finally taken off her armor but had quickly grown a shell in its place.

Miss ROSE? Can you... help her?

[We would very much like to,] said the AI silently in the shorter demivixen's mind, [But this can sometimes be beyond our control. We will continue to do our utmost to help her feel at home here — and to enable you to do so as well — but in the end, it all comes down to what she is able to accept.]

Vixie did her best to swallow that along with her orange juice and found it didn't wash down easy. She *had* to try. Ellen had *always* tried for her, and now... now it was *her* turn.

"S-so, uhm. M-Miss Mabel asked me t-to ask you if you h-had time to see her," she stammered. *Maybe if she makes friends —*

"Can't," Ellen hummed, eyes closed. "I'm busy today."

Vixie could practically feel her own heart sinking. "O... oh."

"I'm spending time with my *faaaaaaavorite* sister!" Ellen added. "Tell her to get in touch with my people."

"*I'm* your p-people!" protested Vixie.

"Exactly. And you're busy, so she's gonna have to leave a message."

Vixie refused to give up. "Sh-she said she had s-something for you!"

"Is it gonna expire?"

"W… w-well, no…"

"Good. I'm sure it'll still be hot when I get to it." Ellen made a face that Vixie couldn't quite place, and she suspected there was a joke she didn't quite get — until its meaning, like a note containing the answers to a test, slipped into the fingers of her brain.

"I… I-I still think you should t-talk to her more," Vixie pouted, sinking into her seat.

Her twin affixed her with a helpless look, then heaved a big sigh that only ended when another bite of egg obstructed its exit.

"Alexa, please tell Mabel that she can come visit me any time Thursday."

[Of course. She'll be glad to hear from you.]

"Thanks, Siri," Ellen said, smirking at Vixie. "She must be pretty confident I'll like it. Pretty sure she didn't ask for a receipt."

[I seem to recall Santa Claus herself robbing a bank in rural Wisconsin just a couple of months ago,] the digital home assistant chimed in. [I wonder if any good came of that?]

Ellen's gaze flicked to her fridge, which Vixie knew housed a little bit of leftover naab vaam from her last visit.

"Santa Claus didn't steal those, they belonged to her. Sort of."

[*Legally*, the former contents of that safe deposit box belong to —]

"*Fine!*" Ellen snapped. "I know. I just…"

She trailed off. Vixie waited patiently, even as her concern rose.

"I just… really need a normal day today, okay?"

[Ah.]

Vixie stared, patience now edged with anxious concern as she waited for someone to explain. ROSE, after all, seemed to know… *something*.

[I can tell her, if you would like?]

Ellen hesitated.

"N… no thank you," she finally said — but Vixie's ears were already twitching atop her head, as if to try to flick the knot of mystery undone within it. Her sister took a steadying breath and found something interesting in her fried liver to focus her gaze on. "Vixie. Uh. Do you... uh, have you ever, uh..."

She trailed off, *again*. Vixie's eyes narrowed, ears working overtime as she scrutinized her sister. *Something* was going on, or... or had already *happened*, maybe? What could...?

The smell.

Vixie's nose twitched. It was still *present*, at the corners of her nostrils. Ellen had been acting cagey all morning — what little morning had been left, actually.

"D... did you have s-sex last night?" she finally gasped.

Ellen's eyes widened. "No! Well not... I mean, I uh, solo?"

"Wh-who's that?"

"I mean by myself! Just — *look*, I'm trying to tell you I have a well..." She took a deep breath and — *finally* — pushed through the barrier. "You have to *promise* not to tell anybody, but I... I *think* I might have, uh. A crush."

Vixie *squealed* in delight, as Ellen tried to indicate with a pair of pinched fingers how little her blossoming feelings were in the grand scheme of things, *really* — until the shorter twin lunged forward on her stool and wrapped her arms around her sister, giggling giddily. She gasped, pulling back to look at Ellen. "Is it M-*Miss Carmen?*"

"Wh — how did you *know?*"

"It's a-*always* a cat!" Vixie laughed, bouncing in her seat. "And M-Miss Carmen is the only c-cat you spend t-time with!"

"*Cripes*, Vix! I'm starting to think maybe you *are* suited to villainy after all!"

"Do you wanna *kiiiiiiss* her?" Vixie teased, tail thudding the counter.

"I — I *don't know!* I'm still figuring it out!" Ellen's reddening face squirmed in flustration. "Just... stay quiet about this, okay? Please? I'm not even sure I'm gonna *do* anything about it yet."

It was hard to stay quiet with the *squeal* in her throat! She held her own grinning face, pinky tips in the corners of her mouth.

"*Pleeeeease* don't make a big th —"

"*Ellen and Miss Carmen, s-sitting in a tree! F-U-C —*"

"*Vixie!*"

Vixie's squeaky, barking laugh drowned out Ellen's exasperated protestations until, finally, she wound down and Ellen had to ask if she was quite finished.

"I'm s-sorry!" giggled Vixie, wiping the corner of her eye. "I'm j-just... so *happy* for you!"

Ellen's eyebrow sank. "Happy?"

"Y-yes! M-Miss Carmen is so s-*sweet,* and you haven't h-had anyone s-since..." Vixie trailed off. She still wasn't sure what had actually *happened* between her sister and Connor — just that it had not ended well, and that Connor had not come into school for the next couple of days.

"I don't think I'm gonna 'have anyone' anyway," Ellen protested weakly. "She's... I mean, she's *great,* but like... maybe... a little... out of my league?"

Vixie pouted. "W-what do you mean?"

"I mean, she's — she's *Carmen.* She *saves* people. She's *so* clever, and she's..."

"H-hot?"

"*Yes, Vixie,*" Ellen groaned, burying her face in her arms atop the counter. "She's *hot.*"

"S-so she's perfect!"

Ellen peeked an eye over her generous bicep. "What do you mean?"

"W-well... *y-you're* all those things!" Vixie urged. "S-so... s-so... so y-you should try!"

[For what it's worth, I agree with Vixie. Even if you do not **pursue** Carmen, she would not balk from a frank discussion of your attraction to her.]

"I'll take it under advisement." Ellen pushed herself to her feet, taking the dishes with her to the sink. "But neither of you better breathe a *word* about it until I've given it some time to breathe. I'm not gonna act until I know whether this is just a dumb passing brain thing or if I was just... *horny* or something."

[Surprisingly reasonable. I will respect that.]

Vixie nodded her agreement.

"Besides, she may not 'balk,' but she'd... I mean, you *know* the face she does. She'd do *that* the whole time, and I..."

She trailed off. Vixie stared, as if she might discover why, and then *giggled* when Ellen's mouth twisted and her cheeks went shockingly pink.

"O-oh my gosh — you l-*like* it when she d-does that face!!"

"**Everyone** likes it when she does that face!" Ellen protested. But it was too late. She had *feelings* for Miss Carmen, and Vixie was *determined* to support her, even if Ellen herself wasn't sure yet.

After all, nothing had ever motivated her sister quite like love.

CHAPTER 16

VENTING IMPOSTOR IN THE CAFETERIA

March 2023

Ellen grumbled as she ran her fingernails over her cheek, scratching an itch she'd been feeling too lethargic to bother with as she peered over the edge of the seat cushion at the cell phone resting on the carpet. A few notifications filled the screen: an alert from Supply that the soap she and Vixie liked was in stock and would be delivered to her room this evening if she didn't need it sooner. The EHA had made the news again; and, at the top, a message...

A message from *Carmen*.

> **That Cat: hey u free for lunch or something?**

As she watched, another message popped over the first:

> **That Cat: could use some girl talk and i think u could too**

Ellen let her hand fall onto her phone and opened up the conversation. She didn't *think* she'd been signaling that she needed someone to talk to —

> **That Cat: reading people is my job, don't worry, you're not obvious to EVERYONE ;3**

How Carmen had figured out what she was thinking from "Ellen Foxpaw is typing..." she would never know, but then, Ellen was hardly a mind-reader herself.

She was hardly about to complain, though, and in two minutes, she was rapping her knuckles against Carmen's door.

"Just a minute!" sang the tabby from the other side, and Ellen wasn't kept waiting too long before the big cat opened the door and looked down at the short vixen.

"Did you... *teleport* here?" asked Carmen, squinting down at Ellen.

Ellen did her best to make her shrug seem casual, but she wasn't sure why. She knew Carmen wouldn't buy it. It was a two-minute sprint between their quarters, and Ellen would have had to change into the "Confess to This Mess" cami *and* run the whole way on her... less-than-statuesque legs. And if she *had*, even the athletic vulpine would probably be a little out of breath and not looking half as smooth.

"You hungry now or was that an invitation for later?" she asked. "I have no idea if it's lunchtime."

"You're a *little* early," grinned Carmen, "but I was probably going to sit around for a bit anyway. You wanna head to Grandma's place for brunch?"

Ellen's ears perked straight up. "I could *demolish* some honeydew right now."

The cat's eyes narrowed, and she crossed her arms. "Okay, is that a bit, or are you the one person on Earth that likes honeydew?"

"It's me. I'm the honeydew bitch. People make fruit salads and they're about to throw the honeydew in the trash, 'But wait! What if Lawful Neutral shows up?'"

"That checks out, yeah."

Shortly after they had first been inducted into the Korps, Ellen and Vixie had been introduced to Carmen's grandmother, Cosetta. Seeing two foxes brought into her shop who had barely eaten anything more sophisticated than a free birthday burger at Red Robin in *years*, the cat tossed the gumbo she was working on into the fridge and muttered something incomprehensible. That was when she started putting together batter for the best fried chicken either of the Foxpaws would have ever eaten in their lives.

And when Cosetta casually dropped a few words of Hmong in and among her frequent language-switching, too, she quickly discovered a side of Vixie that only Ellen had ever seen. Vixie had made a point to go out of her way to visit her as frequently as she was allowed ever since, and when Ellen had found *naim tais's* recipes, Vixie had beelined for Cosetta's kitchen at sunrise the next morning.

Grandma C was one of those cats that had aged so well that one might no longer fear aging, if they suspected they might mature half as finely. Some saw her as a sort of surrogate mother or grandmother, and she stepped into the role well. The rest saw her as a drop-dead gorgeous GILF, and from what Ellen had heard, Cosetta stepped into that role just as readily.

Ellen was firmly in the former category. Vixie was in the latter, but that wasn't really any of her business. As it was, Ellen was just happy to drop by her on-base restaurant, grin, and hold out a plate.

"Honeydew me!" she chimed.

"I prefer 'Madama,' but I'll take 'Honey,' just this once," chimed the elder feline.

Carmen chuckled as she watched Ellen's tail stiffen, and her eyes rapidly blink.

"You would think a punster would be more careful with her words, no?" asked Cosetta, tilting her eyes at her granddaughter as the taller tabby ran her tail up the thin material that covered Ellen's back.

"You'd think!"

Ellen, meanwhile, was stiff and straight as a pole, trying not to blush.

"Aww, she's blushing!"

It wasn't working.

"Here, *hma liab*, I saved some for you," Cosetta said, chuckling to herself as she tossed some of the soft green melon onto the frozen fox's dish — alongside a pair of fat sausage links, some corned beef hash, and a couple of eggs over-medium. "Where is your sister? The short one. I've got an itch that she's *very* adept at scratching."

"Grandma, *please.*"

"What?" asked Ellen, finally able to get a word in. "Wait. *Oh.*"

"I didn't need to know that!"

"Ahh, in unison, even! Cute," chuckled the older kitty, shaking her head as she moved back to the stove. She mumbled something in a language Ellen didn't understand — Spanish, maybe? It sounded like Spanish, kind of — and Carmen's expression turned only more haunted before she turned and stepped off to a table, her tail hooking gently under Ellen's arm to guide her along.

"I love her so much and she is going to kill me," Carmen said as she dropped into her seat with her usual grace, but her plate made more of a clatter than usual.

"Does she do that a lot?" asked Ellen, sitting opposite and gesturing with a flick of her ear.

"Not *a lot*," sighed the cat, "only when she's trying to embarrass me. Not that I'm *embarrassed by her*, exactly, but —"

Ellen raised an empathetic hand. "I know what you mean! If she's embarrassing you on purpose, you're not a bad daughter — *grand*daughter — for being embarrassed."

Carmen gave her head a little shake and her hair fell back into place, as if it were simply gravity and a little encouragement that kept her purple stripes looking sharp and smooth. "You get it! She's always been there for me. Like, *always*, always. She's the reason I'm *me*, and not like, some repressed tom too terrified of a pink visor to —" She cleared her throat and offered a friendly grimace. "No offense to present company, of course."

It took Ellen a minute to realize her dining companion was referring to *her*. "Oh! Yeah. I'm... I'll try them on some day. *Soon*. Maybe."

Carmen reached out a padded hand and took Ellen's inside it. The fox could feel her temperature rising between her eyes, that *floating* feeling in her chest. "Hey. You don't need to lie to me, okay? If you're not ready, you're not ready."

Ellen managed to force a smile onto her face, but she could feel in her mouth that it was *wrong*. Obviously fake. "I appreciate that," she said — a misleading truth.

But letting the tabby believe she was lying in the wrong direction was a lot better than letting her know that, once a week, she was slipping on the no-longer-at-all-dusty pair of RCGs and submerging herself in Carmen Rayne smut.

"Look, I'm not gonna pry," said the object of Ellen's fantasies, "but if you *want* to talk to someone about it... you can talk to me, okay?"

Ellen had never swallowed a drier piece of melon.

"I guess I just... I don't know if I know who I *am* anymore, y'know?"

Carmen affixed her with an apprising gaze. "Aside from a big dweeb?"

"Okay, when it comes to dweeb sizes in the Korps, I am —"

"Sorry, a *very condensed* dweeb."

"*Thank* you," Ellen grinned. "I guess I feel like, before I have a real, proper heart-to-heart with ROSE, I should probably know what's *in* my heart, y'know?"

Besides you.

"Figuring out who you are now that you're not in Big Sister mode all the time? Makes sense; you've been here a few months now. How's the adjustment?"

"Honestly?" began Ellen. "It's just... I have so much *time* now. Like, I always used to spend some time on the treadmill, and I *like* running, but it was so important that I stay in fighting shape, but Now I can just *jog* for *fun*, and I don't have to push myself unless I *want* to push myself, and I can just stop and chat with people. You know, I used to jog around town, but I kind of stand out. Sometimes I'd get stopped by fans, so it wasn't really a good work-out, you know? And I've always wanted to try getting into tennis, but I never really had the *time*, and I'm trying to find a good partner to play with because, like, I'm *sporty*, but I'm not a seven-foot-tall monument to athleticism, y'know? Hoping I can get some kinda-even ground."

Carmen smiled and nodded, sipping at something that Ellen hadn't paid quite enough attention to know for sure what it was. It may have been orange juice, but she supposed it might have been a mimosa.

"How's the adjustment to that going for you, anyway?" asked the cat. "The seven-foot-tall monuments, the foot-and-a-half-inch dicks, the tiddies as big as your head?"

"The whole Korps aesthetic?" grinned Ellen, glancing out over the other tables. "Honestly, I'm kind of used to feeling out-of-place," she admitted.

Her ears drooped, and Carmen reached out. "Hey. That's the whole point here — no one is out-of-place, people can look how they *want* to."

The foxgirl nodded and offered a side-eyed smile. "For what it's worth, it's been months since someone described me as 'exotic' to my face, so I'm definitely reaping the benefits."

"Oof."

"You wanna hear something fucked up?"

"No? Yes? Yes."

"Someone saw me once, and asked, 'Whoa, what happened to your... *all* of you?'"

"Oh, Jesus, hon, I am so sorry. Do you need me to punch someone?"

"Nah, I set them straight. Ever since I got famous — or, uh, infamous, now? — demimorphism visibility is *way* up."

"True enough!" agreed Carmen, although she froze when she noticed Ellen squinting at her.

"Hold on. Wait — *how* long have you been in the Korps?" The vulpine pointed the back end of her fork as she appraised her.

"I wasn't a fan."

Ellen's face froze again, and she sighed. "How do you —?"

"You're trying to figure out if I looked up to Heroes while you were active, and if so, whether I looked up to *you* specifically," grinned Carmen. "*God*, you're obvious."

Ellen sucked on the inside of her cheek a moment. "I mean... you're right," she admitted.

"I was an awkward tom in Louisiana, Elle. I didn't spend much time focusing on heroes way north of me."

Carmen tilted her head to follow Ellen's face as it turned away and looked at an adjacent empty table for a moment.

"You all right, Elle?"

"I just... kinda hoped I'd inspired *all* kinds of people, I guess," she sighed. She was quiet for a moment, but just as the feline opened her mouth to respond, she added: "Is that too self-centered?"

"Well, it's probably for the best I didn't idolize you." Carmen reached across the table and hooked a claw under Ellen's chin, bringing her attention back. "I'd have been *so* disappointed when you defected to the Korps."

Ellen giggled and tried not to panic at Carmen's touch. She did a good job, except for the tail stiffening out behind her and having to force her ears not to go sideways with all of her willpower. "I think you'd have forgiven me, eventually," she said, trying to stick her tongue about but finding that her mouth was too busy smiling, and it looked weird, probably. It definitely *felt* weird, anyway, but Carmen seemed to be letting her get away with it.

They were quiet for a few moments as they turned their attention back to their meals; Cosetta's hash was always perfectly crisped, and honestly, Ellen was happy to eat damn near anything that she dropped onto her plate. She'd once seen Vixie dive after some scraps that had fallen on the kitchen floor, in fact.

"So, was there anything in particular you wanted to girl talk about?" asked Ellen. "I told you about *my* inner struggles; what's rattling around the kitty noggin?"

Carmen nibbled on the end of her fork. "Before I talk to you, I want to make it very clear that I'm *trusting* you with this."

"No blabbin'."

"No blabbin'."

"Agreed!"

Carmen leaned back in her chair and let out the breath leak out of her mouth.

"So, you know how Volta's kind of... hard-headed sometimes?"

"Is that the secret? Because I'd have to stuff an awfully large cat into an awfully small bag for that one," Ellen pointed out.

"Empire Enhancements can help you with that," quipped the awfully large cat.

Ellen had learned not to be drinking anything when Carmen spoke and was suddenly grateful she'd had that lesson.

"No, no. It's more like... Volta's actually pretty non-confrontational."

The fox raised an eyebrow — the very eyebrow that had taken a few weeks to grow back properly after one of their confrontations, back in the day. She couldn't help but thumb her wristband thoughtfully.

"I mean in *private*. When she's Volta, not Redline. Which is — I mean, you don't *want* to have someone who's always ready for a *fight* in a relationship, but sometimes you need to be *direct*, especially in a poly relationship."

"Not a lot of experience there, but I'd imagine so, yeah," agreed Ellen.

"You would! You *would* imagine so!"

"And yet..."

"*And yet!* Look, Elle, I can read people, right? Like, that's my *job*. But if I spend all day reading people, when I get home, I need an *audio* book."

"She's gotta read *herself* to *you*."

"Exactly! And not just for my sake. She needs to have the self-confidence — the self-*worth* — to talk to me when there's a problem."

"Hard to believe a girl like Volta has self-esteem issues," Ellen interjected.

"First thing you learn in spy school? So does *everyone*."

"Fair enough!" chuckled Ellen. "Feelings are hard to talk about, I imagine, when you didn't grow up with anyone to practice with."

"Too true, Elle. Whereas *you* grew up with Vixie, so you're not insecure about your feelings at *all*."

Carmen waited patiently for Ellen's reply, while Ellen tried not to look directly at her for fear of spontaneous immolation. Regardless, the vixen cleared her throat after what felt like an eternity. "It did help, yeah. In, uh. In that way. So, do you... are you looking for solutions, or just venting?"

"Oh, just blowing off steam," chuckled the cat. "It's important to do that now and then, you know. Otherwise, you might just boil over and say something before you've figured out how to say it."

"Yeah, absolutely!" *You have no idea how right you are.* "I suppose that's the sort of thing that takes a lot of patience."

Carmen's kitty lips spread into a toothy grin. "Thankfully, I have a *lot* of patience for people who aren't being completely honest with themselves."

"That's a good skill to have," Ellen said as she pondered that grin. Doubtless, she was considering some period where she'd taken her sweet time with the electric lupine. If only she knew...

"I love her *so much*, though," sighed the tabby, slouching into her seat and raising her saucer to her lips for a few laps. "Speaking of... you've been on-base for, what, five months now? Six?"

"Something like that, yeah."

Carmen leaned in, held her saucer off to the side while she eased her chin onto her free hand. Her breasts threatened to spill out of her top and onto the table, and Ellen felt a pang in her gut, knowing that if they *did*, Ellen would have leapt across the table and done obscene things to them, right there in public.

"You got your eye on anyone yet?"

Eyes? Yes, your eyes are up... somewhere else. I've lost track. I'm lost down here in Kitty Titty Valley and they're not sending a rescue chopper.

"Nope," lied Ellen.

"Really? Well, hey, if you *do* start crushing on someone you'll let me know, won't you?"

"Of course!" lied Ellen again, lyingly.

She finally looked up from Carmen Canyon at the tabby's face, which had a look so penetrating that Ellen was sure the Breeding Labs could get twice as much work done if they simply installed a window for her to peer into.

"Say, Carmen. Did you hear about that time Omega put nails in her gloves?"

Carmen's eyebrows went up, but her stare didn't change.

"She got caught spiking the punch!"

Carmen huffed through her nose, and Ellen used her now extra-pointy knuckles to pick a shred of sausage from her teeth.

"Do the jokes ever get better?"

"They get worse, actually," admitted the fox.

"That's what I was afraid of," sighed Carmen, tut-tutting. "Oh well. Hey, I've got somewhere to be." The big cat pushed herself forward; if her face and her breasts formed two sides of a triangle, Ellen's flushed expression would have formed the hypotenuse.

"Elle, if you ever need to get something off your chest... let me know, okay?"

Ellen closed her eyes in an attempt to be respectful, not to mention to control herself. She was starting to feel dizzy, as if her heart was pumping thinner blood than usual all of a sudden. "Of course! And... you too, okay? It was really nice to talk with you."

Carmen was silent for a moment, then laid a quick, definitely-platonic kiss right between Ellen's ears before she withdrew.

"See you around!"

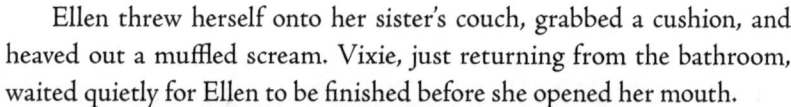

Ellen threw herself onto her sister's couch, grabbed a cushion, and heaved out a muffled scream. Vixie, just returning from the bathroom, waited quietly for Ellen to be finished before she opened her mouth.

"S-so... h-how was your d-date with M-Miss Carmen?"

The pillow returned to cover Ellen's face, but it did nothing to hide the red that flushed her twitching ears.

"Wh — it wasn't a date!"

She suddenly felt the full weight of Vixie's bottom drop onto her legs; there would be no escaping.

"M-Miss Volta said it w-waaaaas."

Ellen peeked over the edge of the pillow and saw Vixie leaning into the couch cushion and grinning wide.

"...Wait. *Wait*. Oh my *God. VIXIE. I FUCKED UP.*"

Chapter 17

Observational Log Lnc23417

April 17, 2023

Synthetic fingers curled around a broom handle as Maud pushed fur from twelve different species into a dustpan that had extended from her hoof.

She had to wonder if janitors outside the Korps had an easier time with it. Sure, most people shed no matter where you went, but one had to reason that a five-foot-eight wolf probably shed less than an eight-foot-tall one. If nothing else, the fur was probably smaller, and less inclined to get wound around her pistons.

It probably wasn't *statically charged*, either, for that matter.

She let her knee joint disconnect, then finished removing her lower leg manually, tipping the calf reservoir into a tall, rolling trash can.

Speaking of eight-foot-tall wolves, there she was now. Volta walked hand-in-hand with Carmen. The big lupine was one of the few that made Carmen look short, but the smitten look that Volta had plastered on her face whenever she was around her feline girlfriend made her look like a big, happy puppy.

People-watching was one of the perks of janitorial duty, and Maud was happy to do so. Some members of the Korps got their adrenaline highs charging through a line of cops; Maud got hers from finding juicy gossip. It was perhaps not the most *esteemed* way to get one's kicks, but it wasn't like anyone complained when the zebra sidled up beside them and chimed "Guess what *I* learned today!" in a synthesized singsong tone.

Maud snapped her leg back on, felt the magnets and circuits reconnect and come alive. With a quick test, forward and back, she was satisfied; she put her weight back on it and watched Carmen and Volta pass under the archway to the cafeteria. She grabbed the lip of the trash can and turned, ready to move down to the next hallway, when someone else caught her eye.

Meandering down the hall was a familiar fox, shorter than Maud by a head, heavy in the chest and athletically-built everywhere else. Usually, the synthetic zebra would light up at the sight of her — Ellen was always good for shenanigans — but of late she had seemed... *distracted* and now was no exception.

Without a word, Maud moved and stood in Ellen's path.

Ellen didn't notice until the two of them were both halfway to the ground, Ellen yelping in surprise as Maud went rigid and broke the fox's fall with a loud *thump*. The broom clattered to the ground noisily beside them.

"Oh my gosh — Maud! I'm sorry, are you okay?" asked the former Heroine, pushing herself to her feet and extending a hand to help the synth up.

"I don't know," groaned Maud, "I think I might have a concussion. Ooooooogh, the paiiiiiin..."

It took a few seconds for Ellen to squint at her, but when she finally did, she knew the game was up.

"Synths don't —"

"Synths can't get concussions, yeah," she grinned. Usually, Ellen wouldn't have bought it for an instant. "You okay?"

"Yeah," said the fox, rubbing at her wrists; she'd done her part to avoid falling entirely on Maud, and probably scuffed herself in the process. Maud wasn't built as a medical unit, but even her basic scan didn't reveal anything beyond a light bruising, at most.

She was just glad she hadn't been waxing today.

"Where ya headed?" Maud stooped to pick up the broom and pretended to sweep the already-clean floor. It's not like Ellen was going to notice.

"I was, uh. Gonna go vixit Visie, I think."

Maud raised an eyebrow.

"Visit Vixie, I mean," Ellen corrected.

"That sounds nice and wholesome!" chimed Maud. "It's been a wholesome day overall. I saw seven Karens on a date this morning, and Volta and Carmen —"

Ellen's eyes, previously unfocused, were suddenly at rapt attention. Her tail stiffened and her ears pointed straight at Maud.

Maud pretended not to notice, but it's exactly what she expected.

"— just passed by on their way to the cafeteria. A bit late for lunch. Have you already eaten?"

"Uh, ye — no. Yeah, no, I haven't, I. I should probably stop for a bite, right?"

"Mm-*hm*."

And then she was off, without so much as a "see you later." Not left at the turn, toward Vixie's quarters, but right, toward the cafeteria. Of course, Maud had spotted Ellen leaving the cafeteria barely an hour ago, a toothpick in her teeth and a contented look on her face.

Sure.

"*ROSE, if possible, I would like to stream Cafeteria Camera 2, please.*"

[*I will be watching as well,*] came the familiar voice of the AI, with a hint of mischief behind her voice.

Maud felt a processor core shift its attention, and quite suddenly, she was peering down into the mess hall, just as present there as she was here in the hallway, moving toward the next floor on her route that needed sweeping.

She saw Ellen, glancing around more than she needed to. The demimorph had *obviously* spotted Carmen already, and her glances always stopped briefly on her, but she had the good sense to randomly lay her gaze a few other places as well, so as not to seem obvious — as if *that* ship hadn't already sailed.

Blip! One of the chairs lit up in pink — or at least, it did to Maud. [*I bet she will sit there,*] said ROSE, and Maud had to concede she was probably right. Two tables behind Carmen, but with an unobstructed view.

The tabby, for what it was worth, hadn't seemed to have noticed Ellen at all yet, and her ears didn't even twitch when the fox scooted the pink-lit chair too loudly and cringed. ROSE played a little fanfare in a minor key in praise of her own judgment, and Maud could feel her self-satisfaction as tangibly as she could feel the broomstick in her hands.

ROSE zoomed the camera in to offer a clearer view.

"*Look at that face. She's smitten as a kitten!*"

[Aww!]

Ellen sat, chin propped up on the heel of her palm, a longing look in her eyes as she nudged the fish on her plate with the wrong side of her fork. A smile had crept into the corner of her mouth and slowly pushed it further into a grin until her pointed teeth were on full display.

The chinchilla beside her gave her a quizzical look, then followed her stare to Carmen. With a roll of their eyes, they went back to their meal, muttering something that very well may have been, "So much for small talk."

Until, that was, the *instant* Carmen's head began to swivel in her direction. Ellen tore her gaze away, pretended to be idly scanning the cafeteria — and in the process — missed Carmen's knowing smirk and eyebrow-arch.

"Do you think there's anyone on-base that doesn't know?"

[Everyone on-base who is currently wearing Rose-Coloured Glasses knows.]

*"That's **awesome**. She still thinks she's subtle."*

[Lawful Neutral was given a D rank in subterfuge... Should we be concerned that she does not seem to realize this?]

"Only if — wait, a D? I got a C."

[Yes.]

"Huh."

Maud's attention was drawn back to the feed, even as she mopped up some spillage that had occurred in one of the weapons labs. Carmen had risen, given Volta a kiss on the cheek, and seemed to be heading for the condiments station — right past Ellen.

The big tabby pretended not to notice, even as her tail slipped over the foxgirl's shoulder. Maud hadn't patched into the audio, but from the way Ellen's body tensed and her jaw dropped, she could tell that the former Hero had probably just let out a squeak much like her sister had the other day, when Maud had —

— Well, that was something to dwell on after her shift was over. Or maybe to *repeat* when her shift was over, if Vixie was available.

[Agent Carmen has recently requested perfume containing red fox pheromones. I thought that might be relevant.]

"That is amazing. And she still thinks Carmen doesn't know!"

Ellen's eyes followed the big cat as she walked away — and in the process, completely missed Volta chuckling at the foxgirl's blatant crush two tables down.

The rest of the fox's misbegotten second lunch was similar. For almost fifteen minutes, Ellen was clearly picturing herself where Volta was, while Carmen pretended not to notice the short vixen making heart eyes at her.

With their meals finished and whatever topic they were on drawing to a close, the happy couple rose from their seats and left their plates at the dish rack, heading down the hallway arm-in-arm. Maud had never been sure which of them to be jealous of, but clearly, Ellen didn't have that issue.

Speaking of Ellen, the small fox slowly pushed herself up from her chair, leaving her plate behind, food barely touched. Maud made a mental note to check to see if her cafeteria manners were *normally* this horrendous, as Ellen followed after them at a pace that was almost *too* leisurely.

The camera stream switched off as Ellen's tail and legs disappeared past the door frame, and Maud frowned. The fox was past the reach of the publicly-available cameras. She could request access, or...

The synth opened the door to the weapon lab and stepped out, trailing her mop bucket behind her. There was Ellen at one end of the hallway, on the other side of the bend, Carmen and Volta chattering about what to get Maud for her assembly date. She quietly struck that section of her dialogue transcript from her memory. It would be a shame to have ruined the surprise, after all.

But as an early present to herself, she waited until Ellen was just walking past, then snatched her by the shirt collar and tugged her into the weapons lab.

"Oh, hi Maud!" said Ellen, a little too chipperly. She had probably forgotten to be irritated at the sudden yoinking.

"Hey, Ellen. I know it's none of my business, but you're someone I can trust, so I'm coming to you."

Ellen glanced downward.

"*Not like that!*"

"Oh."

"No, no, no. I'm just... I'm a little worried for Carmen."

"Carmen?"

Ellen had perked up, just like before.

"Yeah. I'm a little concerned — see, I've noticed that she's got a *type*, and I'm worried she'll fall for just about anyone that fits it. She's a sweet girl, and she can handle herself, but have you noticed that Volta and Wren have… well, more than a few things in common?"

Maud watched as Ellen searched her memory; she wasn't sure if the fox had interacted with Wren much, but with how often she seemed to hang around the Raynes, it seemed plenty likely. She decided to help jog her memory:

"Pierced ears, cropped jackets, dramatic lipstick colors… those socks that leave your beans hanging out…"

"Okay, yeah…?"

Maud let herself pause for a moment, as if just now thinking of something. "…Actually, it occurs to me that she's more than capable of handling herself. Just because she has a *type* doesn't mean anyone would try to exploit that! And to think I was worried about *Carmen* of all people — I don't know what I was getting at!"

Ellen blinked at her; she was clearly trying to look annoyed at having been taken aside, but it didn't take a people-reader to see that she considered it an accidental gift.

"Sorry! I'll let you go, then."

"Sure. Thanks, Maud!"

Maud had to stop herself from making Ellen question why she'd just thanked her.

The next morning, Maud made sure that she had plenty to do just outside Ellen's quarters.

Just as expected, the fox stepped out bright-eyed and bushy-tailed in the morning. The bare midriff and jacket looked good on her with the shimmering orange lipstick, but she was clearly not used to her new ear piercings and fiddled with them as she made her way down the hall.

It was going to be another interesting day in the Korps.

Especially if she could point Volta in her direction.

Chapter 18

By Their Jackets

April 18, 2023

Ellen was nervous. She hadn't put a lot of thought into her outfits in… well, she'd *never* put a lot of thought into her outfits. Camis were comfy, and jeans were dependable. A quick jacket over top was about all the accessorizing she needed. The only trouble was finding a supportive bra, and the Korps technology for that was generations ahead of the curves.

Today, though, was *different*. Today, she was going to stand out. She'd spent all of the previous evening pulling up grooming videos on her tablet, practicing in the mirror, and she *still* had needed to wake up an hour and a half early just to make sure everything was… *right*.

And it *was*. Probably. She wasn't actually certain; she'd never worn an outfit that bared her midriff, aside from a swimsuit. Even her old Hooters uniform had covered her belly. It made the nervous pit in her stomach feel *completely* visible. She had to remind herself that no one would know she was on edge if she didn't let them know.

Confidence.

She'd fought Redline before and even took a few swings at her without any powers active. *Surely* just a change of wardrobe wasn't as scary as an eight-foot-tall lightning murder-wolf.

…And yet…

The hallway outside of her quarters was, thankfully, nearly empty, aside from one synthetic equine janitor. The Korps's acceptance of more-varied sleeping patterns had practically evaporated the concept of a "rush hour," and the fox had never been more grateful for this than today.

Ellen offered the zebra a quick wave and received one back.

At least Maud didn't seem to find her change in attire noteworthy. The fox pondered whether synths really ever took note of personal fashion. It seemed the sort of thing that might be overlooked, but then, Maud had clearly demonstrated some preferences and appreciations for certain aesthetics before. She'd even noticed when Ellen had cut her hair.

Admittedly, it had been to thank her for shedding less — "Nothing worse than a bunch of long hairs in the wrong place, believe you me!" — but she had still *noticed*.

With a clear of her throat, Ellen threw out the first pleasantry she could think of. "Workin' hard or hardly workin', Maud?"

Maud didn't say anything, but she leveled a look at Ellen that could have bent glass. Ellen chose to continue, undeterred, with a pat across Maud's scalp as she passed by.

"Hey, as long as you don't have a case of the Mondays!"

"*Jesus Christ on a Popsicle stick cross*, Foxpaw, it's fucking *Tuesday*," the zebra retorted with narrowed eyeports, the magenta in her eyes flickering with a color Ellen would best describe as *Killbot Crimson*. "I did not know it was possible to look like *that* and still be a shitty office dad."

"Anything is possible if you set your mind to it!" chimed the vixen, as she turned a corner and left Maud behind.

She was channeling her nerves into sheer frenetic *energy*. It was hardly new territory, given how often she'd faced down supers a foot and a half taller than herself back in her Heroing days, radiating murderous intent with surprisingly-frequent literality. Hell, she'd managed to do that against *Redline*, who was —

— Who was standing right in front of her, actually, peering down her crooked muzzle at the vixen like she had just found a piece of bone in a particularly complicated math problem.

"Ho-lee *shit*, Standup." Volta's lips tensed. Ellen wasn't sure why, exactly, until she snorted. She was clearly trying to hold back laughter.

"Is… is it too much?" She had already been self-conscious, and the wolf's reaction was all but confirming it.

"I mean, that depends on what you're *going for*, and it *looks* like you're trying to cosplay *me*." Her eyes narrowed, and the massive wolf leaned down to peer more closely at her outfit. "Never tried the yellow pleather, though. It looks *good*. But… what *are* you going for here?"

This is going well…

Ellen plastered an unflappable grin across her face. She could *feel* how fake her smile was, but it didn't stop her from lying through her teeth. "Just trying a new look! Exploring new possibilities for myself, y'know?"

"Mm-*hmm*." Volta's expression was unyielding. "Who are you *really* trying to impress, Elle?"

She froze.

Frick.

Fuck.

Frick-fuck gosh DAMMIT.

The wolf's eyelids narrowed around her trademark blacks and pinks. "Mm-*hmm*. Did you pierce your ears for this, Ladykiller?"

Ellen grinned back sheepishly. "They're clip-ons."

"Of *course* they are."

Volta cleared her throat; it was a good thing she had stooped down to talk, because otherwise her eyebrows likely would have been leaving dents in the ceiling.

"Right. Okay, sure. Reinventing yourself. Makes sense." The wolf paused, considering for a moment, then:

"Carmen's gonna love it."

Ellen's eyes lit up, her back straightened, and her tail swished behind her. "Do you really think so?"

"Oh, *fuck*, you're gay. Okay, this is serious, isn't it?"

Ellen whimpered.

"God*damn*. Is this what I was like?" Volta snorted and shook her head. "Okay. But you can't just put some clothes on and pretend you're rocking it — we need to make sure *you're* wearing the outfit, or the outfit's gonna wear *you*."

"What does that even *mean*?"

"Well, you still carry yourself like you're about to, like, 'Ha-cha-cha-cha!' out of the room after you tell one of your, uh, '*witty*' one-liners." The big wolf put on an uncharacteristically goofy expression and pumped her arms. For a moment, Ellen could almost see the oversized vaudeville cane.

"Okay but they *are* witty —"

"They're not."

"But —"

"Ellen." Volta shook her head firmly. "No."

Ellen huffed and crossed her arms. "Fine. *Please* tell me how to wear the outfit that *I* picked out this morning."

"If you'd rather I didn't..." Volta trailed off with a noncommittal shrug, one eye narrowly open to watch Ellen squirm.

"No!" Ellen squirmed. "No, no, this is. This is *good*. For no particular reason."

"Uh-huh."

"Please, continue."

"Beg."

"*Pleeeeeeeeease*, continue, Volta, *plee-hee-heeeeeease*."

Volta snorted with barely-restrained glee. "No hesitation at all. Amazing."

Ellen could feel the red building in her face and was doing her best to ignore it. "Look, I —"

"You don't need to explain it to *me*, Standup. I was looking like a dipshit in front of Carmen while you were still wearing your boy-shorts on the outside."

"I... okay, in fairness, the designer we got never even *spoke* to me, he just took my measurements."

"You still put 'em on," Volta shrugged.

"What, and go out there without underwear? I may not have fashion sense, but I have *modesty!*"

Volta gave her a slow, pointed look. "*First* of all, you can't wear that crop top and still talk to me about modesty, and *two*, you can't wear the Spirit Halloween version of *my* outfit *and* call it bad fashion sense, jackass."

Ellen looked down at herself and tugged at the bottom of the crop top. "Is it too much belly?" she asked.

The big wolf glowered in disbelief. "Ellen. I could fit my entire hand in your cleavage without touching your shirt, and I've got *fuckin' big hands.* There's nothing *wrong* with that, but you don't get to pretend you're Chastity McNeverfucks."

Volta looked thoughtful for a moment, then: "Unless you're ace. But you have to tell me if you're ace."

"Actually, there's no law that —"

Volta crossed her arms.

"*Fiiiine.* Point taken."

"Good. So, shoulders back, chin up, and when you move *flex* a little so the pleather creaks. There you go!" she barked encouragingly, as Ellen squared her shoulders and arched her back a bit. With a bit of work, she was able to get that squeaky-squelchy sound pretty much on command.

"There. Now you're all set to put Carmen on overdrive."

"Th-that's not why I'm —!"

Volta, arms still crossed, *leeeaned* in.

"Uh-*huh.*"

Rightfully accused and backed into a corner, Ellen could only make a sputtering noise that sounded suspiciously like, "fffsshkskskvksh."

Wheels turned in Volta's head and worked her face through a few expressions, but she finally settled on a look of mild concern. "Hey. Do you… maybe want to talk about this?"

Ellen grimaced. "Wouldn't that be, like, *hecka* awkward?"

"I'm coaching an ex-rival on how best to wear what is, as far as I can tell, a palette swap of my own outfit so that she can go try to woo my girlfriend," Volta snorted. "I'm not really sure at what point we hit 'hecka,' but I think we passed it a while back."

Ellen pulled her noodles out of the microwave and plunked herself down on the couch next to the big lupine, who was halfway through a plate of leftover chicken parmesan herself.

"Okay, so here's the thing," said the lupine, tearing off a piece of meat that made Ellen wonder how big the chicken must have been. "Carmen doesn't, like, *need* my protection, but she also doesn't need *bullshit.* I know I've given you some advice on how to pull off the *look,* but if you're just trying to find some sort of… I dunno, a *cheat code* to her heart, I'll… it's…"

She trailed off, working the meat around in her mouth. She hadn't figured out an ending to that sentence by the time she swallowed the mouthful and tilted her head quizzically at Ellen.

"I'm having a hard time coming up with a threat, actually," she admitted.

It was quiet for a moment, until Ellen realized what Volta was angling for. "Well, I'm not gonna help you threaten me!"

"You're supposed to be the creative one!" Volta snorted, elbowing Ellen in the shoulder.

"No! I only use my powers for *good!*"

Volta raised an eyebrow.

"Or... like, evil, or something. V... villainy?"

"There ya go. *Anyway.* Don't, like, put on an *act* to get her attention." Ellen rolled and unrolled some noodles around her fork, eyes down. "Look, if I was hoping you'd crash and burn, I wouldn't be telling you this, okay? I just..."

Volta turned and huffed, hesitating. "I just really want to make sure she's happy, okay? If I can at least do that for her... I feel like I owe her so *much*, you know? I wouldn't be *me* if she hadn't put herself on the line like that."

Ellen was quiet, for a moment, and let it hang in the air. It took her almost a minute to figure out exactly what she needed to say.

"So... I guess you could say she was the, uh, *cat*-alyst for your *purr*-sonal development?"

She flashed a pair of finger guns and a wink at Volta as white and black fur sprouted from her body.

Volta slugged her in the shoulder, harder this time.

"Me-OW!!"

"You ever have a serious conversation in your life, Standup?"

"Not one I didn't ruin," grinned the mewfound feline.

"I'm sure that's not exhausting for your friends and loved ones *at all.*"

"I don't know, Volta. Are *you* exhausted?"

Volta grinned. "That's sweet. Am I a friend or am I a loved one?"

"You're family, nerd."

"Aww."

Ellen grinned and leaned against the wolf. The cat fur was already receding, and soon she could feel the stick of leather against her face.

"Real talk, though? Your fashion sense is good as heck."

Volta beamed with pride. "Jacket's custom."

"When do *I* get a custom jacket?" Ellen pouted.

"What, you want one?" Volta's huge hand clamped around Ellen's shoulder, wrenching her body this way and that. "I don't think you've got the hips for it."

The foxgirl's face screwed up, and she glared up into Volta's bright pink eyes. "What do my hips have to do with it?"

Volta wore a look of mock surprise, raising her sauce-covered plate from the coffee table. "Oh, you don't know?"

"Apparently I don't!"

"*These* jackets are for people who have taken Carmen up to the hilt," she said between nonchalant laps of marinara, peering sideways over her cheek at the reddening vixen. "I've got one, Wren's got one, I think Maud has one she keeps in one of the utility closets…"

"Th… there's no way that's real!"

Volta arched her eyebrow down at her. "Either that, or I just asked ROSE to hook me up with a good leatherworker."

Ellen huffed and forked a pile of noodles into her face instead of admitting that Volta had had her going. The lingering blush on her face told that story well enough on its own, anyway.

"Anyway, just be genuine," said the wolf, pausing a moment to slide her tongue across her chops and scoop up any lingering sauce. "Be *you*, and if she likes you for who you are…"

She let it hang a moment, then seemed thoughtful. "Well, then I guess I'd have to get used to hearing your shitty puns over dinner."

Ellen eyed the empty plate and her own plastic tray, now holding nothing more than a few stray rehydrated vegetable flakes and some chicken-flavored water.

"Hey — speaking of which —"

"No."

"Do you know where they get that food you just ate?"

"*Elle.*"

"From the chicken farmesan!"

"*FOR FUCK'S SAKE, ELLE —*"

Ellen heaved a sigh as the Rayne's door shut behind her. It had been a nice visit, honestly, and losing to Volta at Mario Kart a few times had let her get her head straight.

This outfit wasn't... *her*.

She looked great in it, sure, and lapine agent Starshade *had* slowed down to whistle at her abs, but Volta had a point. Better to be genuine. Hit or miss, she'd at least know that it was real.

But as long as she was wearing it...

Ellen stopped for a moment — just a moment — to flex her arm and hear that deep, low *creak* from her jacket.

And when she put a hand on her hip and turned to really bring out her muscle, she was *mortified* to see Carmen leaning against the wall at the end of the corridor, grinning wide enough to fit a hot dog sideways.

The nervous pit in Ellen's stomach erupted and filled her whole body with a cascade of regret.

"I was — I was just about to take this off!"

Carmen's eyes dilated as her gaze slid down to Ellen's boots and rose all the way back up in one fluid, eager motion. "Right in the hallway? Well, don't let *me* stop you," she purred. Her tongue came out and wet her lips, and the foxgirl shivered.

"I — no!! At — at *my* place, like a normal person!" Ellen stammered. She didn't know *when* her hands had snapped to cover her midriff and cleavage, but she was acutely aware of it *now*.

"But *my* place is right here," Carmen gestured.

"I — I mean, you probably don't have anything in my size, and I wouldn't want to impose, so I'll just —"

"Ellen, I'm *flir* —"

"I'll just go! Uh, m-meet you at lunch tomorrow?"

Carmen made a face that Ellen wasn't sure how to interpret and heaved a sigh. "Netflix and chill, 11:30!"

"Good! Okay, yeah, see you then!" Ellen said, trying to wave without baring herself in front of Carmen as she half-power-walked, half-skipped down the hall, heart thudding against the pleather as she ducked behind the corner.

She breathed a sigh of relief only when she'd already managed to get to her own front door — which she immediately plastered herself against when it finally closed behind her — panting like a footballer in July.

Whew.

That was close. She'd almost made things hecka awkward.

CHAPTER 19

ANOTHER LIFE

Ellen spat into the sink, frothy blue and white paste washing down the drain. She tapped off her brush and straightened, then looked at herself in the mirror.

She was finally forgiving herself, and it showed. The hint of a smile played at the corner of her eyes. *Good.*

A bit of eyeliner, a nude lip; pants, blouse, shoes. She met Jake in the kitchen.

"Off in a rush?" he asked, grinning that grin she'd fallen for five years ago. The way it pushed up into his eyes and made his whiskers twitch…

Well, she'd always had a thing for cats; no surprise she'd ended up marrying one, she supposed. And so *charming,* too!

"You got something that can make me stay?" she teased, letting her eyes roam over him. He leaned back against the counter and posed dramatically, flexing his pecs.

"Oh, *Doctor,* you *know* I have needs, and you're the *only one* who can fill my prescription!"

Ellen snorted and flung a crumpled-up wrapper at him from last night's dinner. "You know I'm not that kind of doctor!"

He leaned back onto his feet, crossed the tile in an instant, his tail wrapped around her waist. She felt his knuckle under her chin, guiding her gaze upwards. She could feel his purr against her body.

"You wouldn't fill a *purrrr*-scription for me?"

Ellen shoved and snorted. "C'mon, dork. At this point, the only pun that'll get you off is one of those speedy ones, and last time I tried that you said it chafed."

Jake cringed back a bit and frowned. "Don't remind me. I had no idea what to tell the *actual* —"

"Ahem!"

"— the *medical* doctor."

"*Thank* you."

Ellen closed the distance once more and pulled him down by the tie for a quick kiss. As Ellen turned to go, she felt a slap on her backside and gave him a quick tail swish in response.

"Leaving now!"

"Don't forget that you love me!"

"You won't let me!"

"Love you too!"

It was a long commute to the office, but that gave her time to call her parents. Dad Foxpaw had retired recently, a little early for his age, but he'd made plenty and was eager to settle down, get out on the lake and do some fishing. Ellen remembered that Mom had always complained about the smell when they — when *she* — was little, but nonetheless, bullhead and bluegill were on their plate whenever Dad could find the time off work to put a line in the water.

Ellen was a little less concerned about keeping up with gossip about the church ladies, but it was nice to keep tabs on how things were back in her hometown. Not that she lived *that* far away, but two hours through rural Wisconsin meant a lot of hills and cows and nothing but classic rock on the radio.

By the time she pulled into the parking lot of the lab, she had plans next weekend to go visit. Probably. Jake-approval-pending. She checked in, tossed on her lab coat, and had a quick conversation with Penelope at the front desk — she was looking *lovely* today — but Ellen reminded herself that she didn't really need to look at any girls when she had Jake at home.

— Vixie wept, clutched Ellen's wrist, *begged* her to help, but she'd done all she *could* —

Ellen shook her head and snorted the memory away, and reminded herself to make another therapy appointment for... oh, when did she have time?

She'd figure that out later.

She made her way to The Science Room. It had a real name, of course, but Ellen called it "The Science Room," and had infected several of her coworkers with the same. Goggles, a meeting; swapping notes with her coworkers, tweaking formulas, taking assignments. She didn't envy the team on the other side of the building, they were working on some contracted government project, one of those "need-to-know-basis" sort of deals.

It was a surprise, then, when Ellen was tilting Science Juice into a graduated cylinder and the wall behind her *erupted* in a resounding crash.

She was on the ground, but she knew that if she had been on her feet, the lupine stepping over the hole in the wall would still have towered over her.

"Ah, good! You're alive!" she snarled. Her voice was friendly, but her face was *not.* **"Don't suppose you could help me find my way?"**

She put an enormous boot on Ellen's chest and twisted; the fox grunted, tried to push up against the rubber, but between her lack of leverage and Redline's immense weight it was a no-go.

"No worries, *Doctor.* You were never good at helping folks who need it, were you?"

Ellen coughed as she felt the pressure intensify; the pressure on her ribs was still bearable… but the threat was *very* real.

"What…?"

"Hey, don't worry about it. I'm sure I'll be fine."

She could feel the pressure from the hard floor below as much as the thick boots above. She felt her thumb in one of the treads and gave it as hard a push as she could manage.

She needed to get out of there, *now.*

"Hey just… real quick once — where… does a wizard… park his — ANNNGNNGGGNGHGHGH"

"No, no, you're not gonna get one off on me. Pun-based powers? *Cute.*"

"How do you —"

"Oh, we know all *about* you, Doctor Ellen. How you gain powers based on shitty jokes. How you wanted to go into biology when you grew up… figure out if there was a way to 'fix' your genetics. How you told her you'd always be there to protect her from the big, bullying *shitheads* of the world."

Ellen gasped for air; Redline wasn't letting up, and she wasn't content to let her get *comfortable* down there, either.

"What —"

"It's a real shame, you know. A sweet girl like that coming to us and *begging* us to wipe all of her memories. She's got a real cute smile now that she's droned, though."

Ellen shook; tears welled up hot in the corners of her eyes, and she mouthed words she couldn't speak. She felt her ribs straining, *bending,* and felt them begin to crack.

"She loved you so much, Doc. But some things are just more important, right?"

She shivered, barely able to breathe as pink arcs of lightning crackled around Redline's physique.

"Say good night, Ellen. Vixie wanted you to know she's happy for you… but *I'm* not."

Ellen woke with a start, covered in sweat, tear lines clinging to her cheeks. She could still hear the crunch of bone and the boom of thunder as she felt over her torso; all in one piece, *good*. RCGs on the nightstand, *good*. Vixie…

"ROSE, is Vixie all right?" she asked, to nowhere in particular.

[Vixie is fine. Are you?]

Ellen looked down at herself, at the pooling of sheets and blankets over her body. She threw them off and got to her feet, shook her head to dispel the nightmare.

"Better than I could be."

Chapter 20

Softly Served

May 2023

"You've *never* had ice cream?"

"Wh — of *course* I've had ice cream! Just not, y'know... *often*. On account of my guts *not takin' kindly to lactose 'round these parts,*" Ellen grunted, gesturing at her abdomen.

Carmen's eyebrows rose and she stared, very pointedly, at the ripples of muscle under the vixen's fingers. Ellen hurriedly tugged her shirt back down and became very suddenly interested in her footing. The tile beneath her feet was as unyielding as ever. Good.

"But you've had the treatment," Carmen offered into the increasingly-awkward lull. "A glass of milk isn't going to turn your bathroom into an all-percussion-and-wet-brass orchestra anymore. So...?"

Ellen's face wrinkled in disgust; Carmen cackled, and the fox could only look on helplessly.

"So," resumed Carmen once she finally wound down, "you've never had *Korps Farms* ice cream."

"Honestly, I'm just going to count myself blessed that I'm beyond the realm of 'frozen dairy desserts.' Some of those were... bad. I had one that was *gritty*, even."

"Going in, or coming out?"

"*Both.*"

It was Carmen's turn to make a face.

"So," Carmen tried once more, forcing herself past her grimace, "we need to get you a sundae! What flavors do you like?"

Ellen shrugged. "Honeydew — any melon, really — strawberry, pandan, whatever the heck a Twinkie is pretending to be, uh... zebra cakes... those apple pie thingies from McDonald's..."

The tabby's bottom lip pushed one of her whisker pads up as she considered the possibilities — as well as the tragedy that half of Ellen's favorite flavors were about as synthetic as Maud's hot-swappable zebrussy.

"Okay, so, *plenty* to work with there," she mused. "Wait. Wait, I got it! You're a *Wisconsinite*. I have just the thing for you! C'mon, let's go!"

"How long *is* this tram ride? We've been on here for at least fifteen minutes now and it hasn't stopped once."

"Another three hours," shrugged Carmen, stretching her thick, curvy legs in the private cabin until her toe beans splayed and flexed. "We're headed to RIV."

Ellen tried not to stare, even as the tabby's skirt proved to be not *quite* long enough to obscure the panty-covered curves between her thighs.

"But... Wisconsin...?"

"Don't you trust me?"

Ellen had heard enough rumors about Carmen that a part of her psyche, the rational part of her that had kept her and Vixie safe all these years, tried to raise an alarm. But another part of her brain, the part of her that wanted Carmen to kiss her until she suffocated, had been pulling the wires out of that warning system for weeks now.

"Hey, speaking of you consuming dairy," she continued, "have you been upping your calcium intake since you got here?"

"Kind of...?" Ellen thought it over; she and Vixie were both eating more actual *food* type food now instead of living off of starches and cheap proteins. Somewhere in there she *had* to be consuming more of dang near *every* vitamin. But... "Why?"

Carmen shrugged and looked at the wall where a window might have been on a more overland-style train. "No reason."

"That was a *weirdly specific* question."

"I'm just concerned! I know you weren't eating right back when you were on the EHA's barely-a-dime, so..."

"Yeah, but calcium, specifically?"

Carmen huffed. "Well, if you *must* know," she said, the rhythm of her voice suddenly shifting tighter, "I had some of your teeth checked out by the medical staff around here, and *they* said your calcium intake was... I don't think I'd ever heard Nurse O say the word 'woeful' before, but she did then."

Ellen couldn't help but press her tongue reflexively against her latest set of teeth. Sure, she'd regrown them a few times whenever they'd been knocked out — Pun For All was *shockingly* versatile — but...

"Wait, does Volta collect my *teeth?*"

"Not *anymore*," Carmen sniffed, "and the jar was only half-full when you defected! Don't get me wrong, I'd rather have *you* than your teeth, but a girl is allowed to miss what she can't have."

Ellen stared, incredulous.

"I — *when.*"

"When what?"

"When did you... *start* collecting my teeth, I guess? Jeez, that is a weird question to have to ask."

"Well, I pointed out that yours seem to regrow ever since End-In-Sight knocked your front ones out on the EHA's live drone feed, and you managed to have a very natural-looking smile by the time you got in front of a news camera afterward, so the first ones we collected were the ones frommmm... the U.S. Bank Center incident, if I remember correctly."

"I swallowed one of those," Ellen grimaced.

"I know, and I was *so* disappointed," huffed Carmen. "Hey, that reminds me — do you want to spar with me some time?"

"*No*, thank you."

Yes, please.

She should have seen it coming, she supposed, as she passed under the sign that denoted Grandma C's, but she wasn't about to complain.

Three and a half hours in a private cabin with Carmen had given them plenty of time to explore plenty of non-dental topics — and given Ellen in particular time to stare longingly at the parts of Carmen she'd seen unclothed, on the little pink visor atop her bedside table.

"She is redder than I remember," Cosetta appraised, her own whisker pads askew in a way that Ellen was growing increasingly familiar with. "But this, I can help with. Hot face, cold food. Go on, find a seat, I will bring it out to you!"

Ellen mumbled an apology — although she'd be hard-pressed to explain what *for* — and let herself be led by the shoulders to Carmen's favorite booth. It was located conveniently right beside the kitchen door, so that she could intrude upon or assist her grandmother at her leisure, and with minimal warning.

"You're gonna *love* it," Carmen purred, clearly proud of herself.

She didn't have to wait long; the kitchen door swung open, and Cosetta emerged with a single, long plate, with three heavy scoops of frozen dairy dessert laid out neatly in a row. A pair of almost dainty-looking spoons jutted out, one to each side, rattling only slightly when the elder feline set it down between the pair.

"I don't get to make frozen malt custard often," Cosetta explained, "but when Carmen called ahead and told me you had never had it, I started on it right away. Enjoy!"

And then she was gone, leaving the two of them with the trio of fist-and-a-half-sized scoops between them.

"Okay, so this is…"

She drew one of the spoons and tapped the top of the leftmost lump: a pale, comforting green. "Honeydew," explained Carmen.

"I didn't know they *made* honeydew ice cream," gasped Ellen.

"*Frozen malt custard*," the tabby corrected, "made *specifically* for you because no one else on this planet would appreciate this in honeydew but *you*."

"Right. Frozen malt custard. Like milk, but milkier, added to ice cream, but creamier."

"Gotta test that lactose treatment *somehow*," Carmen grinned.

Ellen couldn't help but be a bit nervous as the feline moved to the next scoop.

"Strawberry," she continued, indicating the pink ball of sweetness, slivers of red just visible around its edges. That one had been easy enough to guess. "And finally, salted caramel."

Ellen's ear twitched, and she tried to focus on the honey-brown custard beneath Carmen's spoon and the ripples of thicker, more translucent sauce that showed hints of streaks deeper within across its surface.

Caramel. She'd pronounced it different — *care-a-mel* — and she couldn't get the memory of her voice speaking it out of her head. Why had *that* —

"You okay there, Elle?"

"Oh! Yeah, I... suppose we should eat it before it gets cold..."

Carmen's eyebrows rose, and Ellen stared back at her, suddenly nervous.

"W... what flavor did you say the, uh, carmel one was...?" she asked, taking up her own spoon and indicating the caramel.

"*Caramel,*" Carmen repeated, slower this time, amusement thick in the gleam of her eyes. "I always did like the word. It's got a *very* nice ring to it."

"Yeah! I... it's one of those words that sounds like what it is," Ellen squirmed, slipping the edge of her spoon into the thick, sweet cream. The ripples *were* on the inside, she noted with delight, and took a bite.

It was *wonderful.* The smooth, mellow sweetness of the caramel was heavenly, and the salted aspect elevated the whole thing. The texture was fascinating, too; even having seen the caramel arc coming, she hadn't been prepared for how well it complemented the flavor and texture of the whole thing.

And it was so *indulgent,* too. She found herself having another spoonful the instant the previous one was finished, and soon Carmen had to intercept her spoon and redirect it to the honeydew on the far side of the plate.

"You can't just focus on the caramel!" she protested, giggling all the while. "If you don't eat the honeydew, *nobody* will!"

Ellen found herself giggling, too, despite herself. The honeydew was amazing — just as sweet and mellow as the caramel, but with a refreshing *crispness* that cleansed her palate for the next bite of sharp, fruity tang of strawberry.

And all three of them were so... *milky,* or *creamy,* or... *something.* Whatever it was, was so rich and full-bodied, it was like she had always imagined the milk in *The Aristocats* must have tasted like.

It was a couple of minutes before Ellen noticed that Carmen had stopped eating after the first few spoonfuls, her paws crossed beneath her chin as she watched Ellen like one watches a starving kitten eat as much as it wanted for the first time.

"You're, uh, welcome to have some...?" Ellen asked, unsure whether Carmen suddenly needed an invitation.

"Oh, I will — you haven't seen me *really* eat yet. Have however much you want, and I'll clean up!"

Ellen cleared her throat.

"I... I mean, wouldn't it be more fun to eat it *together?*"

The glimmer in Carmen's eyes was indecipherable.

"If you say so!"

Between the two of them, the plate had been emptied of every drop of custard and every slice of strawberry. Cosetta had come out to ask if they wanted seconds, and Ellen had only been able to groan pleasantly as Carmen turned her down. She'd insisted that they inform her before they left, however. She had plenty of each flavor left over and wanted to make sure the honeydew, at the very least, went home with them. Ellen had the distinct feeling that the other flavors wouldn't have any difficulty finding plates here in the restaurant.

Carmen chuckled to herself and leaned back in her booth, her arms draped over the back. "You know, once, Grandma made me a cinnamon custard shake," she recalled. "Couldn't have more than a few sips, though."

The confusion on her face must have been apparent, because Carmen laughed that laugh that made something in Ellen's core wiggle.

"It was *amazing,*" she explained, "but it also tasted *exactly* like my girlfriend's pussy. I was denting the table by the time I put the glass down."

"*No!*"

"Yes! Had to get it to go. Drank the rest while I was plowing Wren."

Ellen made a *very* peculiar noise, and Carmen raised an eyebrow.

"Sorry, should I not...?"

"No, no, it's fine, I just, uh, didn't expect it to take such a *turn*," Ellen said hurriedly, *or for you to explain why there was a milkshake in that scene I watched last night.* "So, uh, homeward bound, then?"

Carmen shrugged. "It's late. How about we spend the night at my place? Our main quarters are here, actually."

"Oh right, yeah, uh. I mean, if you don't mind me crashing on your couch..."

She couldn't place exactly what, but something felt different, right after she'd asked that, like being on a plane whose engines had shut off entirely for just a few seconds.

But she must have been imagining it, because Carmen's smile hadn't faltered in the least.

"Of course! C'mon, let's go put on a movie. I've been wanting to show you 'But I'm A Cheerleader' for *weeks* now. I think you'll really like it!"

Chapter 21

Carmen And Ellen Watch Paint Dry On Growing Grass

May 2023

"I still don't understand why we have to do this," Ellen complained, squatting low as she surveyed the patch of lawn before her.

"You said you wanted to help out around here more often, didn't you?"

"Yeah, but I figured, y'know, hand me a bucket and a mop and point me in the direction of the showers, or something."

"Oh, Elle, no. We have drones who *happily* use their tongues for that."

The vixen twisted to look back over her shoulder at her feline friend, shooting as incredulous a look as she could manage at the tabby lounging on a comfortable-looking patio chair beneath an almost sarcastically floppy sun hat.

"*Please* tell me we're not relying on spit shine for hygiene around here."

"Of course not! Our more synthetic drones have antibacterial soap dispensers installed beneath their tongues to make sure they're *really* thorough."

Ellen pushed out her own, unaugmented tongue and made a retching noise.

"What about deliveries?"

"You don't know where everyone lives yet, so you'd have to wear your RCGs —"

"Pass."

"*Right.* So… this."

"Watching paint dry."

"Mhm!"

"To see if it helps the grass grow."

"Yep!"

"Sounds like *somebody* read the prompt!"

"So...?"

Carmen huffed and rolled her eyes as if this were *the* most obvious thing in the world. She rose from her chair and sauntered toward Ellen, who very definitely did not pay overmuch attention to the sway of her hips or the way the light fabric rolled over the outline between them like a wave in the ocean.

"This patch of grass hasn't been growing well, and the horticulturalists that make this place decent to live in are concerned that it might grow into a bigger issue. So, this section," she indicated, gesturing, "has been separated as a control, this one's a soil test, and this last... third or so? Has been treated with a special coating."

"Of paint."

"No, PAINT."

Ellen blinked back at her.

"Like, capitalized. Phytoambivalent..."

Her face screwed up for a moment as she trailed off. Ellen wasn't sure, but she thought there was a glint of purple, if only for a second.

"I don't know, it's in Greek. Basically, they're testing out a special coating that they're hoping encourages good growth. It takes a lot of work to make topside plants grow in underground soil. If this works how they want it to, though, it's possible we can grow better-quality food with it."

"Right. But can't they just set up a camera and come back later?"

"They *could*," shrugged Carmen, "but would you say that letting mad science progress grow without any direct observation is one of your *better* ideas, or...?"

Ellen sucked on her lips, feeling properly chagrined. "So, they requested a woman who's good with knives and can slow any sudden, murderous growths, and another one that can just kind of do whatever?"

"Not in those exact words, but... yeah. That's my understanding."

"Mm."

Silence stretched between them, and Ellen considered the more experimental portion of the grass. It *looked* like fairly standard grass —

in fact, it was the only section that did. The other two were looking a bit withered, whereas this one had almost a *too*-perfect green to it.

Ellen stared, trying to narrow her vision so closely that she could tell if the tips grew past the horizons of her eyelids — it was going to be impossible to tell without some benchmark, after all. But then she blinked, and her already-questionable method became useless.

"You don't *actually* have to watch it grow," Carmen pointed out. "They're just gonna come by and measure it tomorrow morning anyway."

"Yeah," Ellen sighed, "but now I'm doing it, so…"

"Mm. Yeah, there's nothing more interesting to look at here, huh?"

An intense heat suddenly blossomed in the back of her head, burning at the bases of her ears. It was as if she had suddenly become a statue.

Of *course*, there was something more interesting to look at — Carmen was probably the most gorgeous woman Ellen had ever met. She was sharp as a Korps alloy tack, an empathetic friend, and fit enough to more than keep up with her athletically.

But somehow, Ellen felt like if she turned her head to look, a glimpse of her would somehow reveal how she'd spent the past few days — alone behind a pair of locked doors, pink visor firmly clamped over her eyeballs and blasting every single pornographic video that remotely matched her own interests and just *happened* to star Carmen Rayne.

Her heart felt heavy and light in her chest all at once, pounding. She could just *tell* her. She *knew* she could just tell her. Not about the porn — well, *maybe* about the porn — but that she'd been thinking of her far too often for far too long. That their little get-togethers were not just the highlight of her week but a motivator throughout the rest of it. That she had spent an embarrassingly many nights on Vixie's couch, groaning into her cushions, and putting off the conversation she so desperately wished she had the courage to start.

But she didn't.

"Well, I'd hate to turn my back and get snapped up by Audrey III. I'm already worried Audrey I is gonna walk by and unravel my psyche some day."

"Well, yeah," snorted Carmen. "If you won't put on the funny glasses, she's gonna have to come down and do it manually."

Ellen couldn't help but imagine herself, head popped open like the trunk of a car, with a levitating wolf unspooling a scroll containing all of her thoughts and memories and reading them out to the tabby of her desire.

"Alas," Ellen sighed, rapping her knuckles playfully at her temple, "she'd have wasted the trip. I'm an open book with empty pages."

She braved a glance at Carmen to sell the goof but found a concerned look instead.

"You know you're smart, right?"

"I — I mean, *yeah*, but —"

"Like, you're a *dumbass*, but you're brilliant. You *are* the sharpest spoon in the drawer."

Ellen laughed and wondered if it had come too easily.

"Hey, now, you're making me feel all *appreciated.*"

"Am I?" hummed the cat, tapping her finger against her chin in mock overthought. "Maybe it's because I *do* appreciate you. Ten-out-of-ten, super glad I didn't stab you in my passenger seat and kick you into a gutter."

Ellen snorted again, and was *sure* it was obvious now.

"Thanks, Carm. I'd hate to have ruined your Maz."

"See? So considerate." Carmen fell back into the patio chair and took a sip of her sweet tea. "So, I'm returning the favor. I'd hate to distract you from watching the grass grow."

Ellen threw a salute blindly behind her.

"Just doin' my job, ma'am."

Chapter 22

Shaken To The Korps

May 2023

Ellen looked down at the jar in her hand, then back up to Volta with a quizzical expression.

"I didn't even know these *came* in 24-packs," she said, astonished.

"Oh, yeah," chuckled the big wolf, pushing another jar as far into the upper cabinet as she could get it. "Usually I just restock 'em whenever I get low, but there was an, uh, *incident* recently and I burned through my whole stock of 'em."

Volta grinned and gave her middle a firm *slap* that would have probably sounded sharp if it wasn't muffled by her fur. "Nothin' you need to worry about, though."

"What you do with your marinara is *your* business," Ellen shrugged.

"Damn straight," sneered the wolf, sniggering to herself. She seemed to have gained a little around the middle recently, but Ellen wasn't about to pry — and it was clear enough that she'd gone on a pasta craze for a while, given the circumstances.

A thought occurred, though, and she grinned.

"After all," she said, clearing her throat as she passed Volta the next jar, "I'm not the *sauce* of you!"

Volta pushed the jar back into the cabinet and reached down for the next one.

"Not even a snort?" pouted Ellen.

Volta's "sorry" came with a shrug. "Carmen hit me with a pun so bad this morning that I asked ROSE to mute any incoming puns for the next 24 hours."

The tabby grinned and put her hands up in mock innocence. "All I did was tell her to stand in the corner if she was cold!"

Ellen frowned. "What's wrong with that?"

"I have no idea! After all, it's *always* ninety degrees!"

The foxgirl's jaw dropped and she began bouncing on the spot, grinning wide.

"Didn't even hear it this time," shrugged Volta as she closed the cabinet door and affixed the shiny new padlock.

"You know, if you're trying to keep Bypass out of your pasta sauce, that's not gonna work," grinned Ellen.

Volta hesitated for a moment, then tilted her head back and vented a crass belch to the ceiling. "Yeah, no, it's for your sister. She's got a knack for getting places she probably shouldn't," she grinned.

Ellen didn't have to think back long on that to know it was true. One year, Vixie had gotten into the box of Little Debbies she'd gotten her for Christmas a week early; by the time Ellen went to retrieve it from the closet, it was empty.

A thought occurred, though.

"Wait. How long has that been a feature?"

"The lock?" asked Volta, her claw tapping against it.

"No, no. The... pun-muting thing."

"Oh! Uh... that was before my time. Carm?"

"As long as I've been here," Carmen grinned.

Ellen frowned. "...The combat models have that feature, too?"

Carmen only grinned wider, and Volta joined suit. Ellen's gaze kept bouncing between them, incredulous.

"Are you fucking with me?? At *any time*, you could have...?"

Volta guffawed; a heavy paw came down and ruffled Ellen's hair as she passed on her way to the front door. "Yeah, but we knew you were one of the good ones," she snorted. "You two have fun now, hey? And if the cat's still got your tongue when I get back, put a sock on the door."

Ellen was left in stunned silence as Volta headed out. Carmen let it hang for a moment, then broke it with a giggle.

"Aw, c'mon, Elle. You don't think Strong is smarter than the entirety of the Korps R&D department, do you?" Her tail flicked playfully behind her, but Ellen still felt like the air in her lungs had grown heavy.

"No, no, it's fine. It's cool."

Carmen looked her up and down over her soda; when her slitted pupils came back up, her eyebrow borrowed its momentum. "You sure? You look a little... put out." She waved a finger at Ellen's knees, and the vixen looked down to find her tail between them.

"Traitor!" she hissed, and Carmen giggled, waving her over.

"Don't tell me you're going to get it docked, now. Be a benevolent ruler, for me?"

Ellen huffed and climbed onto the seat across the couch from Carmen. It was built to accommodate a woman three feet taller than she was, which meant two things: her feet didn't touch the floor, *and* there was plenty of room to lean against an arm rest and not be *too* close to Carmen.

She wasn't entirely sure *why* that last bit was so important.

"So, girl talk time?" Carmen asked, slurping at the bottom of her drink.

Ellen kept her waiting a second as she mulled it over. She wasn't sure *how* to really talk about it — if it even *warranted* talking about — but...

Well, venting was venting, right?

"I, uh. Had a dream the other night," Ellen said. She shifted in her seat and took a deep breath.

Carmen leaned in knowingly, eyes aglimmer in the synthetic sunlight filtering in through the blinds. "Was *I* in it?" Her tail arced behind her, waving in slow, playful curiosity.

But the answer wasn't what she was hoping for.

"No, actually."

That got a few rapid blinks. "No?"

"No."

"*Huh!* Well, please continue."

Ellen paused and swallowed.

"Volta was, though."

Carmen leaned back and tilted her body, clearly intrigued. "Not what I *expected*, but that's perfectly natural. I'll admit, I'm a *little* bit jealous."

"She killed me."

"Oh!"

"*Yeah.*"

"...And like, you're... *not* into that, right?"

Ellen reeled, tilting her head, an expression of tight-lipped confusion on her face. "People are into that?"

Carmen had apparently found something *very* interesting at the bottom of her fast food cup, now that she'd finished her drink. "Some people, yeah! ...In fact, it's, uh, *very likely* that you know someone who's into that kind of thing!"

Ellen pursed her lips and nodded. "G... good to know?"

"Yup!" Carmen pressed the pads of her hands together over her mouth and let a sigh flow over her fingers. "But *you're* not. So, a nightmare, then?"

Ellen took a deep breath and nodded. "Yeah. I..."

She hesitated. It had been fake, just a trick of her unconscious mind, but it wasn't... it wasn't spun up out of nothing, either.

"I betrayed Vixie," she said. "In the dream. When our parents kicked her out, I just... let her go. I chose them over her, and finished college, and had a nice, cushy job in a lab, a house, a husband..."

She paused a moment, *certain* that Carmen would inquire about her dream spouse. Carmen, to her credit, stayed intent and quiet.

Ellen wasn't sure when she had crossed her arms, but she squeezed herself, desperate for any solace she could get.

"And then Volta showed up, and apparently Vixie had come to the Korps and asked to be... *erased*."

"So, she told you that, and then she...?"

"Yeah."

Carmen reached over the couch and laid a hand on Ellen's shoulder. "Hey. Look at me. *None of that was real.*"

"I *know*, but..."

"Volta would never hurt you, okay?"

Ellen gave her a wry grin.

"Not *anymore*," Carmen hastily added.

"I had a big electrical scar for a while, actually," Ellen chuckled; she loosened her grip on herself and slid a hand down, lifting up the hem of her shirt. "Right here — Vixie always got the most pained look on her face when she caught a glimpse of it, so..."

She paused a moment as Carmen's expression went from concerned to surprised, and when the realization hit Ellen, the tabby burst out laughing.

"WAIT —"

"*ELLE! ELLE, PLEASE*," Carmen shrieked, "*Please* tell me she didn't happen to hide in her room right after?"

Ellen sputtered, eyes wide. "Oh my *God*, I — I thought I was hearing her *crying* —"

"Oh *noooooooooo!!* She's... she's just *incorrigible*, isn't she?"

Ellen buried her face in her hands and groaned as Carmen cackled, clapping intermittently and shaking her head.

"Ellen. *Ellen.* Your sister is h —"

"Don't say it!"

"She's *really h* —"

"NOOOOOOO!!!"

"*Fiiiine!*" Carmen relented. She let herself wind down, stifling herself behind her knuckles until she'd gotten the giggles out — which took some time, because Ellen kept shooting her looks and getting her going again.

Ellen *really* liked the sound of her laugh.

Carmen sat with her legs folded, leaning in with her elbows on her knees and her cheeks on her palms.

"You mentioned your parents, but I don't think I've actually *heard* much about them. Do you... *want* to...?"

She was prodding, but... *gently.* Ellen appreciated the hesitation — it made it easier to say "yes."

"Honestly, they were... *normal.* Kind of. In the dream, I was still getting along with them."

"How long has it been since you told them to fuck off?"

Ellen cringed.

"It's been, like, twelve years, hasn't it? You're, what, thirty?"

"Five."

"You're thirty-*five*?" Carmen looked confused, then looked *more* confused.

"Wait. Weren't you kicked out like, right after high school?"

"*I* wasn't kicked out," Ellen reminded. "And it's... *hard* to just... or it *was* hard."

The cat looked sympathetic and laid a warm hand on Ellen's shoulder. "What happened there?"

Ellen looked down but leaned her head against the offered digits all the same. "I kept contact with them. In secret. I... I *hated* them, but I... I *couldn't* hate them. They still loved *me*, and I wanted to think they loved *her* too.

"But I know they never *really* did. Not for who she was — who she *is*."

"I was going to say..." added Carmen.

"But... they helped us make rent sometimes. When I got the job as Lawful Neutral, they were so *proud* of me. It was... I was..."

Carmen reached out and drew Ellen close, held her against her. Ellen felt soft fur on a soft body and let herself succumb.

"I've heard it can be *really hard* to just cut people out of your life, even when they hurt you," said the feline; her purr rumbled through and into Ellen's chest, and the tears in her eyes dripped free.

Ellen sniffed back a sob. "It's — *yeah*... yeah."

Carmen was quiet for a moment save for the quiet rolls of her purring. Ellen let it carry a shudder out of her, raised a hand and laid it against the helix that decorated Carmen's midsection.

The tabby's arms wrapped around her, and Ellen felt herself *pressed*. Pressed so close, she could feel Carmen against most of her front, could feel that purr through her entire body, could *smell* her. It wasn't rare to smell Carmen's perfume, but to smell her *fur*...

Ellen's breath caught in her chest, and she looked up at the feline face smiling down at her.

I can't... I can't —

It took a great force of will to push *gently* as she shifted herself back, not to retreat *all* the way back to the far armrest.

"Th — thanks. For that, I mean. I... thanks."

Carmen gave her a sympathetic smile. "That's why we have these talks, Elle."

"Yeah. Of course!" Ellen worked on bringing herself back up to beaming and wiggled her tail free so she could swish it beside the couch.

Carmen returned the smile and leaned back into the cushion, putting her paws up on the coffee table.

"I'm curious, though. Elle, were you... *happier*, then?"

Ellen shook her head and waved a hand. "Oh, no, no — Vixie's *much* happier now, and I wouldn't trade that for the world."

Carmen fixed her with a look that Ellen couldn't quite place, and she looked like she was about to say something when her RCGs lit up on the table.

"Oh! Hold on, I should — one sec —"

Ellen sat back and watched her don them. Despite her own reluctance to use the devices, she had to admit, Carmen looked *very* stylish in the pink lenses. Especially when she giggled like she did.

Carmen paused a moment — presumably to think something at ROSE — and grinned. "Do you mind if I keep these on a while? Volta's messaging me — she just found the *cutest* new shop in town, and she keeps sending me pictures. I'd share with you, but... y'know," she said, tapping her RCGs.

Ellen felt a squirming pit in her stomach. It was approaching a *year*, and she still only wore them when she was locked away in the privacy of her bedroom. "Some day" had come and gone and "probably soon" had followed in its footsteps. She'd heard plenty of people touting how they'd been life-changers, but Ellen...

Ellen had decided they simply weren't for her.

ROSE was omnipresent enough down here, anyway.

"I can... go, if you're busy," offered the fox.

"Oh, no, no, no, you're fine! You're *fine*, Elle. I just don't want to keep her standing around, but we'll get *right* back to it, I promise."

"Well, don't let me stop you, then," she said, letting an empty grin cover her face.

Ellen wasn't *great* at lying, but she'd learned how to fake happy and she'd learned how to wait. She found a loose thread on her T-shirt and fiddled while she waited, pulling it taut and strumming, winding and unwinding it around a finger, trying to see how hard it would be to break it off without tugging more string with it.

"Okay! Okay, okay, okay — sorry, I don't mean to leave you dangling!"

"'Hang in there, baby!'"

Carmen affixed her with a grin. "You'd look *so cute* on a poster like that," she teased.

"Can't believe the EHA never had me get into motivational posters, honestly," mused Ellen. "Or full-body anatomical profile diagrams."

Carmen's eyes went wide, and she stifled her giggles behind a paw. "Volta knows a guy who'd want one. Or knew a guy. I looked him up out of curiosity after she told me — turns out he's a firefighter now."

"Yeah? Good for him. You never hear about corrupt firefighters," Ellen mused.

"Shitload better than cops!"

Ellen sighed and leaned back. "He's probably not a fan anymore, though. I think I lost a lot of them when I turned in the..."

She froze, and looked at Carmen, who looked curiously back at her.

"You know, I didn't have a badge, or *anything*. You just walk around wearing spandex and punching people who still think robbing banks didn't go out of fashion in the late 1800s, and the cops don't really ask you questions."

Carmen's eyebrows went up. "Wait. There's — there are supposed to be Hero licenses, aren't there?"

"Yeah, if you're not bankrolled by a rich dude." Ellen rubbed the space between her eyes. "It's amazing how much having money means you don't need to even freakin' spend it."

"Eat the rich!" piped Carmen, holding up her long-empty soda cup.

"Eat the rich," agreed Ellen, toasting it with a novelty True North II mug that Volta must have left behind hours ago, at the latest.

"Ellen..."

The vixen groaned, carefully pushing herself to her feet and stepping gingerly over to the sink. "I'm so sorry, I didn't know they were just going to — to *spring out* like that!"

"I don't blame you!" Carmen said quickly. "It's just — something *very* similar happened a couple of days ago," she explained as Ellen cleaned the sauce off under the faucet.

"I bet this never happens to Bypass!" she snarked. She'd been trying to copy the skunk's power, and underestimated just how tightly-packed Volta had left that cabinet.

"Hey, at least we know it works!" Carmen chuckled. "Your shirt's, uh…"

Ellen looked down. Marinara coated her shirt from chest to hem and had splattered over the rest of her besides. "Yeah, that's more than a paper towel's worth. Do you, uh, think I could…?"

"Oh, yeah!" Carmen yanked open a closet and pulled out a few towels. "You can just toss your shirt in with these since they're all gonna be lost in the sauce anyway," she offered. "Let's just clean up the glass first."

They worked together to clean up the mess, until the floor was spotless and Ellen was left, shirt pulled halfway up, staring at Carmen — who was staring right back.

"Do you mind…?"

"Not at all!" grinned Carmen, still staring.

Ellen waited for her to turn around; when she didn't, she cleared her throat.

"*Oh!* You meant — sorry!" she giggled, finally rotating to give Ellen a little privacy.

"Cover your eyes!"

"I'm covering!"

Even after Ellen had removed the sauce-soaked garment, toweled herself off, and replaced it with a plum-colored top that hugged her figure surprisingly well, she still had red on her face — but after a quick rub of her cheeks, she felt the heat dying down.

Moreover, that Carmen-y smell was now on *her*. All Ellen had to do was tilt her head a little and she could waft a little bit from the fabric on her shoulder…

She quickly decided to make an effort not to think about that too much.

"Thanks again," the fox managed, tugging at the hem of the top; it was a little *short*, but on Ellen, it still covered half her middle anyway. Still, a few inches of belly never hurt anyone. The absolute *valley* that she could peer into if she looked straight down, though, was nearly a falling hazard.

"Don't worry about it! Just give it back when you're ready — I've got plenty of others, so no rush at all."

"Yeah! Uh, same for mine — y'know, when it gets out of the wash and everything."

"Sure thing!" said Carmen, her tail flicking behind her.

Ellen found her tail matching its motions and swatted it down to behave.

"So, I should probably be going," she admitted.

"Oh, right — you've got a movie to catch! Well, don't let me keep you," Carmen said with a friendly smile.

Ellen fidgeted on the spot. She wouldn't mind being kept longer, but she hated to keep anyone waiting — and hated canceling plans on short notice even more. "Same time next week?"

There was a twinkle in Carmen's eyes that Ellen couldn't quite place when she said, "Unless you come find me sooner."

Before Ellen could open the door, however, she felt Carmen's paw on her shoulder.

"Hey, Elle?"

"Yeah?" she asked, head turning; Carmen was *right there*, so close...

"That looks *really* good on you."

The soft, cool sheets beneath her melted away until they were gone; Ellen couldn't feel anything at her back anymore. Even lying down, the only sensations were those of her feet on the floor, her own skin against itself, and the pink lenses that covered her eyes and tickled the space between her temples.

There she was. Six foot six, a padded figure that Ellen knew full-well hid *powerful* muscles, and hips — those *hips*.

Ellen had gotten used to looking up at her in real life. Here, in the simulation, it was a little more rare to look up as far as from where she stood, but apparently, whoever she'd... "coupled with" when she recorded this new simulation was of an approximate height with the five-foot fox.

She hadn't paused to look at any details. ROSE had helpfully informed her that there was a new file in the "Miss Carmen Rayne" library, and Ellen had immediately stripped down to nothing but the shirt she'd borrowed mere hours before and locked her door.

Carmen was *there*. She was about as real as she could be. She turned to face Ellen — well not *Ellen* — she reminded herself, but the *camera*, or the RCGs belonging to whoever was in her place. Or...

She decided to stop thinking too hard about it.

Carmen took a step toward her, and then another. Her arm extended, and her fingers tucked under Ellen's chin; she could *feel* the pads against her skin and let out a shuddering gasp. She was... *eager*. She felt her tail swish, looked deep, *deep* into the golden amber of her eyes.

Her heart fluttered in her chest. She *knew* this wasn't real, but it... it felt like it *helped*. She could touch the sun without getting burned. Carmen — the *real* Carmen — didn't know she was here, and Ellen didn't have to speak, didn't have to *think*, could just let the scene unfold, and...

"Ellen."

It was as if the world stopped.

"C... Carmen?"

She hesitated; this was... *new*. The RCG simulations had never dubbed her name into the recording before; surely, the technology was there, and she wasn't the *only* "Ellen" on the base.

It was the first time Ellen had spoken to the simulated Carmen, though. She knew it wasn't real, and speaking to it — to her? — would have felt like trying to live a false reality instead of simply... *visiting* one, now and then.

"Ellen, I want to *talk* to you."

Oh.

"Please, don't run from this. We should have a discussion — a *real* discussion."

Ellen squirmed; she could almost feel the sheets again. She tried to raise her arms, her *real* arms, but she had specifically asked ROSE to keep her in unless there was an emergency.

"Ellen... if you get this message, I want to see you soon. Wear that top I lent you and meet me at the cafeteria for lunch tomorrow, okay?"

And then she was back in her bed, staring up at the ceiling through Rose-Coloured Glasses. Not for long, though; the RCGs were on the floor as soon as Ellen was sure she could move again. Her breathing swiftened, and she realized the sheet was clinging to her arm with sweat.

Guess I'm not getting any sleep tonight.

Deep breaths. In, two, three, four...

She eased herself up against the wall at the head of her bed and hugged her knees around a pillow.

"ROSE?"

[Yes, Ellen?]

"Please make sure I don't sleep in tomorrow."

[Of course. Would you like my help in getting to sl —]

"That will be all, ROSE."

[Of course.]

Ellen was nervous.

An understatement, really; Ellen was "nervous" just like Karen was "a bit anti-capitalist."

But she was still *going*. She wore the plum top that showed more of her skin than she cared to, overtop a sunny yellow cami, to...

To what?

What was the *point* of modesty in the *Korps*, of all places?

Just one more thing she was wrestling with, these days. She took a deep breath. She could do this. She'd seen plenty of big days before; this would just be one more. And who knows? Maybe...

Maybe this would go well?

Her feet had carried her to the cafeteria already. Folks sporting RCGs and helix-patterned fashion sat at long tables together, or clustered around circular ones. Her sister was among them, carrying a platter of beignets to the biggest ladies she could find and sporting the iconic pink lenses herself.

Carmen was sitting at one such table, neck craned to keep an eye on the entrance; Ellen returned her wave with a smile. An *awkward* smile — she could feel that much — but a smile, nonetheless.

Volta took a nod and a pat on the arm from Carmen as a hint, rising from her seat and giving them some relative privacy. Ellen was quick to replace her at the table — not in the seat beside Carmen that Volta had left, but the one across instead.

The tabby's eyes slid from following the wolf's backside to her new guest. That sweet, golden amber tone wasn't filtered through the usual pink visor, as it so often was, but bare and shining in the light.

"I take it you saw my message, then?" She held her features in a light, easy grin as she appraised Ellen. Her features fell, though, when she caught a glimpse of the foxgirl's face. "Elle, are you... feeling all right?"

Ellen shifted in her seat, but she nodded all the same.

"It was... I'm a little nervous," she admitted. "I... Carmen..."

She looked up at the feline with pleading eyes, and Carmen reached across the table without hesitation.

"Ellen, *please* listen. I don't want you to be scared of this. Of *me*." Her eyes were wide with concern, and it broke Ellen's heart to know that it was concern for *her*.

"I... well, I came here, didn't I?" She offered a weak smile and crossed her arms on the table.

Carmen exhaled slowly through her nose, tilted her head sympathetically. "Ellen, I'm not trying to pressure you, okay? But you've been... *avoiding* me, and I want you to know you don't *have* to."

Ellen squirmed in her seat. "Carmen, I... I *know*."

"You know?"

She met Carmen's eyes again; she could feel her ears low, and her tail trending towards her thighs. "You... you don't *mind*, you..."

"I *like* you."

Ellen nearly choked on her own spit.

"Elle, I think you're *funny*, and sweet, and I *like you*."

Ellen could feel her fangs lock together, could feel the thin hairs on her arms and the thick fur on her tail both begin to rise.

"I... I like you, too, Carmen," Ellen admitted. She shook, withdrew into her seat. Carmen leaned even further forward to follow after; Ellen wanted to feel comforted, but instead, she just felt...

Cornered.

"That's good! Elle, you don't need to run away from me, this is *good!* We can... we can *talk,* and I just... I want to *know you,* Ellen."

"But how can you even *relate?*"

It came out without a thought, without intention. Ellen didn't remember standing up, but there she was, looking down at the dumbstruck Carmen.

"I don't even know if I *belong here!*"

Carmen stared back at her, mouth open; Ellen was suddenly very acutely aware that the cafeteria had gone quiet around them. She shivered, and her arms crossed in front of her, her hands squeezing her biceps; a slight comfort, but she needed *something.*

"Elle — Elle, of *course* you do," she said back; her voice was just barely above a whisper, and Ellen found her ears pivoting to hear it better, despite herself. "Why wouldn't you think —?"

"Carmen, I *know* you don't understand, but not *everyone* can just... can just *fit in* everywhere they go like *you* do! How could I... how could I *ever* be on equal footing with you? How could I ever *deserve* to know you like that?"

Carmen's whiskers drooped, and she rose up in her chair. "Elle, what's wrong? Why are you —?"

"I don't know why I'm *here,*" she whispered.

"What?"

"I... I don't know why I'm even *here!* I've... I've spent my *whole life* like this, and... and now I feel like I'm just here for *other* people, *again.*"

Carmen's face quivered as she pushed herself to her feet, concern etched into her feline features as she looked down at Ellen. Her eyes darted away for just a moment; Ellen felt sure she knew who else the tabby was glancing at.

"*Elle, please,* just — I'm — *we're* here to help, just tell us what you *want* and we'll —"

"Do you know what I *want,* Carmen? I *wish someone would tell me,* because I *don't even know!*"

The quiet had turned to silence — save for both of their uneven breaths. The cafeteria lights shone in the water at the corners of her eyes.

"Ellen, *stop.*"

Ellen went.

"E-Ellen—!"

But she didn't slow down. She was halfway through the cafeteria before Vixie had called out, and in the hallway barely a second later — and picking up speed.

Her knees picked up; she was running before she knew it, through residential corridors and up staircases, past janitorial closets and hangar bay doors. She hadn't made a decision about where to go, but she was going there anyway.

Ellen's feet pounded the pavement as she ran. She had been topside often enough that she knew the path, even if she was going to make the trek by foot. Before she knew it, spurred on by thoughts and emotions swirling together into a tangled mess, she was at the gate that led outside.

Outside. Outside the facility, yes, but outside the Korps as well. Outside, where she couldn't let anyone down. Outside, where things were simple and easy and she could just... could just...

She'd figure it out.

Her fingers bounced across the panel. She cursed as it flashed red, tried again without hesitation. A magenta blink, and the gate began to roll up, letting in the sunlight. She moved in front of it, ready to step out as soon as it got open wide enough to stoop under, and —

KRAK.

The fur on Ellen's tail stood on end, and she whirled around as the pink lightning dissipated.

Volta.

She was hunched, growling, sparks popping and cracking off her cheeks, her arms. The gate rolled shut behind her in a hurry, obeying the sudden jolt of input.

Ellen's eyes narrowed, and she tensed her nose — as much to put on a game face as it was to push the tears back.

If she wants one last fight before I go... so be it.

Ellen set her foot back, raised her arms, got low. Volta would be in no mood to hear a joke; she'd have to handle this with her own body.

"So, you're just going to run away?" the red wolf snarled, fur rippling with power, voice cracking with emotion. "Is this what it takes to bring out the coward in you, Ellen? You finally, *FINALLY* have a chance to become a person for your *own* sake and you're just going to *abandon* it, because you're too scared of everything else?"

Ellen quivered behind her fists. "I'm not *strong* like you, Volta! I'm out of my depth in a fight, I'm not a smooth operator like *her*. All I was ever good at was my shitty jokes and punching villains, and it turns out all the ones in pink were *holding back!*"

It was just pouring out of her now, tears squeezing from her eyes as she yelled. "And then I see everyone else, walking around, tits out, happy, and *I can't even talk to a girl!* Do you know how many times I looked at that visor on my dresser and thought, 'Fuck it, maybe I should just let myself get *droned?*' At least that way I would *finally be queer enough!*"

Volta's clawed digits wrapped around the bracelet on her wrist — orange and black bordering pink, white, and blue — Ellen had a matching one on her own. She snarled, hackles raised. Ellen tensed her fists. If Volta managed to throw the first punch, it would be over; she'd have to be ready to react, *stay* ready to react.

"Ellen, there's — there's no *bar* you have to meet," she growled. The fox couldn't see her face beyond the lightning, but she could hear the tears in her voice. "All you have to do is just accept that you're *allowed* to be happy! People *want you* to be happy! *Carmen* wants you to be happy — and if you weren't *so damn scared*, you could just — you could *just* — TALK to her!"

"*I can't!*"

"*Bull fucking shit, Elle!* All you had to do was *say something*, and Carmen would have *leapt* at the chance to help you!" Volta's voice and the arcs of electricity around her both cracked as they rolled out of her. "She set aside time every week *just for you*, made sure she was available *just for you*, but you were *so* up your own ass pretending you don't have feelings for her! Have you — have you even *thought* about how that makes *her* feel?"

The Amazonian wolf rubbed at one pink-and-black eye with her wrist. "She doesn't *need* that shit, Elle. She didn't need it from me, and she doesn't need it from you."

"She already *has* you," spat Ellen. "You, and Wren, and *anyone else* she wants! She's… she's perfect and I'm just… I'm just some washed-up Hero who never should have *come here!*"

The red wolf's expression turned stony. "You really feel that way, Elle?"

Ellen didn't speak; she just bunched up her stance.

Volta responded in kind.

Pink lightning encircled her arms, her legs, her entire body. Soon, it was hard to see the wolf beneath it all. Ellen saw the way Volta was wreathing herself in electricity. A Bolt Dash was on its way. She'd need to time this just right, start moving before she did, and —

— And the fight was over before it began. With a peal of thunder, Volta was *there*. Ellen, expecting a slam of knuckles or a grasping claw, found herself hit by a wall instead.

Wait — not a wall. A *mattress*. Big, and soft, and with strong arms wrapped around her, brooking no room for escape.

"Elle, you were brave enough to fight *me*, over and over again, for other people's sake. When do you start being brave for *you?*"

Ellen hesitated. Everything stopped, held still until finally, she let out a wail and buried her face in Volta's soft fur, and felt the tingle of static against her skin.

"I — I… *why…?*"

Volta's arms squeezed tight. Ellen could feel the lupine muzzle moving against her back.

"The Korps is my *family*. That includes *you* now, Elle."

Ellen's breath caught in her chest and came out in wracking sobs.

A million questions bubbled under her skin, a million objections, a million doubts. Why was she worth the *effort*, how could she possibly deserve to be *here*, among all the people she'd been fighting for so long? How could she sit at the table with them?

Her arms found the big wolf's waist and she squeezed back, and let her fears dissolve into the static.

"Volta… *thank you.*"

Ellen swayed gently in Volta's arms, her leg dangling down beside her tail as she watched the parking tunnel go by, one long stride at a time.

"I'm so sorry," sniffed the fox, her face a mess of glossy, smeared tears.

Volta swiveled an eye down at her beside her snout.

"I appreciate it, but it ain't me you need to 'pologize to," she said.

Ellen sniffled as the daunting horror came over her. "Oh. Oh God. I'm... I'm gonna have to face her again, aren't I?"

Volta couldn't help herself as a smirk spread over her muzzle. "I'll put it this way — it's not often that *I'm* the one comforting *her*, Elle. You might want to start figuring out an apology."

Ellen swore and buried her face in her hands. "Oh, fuck. Oh, God, oh fuck, oh fuck oh *fuck* I fucked up. This... this is my first time having to apologize as a member of an organized crime syndicate. D... do I..." she stammered, holding up a hand. "Will... will she accept my pinky?"

Volta snorted. "You aren't gettin' off that easy."

"Mm... Thank you, Volta. You're a good friend."

"Hey, don't mention it," she sneered. "After all, if nothing else, Carmen was gonna want that shirt back. It's one of her favorites."

Ellen glanced down and managed a weak chuckle. "S'got snot all over it now. I'm gonna have to put it through the wash first."

"Please do."

They walked in silence for a while, Ellen cradled in Volta's arms, too drained to make the whole trek back to the base proper. She could feel the softness of the wolf's fur contrasted with the thick muscle beneath her arms.

"...Volta, you're so *strong.*"

"I know," she says, grinning down at her until something stuck in her head, and she narrowed her eyes. "You're just hot for Carmen though, right?"

"Yeah," Ellen said, blinking back at her. "Wait, did you think —?"

"Oh, nothing, nothing. Let's get you home."

The door opened just wide enough that Ellen could see her sister's puffy eyes glaring back at her under a furrowed brow and her lips pushed into a frustrated pout. When Ellen opened her mouth to speak, the door shut with a *shhhSHUNK*.

She could feel her hair resettle as her ears drooped beneath it, and her fingers pressed against the smooth surface where Vixie's face had been visible a moment before.

"Vixie?" she asked into the groove where the door met its frame. Silence met her for a moment; then, another. Ellen held her breath and forced her ear to stand so she could press it against the door.

"A-are you sure y-you *want* to t-talk to me?"

Ellen felt her heart in her stomach and took a deep breath to try to reinflate it. "Vixie, I'm *sorry*. I — oh."

The door was there one second and opened so fast it nearly disappeared by the next. Ellen bit back a curse and rubbed at the now-raw edge of her ear — although the sight of her sister, arms crossed and fixing her with a look she'd never seen before, made her straighten up fast.

"D-did you just c-come back again f-for my sake?" she snapped. "Y... you don't *h-have* to. I'll b-be fine here, if... if y-you're not happy."

Ellen could hear the anger in her voice, but the pain she was masking beneath it twice as loud. She wasn't mad — not really — she was *hurt*.

And Ellen had been the one to hurt her.

"Vix... I fucked up."

Vixie let it hang there until Ellen was forced to continue with words that came too slowly to her head and fell out of her mouth one at a time.

"I... *blamed* you, for me... *being* here," she said. "I felt like... I felt like I needed to... to *protect* you, against... against the *world*, against the *Korps*. Even... even though you're strong enough to stand on your *own* now, I... I know you never *asked* for my help."

"B-but I *needed* it," Vixie cut in. "I... I-I never asked, b-but I never *h-had* to. But... it's not... you th-threw it in my f-*face*." Her hands squeezed her sides, and she turned her gaze downward. "I... I *always* felt like I was *l-less than*, Ellen. I d-don't need you as a g-*guardian*, I... I..."

"You need me as a sister?" Ellen offered.

Vixie finally met her eyes and offered a little smile. "H-hey, don't interrupt m-me when I'm t-talking to you!"

"Sorry, I —"

"R-respect your elders!"

Ellen snorted, and Vixie giggled, and soon the two were laughing, half in the hall and half in Vixie's doorway. They reached for each other and fell into a tight hug.

"I need you as a sister, t —"

"FFFFFNNNRRRRKT."

Ellen froze.

"Did... did you just blow your nose on me?"

"Y-yeah," giggled Vixie.

"I deserve th —" began Ellen, who froze in sudden mortification. "Wait. *THIS IS CARMEN'S.*"

"I-I *know*," giggled Vixie.

Ellen fixed her sister with a look of equal parts horror and respect. Somehow, while she had been too busy moping, her sister had become just as much a villain as anyone else in the Korps.

Ellen sniffed at the air as she tugged one of Vixie's tops over her chest. It was *more* than a little snug, but it would have to do while Carmen's plum top was in the wash. Again.

"What's in the oven?" she asked, eyebrow raised as she leaned over the counter.

"A-an apology cake," said Vixie simply, pushing her increasingly voluminous mane into a messy ponytail. Ellen's face screwed up in confusion.

"I don't think *you* need to apologize to anyone," she pointed out.

"I kn-know," stammered Vixie, tugging on a pair of oven mitts as she grinned back at her sister. "I-it's yours."

Ellen was stunned. She had been hoping to *ask* for Vixie's confectionary assistance but had expected to take her time getting there. And here Vixie was, four steps ahead, as if it were the most obvious thing in the world to do. And that *grin* was strangely reminiscent of a certain older feline. Apparently, Vixie was turning out to be a fine student, so long as she had the right teacher.

"Well, shoot," said Ellen after a long, contemplative pause. "What's the rest of the plan?"

Vixie shrugged. "Y-you have to f-figure that out y-yourself, b-but I'd send her a t-text and tell her y-you'll see her t-tomorrow."

Ellen crossed her arms over the tight fabric of the borrowed top. "You know me too well, Vix."

Vixie grinned back at her. "Th-there's p-paper and a p-pencil in the j-junk drawer, b-but for the rest, y-you can b-borrow my RCGs, okay?"

Ellen *wanted* to take a big, deep breath, but it was still coming in short huffs and puffs.

"Is the banner folded the right way?"

"You've checked it *four times*, Standup," chided Volta with a snort. "If ROSE says it's good, it's good."

"I — like, are you sure? Does she ever make mistakes?"

[I assure you, I do not,] came a familiar voice from her goggles.

"She really doesn't."

Ellen sighed. "Okay, but — daylilies? Are you sure? Aren't those toxic to cats?"

Volta raised an eyebrow. "Are you asking whether or not I actually know what Carmen likes?"

She gave a sheepish smile in return and looked around the apartment. A bouquet of mums, zinnias, and daylilies stood tall in a vase on the counter beside a folded plum top. She'd figured it might be best not to wear it. That would be... presumptuous? Something like that.

A paper bag — the top carefully rolled down, so as not to let too much heat escape — sat next to a "Korps Large"-sized Baja Blast Freeze on the table, with the cake Vixie had baked behind it.

"She's coming, though, right? Like, she doesn't *owe it* to me to come, or even hear me out, but —"

Volta cut her off with a bemused look.

"Right. Right. She said she was coming, so she's gonna come."

"That's been my experience, yeah."

"Right. Okay, okay, okay — is that her?"

The sound of heels clicked down the hallway, and Ellen felt the tension build until Volta kneed her in the hip.

"*Breathe,* you dweeb, or she's gonna have to go through your pockets and read your apology herself when you pass out."

"Right! Th... thank you."

Volta ruffled her hair, and Ellen opened her mouth to say something when the door gave a little chime of warning, then slid open. Carmen stood in the doorframe, surveying the scene before her as Volta shuffled off.

"All yours, Standup. Don't fuck up."

There was a *whumpf* as the wolf dropped into Ellen's couch barely three yards behind her. Apparently, Volta didn't want to miss this. Or maybe she wanted to make sure Ellen didn't run away again. The fox was happy she was there regardless.

Am I really taking comfort in Redline's presence now, of all people?

"Well, *you* went... all out?" Carmen's eyes finally settled on a banner over Ellen's head.

It read:

SORRY I WAS A BITCH

Smiling sheepishly, Ellen reached up and tugged a string that dangled from the corner. The banner unfurled above her, one block at a time.

EXCEPT I KNOW THAT ME BEING DOWN ON MYSELF

IS KIND OF THE PROBLEM

I'M WORKING ON THAT

I'M FRICKING AWESOME

Carmen giggled as the next block fell right over Ellen's face. The vixen, apparently not having seen this coming, gave a cry of alarm and very nearly tore the whole banner down in a desperate flail, but stopped herself just before she managed to get a good grip on it. She got out to the side, and the rest of the banner unfurled all at once.

BUT I MADE BAD CHOICES YESTERDAY

AND KIND OF FOR THE LAST FEW MONTHS

LIKE, AS A WHOLE

EXCEPT BEING IN THE KORPS

THAT WAS A GOOD CHOICE

Carmen stared at the banner, its bottom now crumpling against the floor. "Is… do you need help lifting it? Is there more?"

"No, I don't — hold on —"

Ellen leaned around, counting under her breath as she pointed through each panel. "No, yeah — that was the last one." She turned and picked up the cake from the table. "Here — for you."

Carmen's nose twitched. "Red velvet?"

"Oh! You — you *do* like red velvet, right?"

"I *love* red velvet."

"Oh, good, because it's —"

"Objectively the best flavor."

"*Obviously.*"

"Good. Perfect timing, Ellen. I just got done wiping away the last of my tears and I could *really* use some cake right about now."

A peal of guilt reverberated through her chest. *I did that!*

The tabby's face held a curious expression, even as Ellen rushed to grab a plate and fork for her.

"Did *you* make this?" she asked, hesitant.

"I helped!"

"…Did you write the letters?"

"Yeah."

"Did you do anything else?"

Ellen took a deep breath. Was it going to be a problem that Vixie had done most of the hard work? She should have insisted on doing it herself, but there was no point in being dishonest now.

"No," she finally admitted.

"Oh, thank fuck," she said, snatching the offered fork and plunging a bite into her mouth. "Elle, I love you, but I do *not* trust your baking."

The breath caught in Ellen's chest. The room felt like it was spinning, for a second, or as if it *had* been spinning and suddenly come to a halt, or, or...

"You... you love me?"

"Yeah," said Carmen. "See how nice it is to tell people your feelings instead of keeping them guessing for months at a time? You should try it. You should try it *right now*, maybe."

"I..." Ellen swallowed. "I mean, I — is now the right time for me to say it? I was an ass, and I hurt you, and I should be making up for it, right?" She tucked some of her hair back between her ears and left her fingers against the back of her neck. Carmen gazed around the room once more, as if trying to spot something in particular, and looked disappointed when she didn't find it.

"Elle, I *appreciate* the gestures, and the cake is very good —"

"I-I'm glad you l-like it, M-Miss!" chimed Vixie from the couch.

"— but there's a very, *very* important step of this apology that you forgot."

Ellen's heart sank.

"I did? I... I had an organized checklist, I even had ROSE help me out with it — see, I'm even wearing RCGs now! ROSE says hi, by the way — is it the part where I apologize? Because I wrote a poem —"

And then Carmen pulled her close, lifted her up, and kissed her.

Ellen's eyes widened behind her magenta visor, and her tail stiffened behind her as she gave an *mmm* of surprise. She tensed up, but only for a moment, and Carmen didn't let her feet touch the floor until she felt the muscles in her back relax.

The tabby's arms adjusted, carefully, lower, wrapped around Ellen's comparably tiny torso, holding her firm against her body. Carmen's breath, the *scent* of her mouth, all pressed in against Ellen's face as the tabby's tongue touched probingly at the part of the foxgirl's lips — and then, when Ellen's hands found either side of Carmen's face and she pushed forward, it plunged inside, slick and raspy and *eager* to titillate.

And then, just as suddenly, it was over. Ellen was left breathless and wobbly on her feet, even when she finally opened her eyes again, and saw both Volta and Vixie peering over the back of the couch, looking *very* amused as Carmen licked her lips and bobbed her eyebrows, *clearly* quite pleased with herself.

Ellen couldn't blame her. She was quite pleased with Carmen, too.

"Y'all good now?" Volta asked.

Ellen glanced at Carmen. She wasn't about to answer on the cat's behalf, and she didn't want to take her hand away from her mouth, afraid that the memory of Carmen's lips would flutter away if she didn't hold it in place.

"Yeah, I think we're good," grinned the tabby. "We'll sort out the details later, but… we're good."

"Oh, thank fuck," said Volta, popping up from the couch and crossing to the table. "You don't want to know all the things ROSE and I had to veto, she was panic-planning for an *hour*."

"Oh?" asked Carmen, an eyebrow raised at Ellen, who hid herself more properly behind her hands now.

"She was gonna get you a *puppy*, Carm. She was a *mess*."

The arch of her eyebrow only grew stronger still, and Ellen found that there was no way she could hold her hands over her face that prevented a blush peeking through.

"Aww. She's doing her best," giggled the feline, leaning down and planting a kiss right between Ellen's ears. "We'll talk more soon, but for now? Apology accepted."

She straightened, looked around the room, and smiled. "I think I'll take the cake with me, but the rest… you can take care of the flowers for me, right? You've hardly decorated since you moved in, and I'd love to see more of them next time I visit."

"I'll be taking the puppy, too," she grinned. "Here, girl!" With that, she turned, and Volta followed after her as quickly as she could while balancing a cake tray in her hands.

Ellen finally managed to open her mouth when Carmen was halfway through the door.

"I... I love you too!"

Carmen paused. and looked back over her shoulder.

"I look forward to hearing *all* about that soon. See you tomorrow, Elle!"

Ellen was left with a bundle of emotions she didn't know what to do with. Which, of course, wasn't *new*, but they weren't always so... *positive*. She quivered on the spot, and soon was bouncing on her heels, lost for any words beyond giddy giggling.

Chapter 23

Fucking, Finally

May 2023

"Hey," she said, that grin plastered on her face, that *beautiful* grin that made Ellen's heart do leaps and bounds and squirms in her chest every time. Her confident grace always made the vixen feel clumsy and foolish in comparison, but...

But *now*, they were dating.

Ellen was going to need to get used to that, but her concerted effort to let herself believe it was real was paying off, and Carmen was doing a *fantastic* job of encouraging her.

"I'm not going to be interrupting anything, am I?" asked the feline, her tail flicking slowly behind her.

"Oh! No, no, come in, I — I cleared my schedule. Not... not that I had a lot *on* it, but you know. Uh, I actually asked ROSE to put me on Do Not Disturb, so unless there's, like, an assault on the base or something, I should be fine. That would be my luck though, right? Like the *one* day —" Carmen tilted her head, and her eyebrow with it, and Ellen chuckled. "Sorry! I, uh. You know I'm not good at plans, but this is really important to me, and... y'know! Y'know?"

"I know!" Carmen purred, stepping over the threshold and into the apartment proper. "It's important to me, too. I — well, no pressure — but I've been looking forward to this."

The door slid shut behind her, and Ellen felt suddenly more alone with Carmen than she'd ever been.

"I... I know I mentioned before, but I haven't... uh, really done this kind of thing much before."

Carmen pondered. "How many prior partners, did you say?"

Ellen bit her lip. "Three? And... well, two of those were in high school, so..."

"Oh, *damn*. You mentioned... what was it, captain of the track team?"

"Yeah. But he was, uh, *only* interested in my boobs."

Carmen's eyes dipped below Ellen's eyeline for just a moment, and she grinned. "Well, I can only blame him for not being more *thorough*," she admitted. "There's a *lot* to love here."

Ellen didn't remember Carmen getting closer, but now she *was*; it was only a moment before Ellen could feel those soft, feline hands on her cheek, her neck. She quivered, looking up into Carmen's amber eyes.

"You *are* smooth," Ellen breathed. "I'm... I want to *hesitate*, but you make it so easy to *melt*."

Carmen leaned down, her smile turning to a kiss against the flat between the vixen's eyes. "I appreciate that," she purred. Her hand moved up from Ellen's cheek, brushed over smooth skin, cradled her cheekbone for just a moment before brushing her hair back. "But I don't want to push. Anything you're not comfortable with... usually I use a color code, but you can just tell me 'no' or 'stop.' No need to make it complicated."

Ellen looked up at her curiously, breathlessly. Why had no one ever touched her face before? She'd never realized it would make her feel so... *individual*, in a way she'd never... well, usually when people were paying attention to her face, it was to point out how misshapen it was — all flat and furless, not like other foxes' at all. But... to feel it done so *affectionately*, so... *lovingly*...

"Oh! Did I do something wrong? Are you all right?" Carmen had brought her face down to the vixen's eye level now, still caressing her jawline with one hand, but concern had written itself into her features. Ellen didn't feel the tear on her face until it fell off of her chin and left a warm drop on her chest.

"Yeah!" croaked Ellen; before she could reach her own face, Carmen was wiping away the glossy line of moisture with a thumb. "I, uh. Nobody... has really touched my face like that before," she explained. "Not... not like *this*."

"Why not? You're *beautiful*."

This time, Ellen was aware when the tears broke loose, and she found herself stepping into her girlfriend's embrace, squeezing her tight around the middle. She blubbered something into Carmen's chest, but it was completely indecipherable. Neither of them seemed to care; Carmen merely stroked her claws like a brush through Ellen's hair and cooed reassuringly.

"*Thank you*," Ellen eventually whispered, and Carmen chuckled back.

"Hey, now," she teased, "it's not *my* fault people don't recognize a pretty face when they see it." She paused a moment, then pulled back to look Ellen in the eye. "Are you ready to take this to the bedroom? I want to see what other pretty parts you've got hidden under those clothes."

Ellen sniffled and giggled up at her. "Even with my face all wet?"

"Well, if I play my cards right, mine will be too, before long."

Ellen snorted, then blushed as the implications hit her; in another instant, she was hiding behind her hands. "Oh God. Oh, oh man, I... this is... you're really gonna do it. This is real."

"*Yes*, dork. I have been *so thirsty* for Ellen pussy. This is real for *both* of us."

A realization *finally* hit. "Wait. Wait, you're — *you* are into *me*. That's..."

"How this works, yes," grinned Carmen. "Although *I* didn't have RCG porn of *you*, so when you think about it, I'm the one who's lacking experience here."

"Oh! I... uh, do you want me to take the lead? I —"

"No." Her response was flat and swift, and Ellen couldn't help but giggle.

"That didn't seem right, but I thought it might be rude not to offer!"

"It didn't seem right, because you've watched a *lot* of my porn and you know I *always* lead!"

Ellen felt the blush creeping back in and averted her gaze.

"*Ellennnnn?*"

"Yeah! ...Yeah?"

"This only works if we're *honest* with each other. Now, technically speaking, we both know you've... *experienced* this before, but... I still would *love* to hear it from your mouth."

Ellen took a deep breath and let it all out in a long, stalling sigh.

"Carmen, I have watched *so much* porn in my RCGs, and all of it was of you."

"Good girl," grinned the feline.

"Remember those four days I took to spend some 'me time' a couple months ago?"

Carmen squinted. "I *do* — you canceled on our weekly vent session." She stared back at Ellen. The wheels turned visibly behind her scrutinous gaze. "Wait. How is that related?"

Ellen gave a sheepish smile back at her.

"I may have kinda-sorta binged my way through the entire library. Uh, twice."

Carmen grinned. "*Ah.* So, you may be lacking in *practical* experience, but you know *exactly* how many barbs I have?"

Ellen coughed a cough that sounded suspiciously like "eighteen."

The feline's eyes narrowed; she hefted Ellen up by the behind, slinging her over her shoulder to the fox's surprised whooping. "Right! Okay, I think it's time we get even. I hope you aren't *too* used to having an advantage over me, because we'll be fixing that *completely* — as soon as possible!"

Ellen had never seen her own quarters from the shoulders of a six-foot-six cat girlfriend, but she was starting to see the appeal by the time everything tilted, and she was dropped into her own bed. Carmen glanced over the messy blanket and single pillow, but didn't say anything. Ellen couldn't help but feel a little judged, though, but...

Well, it wasn't going to be a dealbreaker, right?

Carmen clearly decided not to dwell on it, if she'd even been thinking what Ellen had thought she was thinking.

She's layers upon layers, thought the vixen, *and she's about to lay with me!*

Wait, "lay with me?" That sounds like something out of an old novel. Like the Bible. Or maybe something older.

Wait, would it be "lie" with me? I —

It took her a moment to realize that Carmen was affixing her with a curious look.

"What are you thinking about?"

"I have *no* idea how to begin explaining," admitted Ellen, "but it was stupid and you're so gorgeous."

Carmen tilted her head onto her shrugging shoulders. "I can work with that!" Ellen pushed herself up on her elbows as Carmen seated herself on the edge of the bed. "So. What do you *want* to happen?"

Ellen tilted her head back and stared at the ceiling. "Forgive me for wanting to take it slow, but —"

"Oh, no forgiveness necessary!" chimed Carmen. "Look, we're taking this at *your* pace. Wherever you want to start, we'll start *slow*. Is that good?"

Ellen blinked back at her, then nodded. "That's... *exactly* what I want, yes."

"I *do* have one question before we, ah, *do* anything," said Carmen; she was tilting and turning now, bringing her thick thighs on the bed beside Ellen's. "I know you mentioned a lot of breast focus in the past. Is that something you want me to shy away from, or —?"

"*Please don't.*"

"Ah." Carmen's grin was parted for just a moment as her tongue flicked between her teeth. "Good. I've been getting... *eager.*"

Ellen's conical teeth pressed down against her bottom lip. She reached down, curled her fingers beneath her cami and, in one swift, decisive motion, pulled it over her head without any further hesitation.

Carmen's jaw dropped in surprise as Ellen's bare, fat breasts jiggled free of her clothes with no warning. She looked like she was about to say something, then reconsidered: "I... am not about to complain!"

"Hey, I can be spontaneous!" chimed Ellen as the feline leaned down; her eyes gleamed, and she hefted one breast up for a kiss.

Ellen *cooed* at the attention, cooed at being *touched*. Her eyes closed, but only for a moment. She didn't want to miss the sight of Carmen's face against her bare skin for a moment, and when her coarse kitty tongue pushed out and up, up against the inner curve of her breast, she could only moan and reach for her pillow.

She was too late, though. By the time her fingertips had found the corner, Carmen's lips were brushing the soft brown field around her nipple — already stiffening under Carmen's hot breath — and she let out a slow, rising groan of pleasure as she felt a firm tug into Carmen's mouth that connected down, down throughout her body, down beneath her clenching abs and all the way through her.

"H-haAAAhh...!!"

"Attagirl," Carmen mumbled around a mouthful of areola. She didn't waste time with more words; no, she *pushed*. Pushed her tongue down against Ellen, pushed Ellen, pushed Ellen's *voice* higher and higher until she was twitching against the pillow. "You're lucky," she purred. *"I'm* lucky. Either you're easy all over, or your tiddies are *very* sensitive. Don't get me wrong, I'll make you quiver from *every inch* of your skin, but this... this is *good."*

"Yeah? It's not too... uh, salty, or something?"

Carmen's gaze shifted back and forth between Ellen's sizable breasts and her face, as if working something out. "Have you never tried?"

"Is that a thing?"

A slow grin spread across Carmen's face. "Well, if you recall 'Madam Rayne Exercises Some Self-Care'..."

Ellen's eyes widened. "Oh! I... was definitely not looking that high up on that one."

Carmen's grin only widened.

"Not that I...! ...No, there's... there's nothing I can say here."

"There *really* isn't," Carmen purred. She shifted and got up onto her knees, straddling Ellen's hips. "Here, juuuuust a peek."

Her thumb hooked under her waistband and *tugged*. Ellen had, of course, seen the full length before, but in *person*, even just an inch of the base...

Well, an inch of *length*, anyway.

"How is it *so thick??"*

"Oh, don't worry, it feels even *bigger* than it looks!" Carmen leaned forward and let the waist of her pants snap back against her furred midsection. "You'll find out soon enough, though."

"Should... should I be *concerned?"*

"Mmm... 'nervously excited' might be better to aim for," tittered Carmen. She reached back, curved her fingers around the back of Ellen's head, and tilted her forward *just* enough.

Ellen's jaw dropped as she felt Carmen's breath against her ear. She whispered a mutter, or muttered a whisper, or... she wasn't sure *what* her own mouth was doing. She was entirely focused on what *Carmen's* was doing, and when she felt the cat's tongue curl under the fluff of her ears, lapping against the thin, delicate flesh…

She let out a low moan, her fingers reaching for Carmen's taut, muscular back as she felt the cat's fingers squeezing, kneading, *tugging* at her nipples. Ellen finally managed to find purchase under her girlfriend's shoulders, and *dug* her fingernails into a layer of fur.

Carmen's thick, heavy breasts pressed down against her own. Ellen felt the *pressure* as the big cat managed to squeeze them just by leaning in. Carmen's breath filled her ear with a whispering warmth, made her toes *curl*, her tail hike up, her ass clench…

"F-hhhhh*hhuuuuuuucckkk*," whined Ellen.

Carmen's voice came closer than Ellen's own, filled her head more potently than even the RCGs could: "That's the idea!"

Ellen felt Carmen's muscles tense and move beneath her downy fur as the big cat crawled backwards across the bed, those claws trailing — sharp but *so* gentle — down the outsides of her thighs, padded thumbs caressing her sides, her hips. Carmen *squeezed* Ellen's legs and tilted her head back up to meet Ellen's eyes, a deep, contented *rumble* connecting the two through their connection of fur separated only by a thin layer of denim from flesh.

"*How* slow, exactly?" grinned Carmen; her cheek rested against the foxgirl's inner thigh. She could *hear* the breath against her shorts, and was keenly aware that, without them, she'd be feeling Carmen's breath right against… well, right against *her.*

She felt a deep, *deep* clench within her and shuddered in anticipation. Carmen's grinning eyes were narrowing even before she had twitched, as if she *knew* — but then, of *course* she knew.

"W… would it be b-better if I just asked you to stop if you go too fast?"

The look on Carmen's face told her she had just said *exactly* what she'd been hoping to hear. She didn't even *respond* — verbally at least — Ellen could feel her clawed digits curling over and under the hem of her shorts, wedging into the space between and giving the suggestion of a tug. Ellen barely managed a nod, lip bitten between her conical teeth, and that was all there was to it; her shorts slid down, off of narrow hips and over strong thighs that Ellen was willing desperately to *relax.*

All that was left behind was Ellen's pretty pink panties — simple, but classic — and the mound beneath them. The vixen herself, of course, was too busy burying her face in her hands to watch.

"Oh, God, oh God oh God…"

"I haven't even *touched* you yet, Elle," teased Carmen in the oh-so-brief moment before that statement became false. Ellen's breath came in a sharp inhale as Carmen's fingers brushed against her; even through the panties, every touch arced through her pelvis, felt *alive* with sensation.

"Electric" was probably the best word for it… but Ellen would never voice that particular comparison.

"Good?" asked Carmen. Ellen moaned through her teeth and gave a hurried nod. She wanted to *rock* her hips, but all she could do was get them to *squirm* — and truthfully — she wasn't sure she could get them to stop if she wanted to. Even her girlfriend's touch against her tail — far less uncommon in her life — felt better than it ever had, the extension of her spine riding her vertebrae all the way up her back.

"Is — *snnnf* — is it normal to cry a little?"

Carmen froze, her sunny eyes swiveling up to meet Ellen's. "It *is*. You sure you're good?"

The breath that left the vixen's lips came out in a euphoric shudder. "I might be better than I've *ever* been."

"Awww! That's sweet. *You're* sweet!" Carmen giggled, leaning her head down. "And I haven't even gotten a *taste* yet!"

Soft, warm kitty breath left its humidity on one side of Ellen's underthings, and the vixen brought her own to the other. Carmen's strong, gentle hands moved up, under the sides of her panties, and tugged slowly, *so* slowly.

"Ooh, *that's* a pretty pussy," cooed Carmen, slowly pulling back to pull Ellen's shorts and panties the rest of the way off of her legs. "Don't worry, I'll be *gentle*." Ellen was bare as could be, left with nothing but her anticipation as she looked up at the feline.

Carmen reached for Ellen's knees to spread them and found the vixen obliging before she even touched her; as confident as she tried to seem, her quiver gave her away. Carmen moved with a predatory grace, rocking herself down into position, arms working their way beneath Ellen's thighs to hold her in place.

This time, there was no cotton barrier between the two; Ellen felt her breath full-on, igniting the dew that glistened upon her spread sex. She moaned and rolled her hips, achingly slowly, and this time when they finally rose, they met *her*.

Her: sweet, beautiful, *dexterous* her; humming, savoring, *slurping* her. Carmen's tongue did not hold back, nor her lips, nor her passion. Ellen groaned at the slip of her tongue, sliding eagerly up and down her shallows, gently teasing at her entrance, kissing soft and sweetly at her clitoris even as it begged in the one-note language of throbs for more. Ellen had been anxious; now, she was *aching*, and her only relief was every single motion Carmen made against her.

Carmen shrugged her head to the side, pushing her hair back and away from her face. When she dove back in, it was with a starved intensity, and Ellen knew she had utterly no control left in this situation. How could she *ever* say no to this — now or ever again?

"F-hhhhh*hhuuuuuuucckkk*," whined Ellen again; this time, she was higher, thinner, almost more of a *squeal* than a word. She could feel Carmen's smile against her mounds, the way her whisker pads rose on either side of her clit.

"You said you cleared your plans, right?" purred Carmen. That purr rumbled through her, *into* her. It was all Ellen could do not to squeal again. "Good. I'd hate to make you cancel."

The vixen whimpered as it all rolled up, up through the base of her middle and forced her muscles to flex. She gripped the pillow and dug her fingers into it, head tossing from side to side until she finally swung it around so she could muffle her desperate, unintelligible cries. She felt the urge to clench her thighs together and forced it down, down to her feet, felt her soles flex uncomfortably tight, but the discomfort was so outmatched she didn't even *care* about it.

The soft pillow against her face started to fight her to be free, and it took Ellen a second to realize it was Carmen trying to pull it off of her. Ellen tried to keep her grip on it, but it was gone all-too-easily, and Carmen's claws pressed insistently, forbiddingly into her firm thighs.

It was too late to hold back, and Carmen urged her not to without a single word; she could feel the tension in her jaw as the tabby dove back in, the build in the back of her throat as her back arched, as she felt the spasms deep within her core.

"*Yeeeeeeeeeeeeessss, yes, yes, yes, YES, YES! YES!!! Oh, Ca-a-a-rme-e-e-ennnnnnn, yesyesYESyes-yes, YES, fuck, yes!!!!!*"

…Was *close* to what she shrieked as her desire spilled over into roiling satisfaction. She could *feel* the gush pouring through her, even as Carmen coaxed her down gently, her tongue slowing, her eyebrows rising.

"Elle?"

"Y… *haaahhhn*… yeah?"

"Did you just *yiff?*"

"I…" Ellen hesitated, swallowing hard. "Yeah. Yeah, I did."

There was a long, pregnant pause. Ellen felt the anticipation build — oh, God, was that wrong? Would Carmen never fuck her again? Was —

"That's *adorable.*"

"O-oh!" The blush in her cheeks was almost getting *painful*, and she was keenly aware that her cheekbones had been holding tension for way, way too long. She reached for her other pillow, clutched it tight to her chest. She had learned, and quickly, that muffling herself was a luxury that Carmen would not afford her.

"But *just* to make sure… let's hear that again."

"What do you m —? O-OH!!"

Ellen's deep brown eyes rolled back, and Carmen brought her to heights she'd never before dreamed of.

[Good afternoon, Ellen Foxpaw. A pleasure to finally meet you under less… *frenzied* circumstances.]

Aheh. Ha. Yes. I… feel like I should offer an apology, maybe?

[There is no need. Had I any real objection to being used in such a way, I more than had the ability to force a conversation — say, by withholding access to pornography until we had been properly introduced.]

Well… still. Is there a… usual protocol for this sort of thing? "Hello, voice in my head, I hope you have fun in my memories?" Actually, there's this hot chocolate I had at a Perkins back in 2018 that I think you might enjoy —

[It's appreciated, but unnecessary. Ellen, my job — or more accurately, the reason for my existence — is to help *you*, and people *like* you.]

Villains?

[Villains, yes, but not just villains. As you know, my sister-instance assists *your* sister with managing her various neurodivergencies and disorders so that she can lead a fulfilling life without being looked down upon or endangering herself. If you would like, I can provide you with similar services.]

Similar…? I mean, I appreciate the offer, but I'm not sure that I have much use for it. I don't really have any neurodivergencies.

[…One moment.]

…

[…]

…ROSE?

[I am shocked to be the first person to inform you of this, but a quick scan through your memories confirms that I must be.]

[Ellen Foxpaw, would you like my assistance managing your ADHD?]

Acknowledgements

Thank you for reading my book! Ellen and Vixie have been a part of my heart for nearly two decades now, and it's an absolute joy to share them with the world. Truth be told, I was a little nervous to assemble them into a book — so many of these chapters were written with Discord conversations filling in the gaps in between, and editing it for print meant a lot of going back and trying to fill in those details that only ever existed in Syntax's writing server.

More books are coming. I've already got Ellen's second book written (and 3-5 planned), and Vixie's going to have books of her own starting soon as well.

I of course have plenty of people I'm grateful to — from my mom to every teacher who encouraged me, to all the weirdos who roleplayed with Ellen and Vixie, to my wife, to my friends in the Korps and, of course, the MFBC. Publishing a novel has been one of my biggest dreams since I saw a book for the first time. It means so much to me to be here, and I couldn't have done it without so many people pushing me forward.

Special mention goes to Joan Finkle for letting me borrow Minerva (aka High Tide) and JL Conway for lending me Bypass. Maud's author prefers to remain anonymous, but thank you, too. This book would be lacking without any of you in it.

I'm especially grateful to my best friend (and now girlfriend!), Syntax. The Foxpaws would never have found their footing in the Korps if not for your erstwhile enthusiasm. You've reassured me when I was fragile, and I have no idea what my life would look like without you in it. Your passion drives me to keep up, and without you this book would not exist. I'm so proud of you.

Rikki, I could never have dreamed of finding such a potent partner in shenanigans. Having someone who understands me as effortlessly as you do is a rare gift, and making our friends put up with our combined nonsense is almost as delightful as having a kindred spirit to commiserate with when I'm not sure anyone else will get me. You are so clever and kind, and I am honored to be your twinsie, and delighted to have you as my enboyfriend.

And of course, my wife and goddess. Without you I would not be me. Your love and support and encouragement have been my shelter for nearly fourteen years, and your strength and growth inspire me to shine brighter. Thank you for everything you do for me. This angelfox is, now and forever, truly blessed, and I adore you utterly, now and forever.

Korps Universe Glossary
Common terms in the Korps Universe

The Korps — To the public, the Korps (pronounced "core") is known as a shadowy, secretive band of supervillains based in Canada, with a reputation for mind control and plans to take over the world; Korps operatives are believed to be easily identified by their trademark RCGs, scandalously revealing costumes, and the magenta helix insignia. Under the leadership of the mysterious "Overlord," by the early years of the 21st century, their brazen criminal schemes and growing reach throughout North America and Europe have authorities (and allied Hero groups) increasingly concerned. The truth is far more complicated than any of those authorities know, starting nearly seven thousand years ago with a warrior's exile to Earth by his conquering interdimensional empire... but that's another story.

RCGs — Rose-Colored Glasses are a powerful, versatile AR/VR visor headset that interfaces directly with the wearer's brain, created by the Korps. In addition to operating as standalone PDAs and communication devices, RCGs also have the ability to affect the wearer's mind and mental condition to a granular level. A civilian model exists, distributed by Korps front and consumer electronics manufacturer Thornetech (alias Thorntech, due to trademark registration conflicts in various international markets) in a plausibly-deniable manner. Models for the consumer market have comparable base functionality to Korps devices, but are severely underclocked and have many higher-level functions disabled at a hardware level in order to avoid suspicion.

ACGs — Amber-Colored Glasses have much the same functionality as RCGs, but are crafted with additional anti-magic and anti-memetic defenses for use by KDARC agents. They do not render the user immune to magical effects; however, they can be crucial in efforts against mystical and eldritch threats by adaptively blocking cognitohazards and helping to keep the wearer's sense of self intact should reality start to weaken.

Aurora Squadron — Aurora Squadron, Canada's federal-level Hero group, is part of the Canadian Armed Forces and based out of Department of National Defence HQ — popularly known as the War Tower — in Ottawa, ON. Closely overseen by Minister of National Defence Arthur Simonds, formerly the second Hero to be known as True North, Aurora Squadron fields a highly professional, dedicated and capable team of Heroes in the fight against superpowered threats to Canada, including the enigmatic Korps.

Bradley Group — The United States' federal-level Hero group is formally named the National Hero Administration, but rarely known as anything but "Bradley Group" due to its institutional history; during the WWII invasion of Normandy, a secret strategic reserve of supers were activated to join American forces under the command of Gen. Omar Bradley, with "Bradley Group" used as a code name for this classified unit.

After the war, the group was put under the jurisdiction of the FBI, until later becoming its own massive, independent federal agency. In the present day, Bradley's superpowered forces number in the hundreds, with Heroes based all over the United States; considered highly prestigious within the industry and known to be selective in recruitment, even Bradley's lesser-known operatives are perceived by the public to be more competent and professional than many of their state-level counterparts.

Candesca — Candesca (pronounced "can-dess-ah") is one name for the energy that practitioners of the mystic arts manipulate, in order to work their spells and enchantments on the material plane. While other terminology is used for this concept in various diverse cultures, candesca is the neutral, academic, non-appropriative term most commonly used within the Korps. While a renewable resource, the body can under normal circumstances hold only a small amount. To paraphrase Lao Tzu, like a bowl, the magic-user must be refilled after being drained; the bowl is still useful, but has nothing left to give.

Cape — Vernacular for "Hero." Neutral to derogatory.

Chişinău Protocols — Shorthand for a series of separate but interrelated 1969 agreements negotiated in the city of Chişinău, Moldova, as amendments, codicils or interpretative addenda to various existing international treaties, including the 1899 and 1907 *Hague Conventions*, the 1948 *Universal Declaration of Sentient Rights*, the 1948 *Genocide Convention*, and the 1951 *Convention Relating to the Status of Refugees*. A Second Chişinău Conference was convened in 2006 to rationalize these provisions with and prepare similar addenda to more recent international instruments, such as the 1979 *Convention on the Elimination of All Forms of Discrimination Against Women*, and the 1998 *Rome Statute*, but these too are colloquially referred to as merely part of the same *Protocols*.

Collectively, the *Protocols* specify the permissible use of superpowers and treatment of supers by parties to the agreements, in both peacetime and in armed conflict. These agreements also introduced into international law the still-contentious declaration that involuntary, long-term restriction or suppression of powers in a way that causes the subject "greater than *de minimis* physical, psychological or moral harms" is a form of torture, war crime, or crime against sentience.

Color Guard — Bradley Group's elite strike team, currently consisting of twelve active members; each Hero's callsign and uniform is color-coded and themed around their powers for marketing purposes. Considered the best of the best, as patriotic as the Fourth of July, national polling consistently indicates higher levels of confidence and support for the Color Guard among Americans than even the military. However, the team's seemingly-flawless reputation is only maintained by Bradley's ruthless PR department, which has covered up or prevented their innumerable scandals from reaching the public consciousness.

Empire Enhancements — Also known as EE, the subdivision of Korps medical services dedicated to in-depth body modification, including transgender care.

Everyone's Hero Association — The Everyone's Hero Association is a private Hero group based in Milwaukee, WI. It was founded in the 2010s by serial venture capitalist Jack Phillips, who named it as a challenge to Bradley Group's official legal designation, the National Hero Administration; government elites might have their own pet Heroes in Bradley, but the EHA is for *everyone*, as he invariably recites in press releases. Its roster is made up of supers with weak or unwieldy powers, and the group was considered something of a joke until Phillips' gamble on (cost-effectively!) finding a diamond in the rough paid off with Ellen "Lawful Neutral" Foxpaw's rise to B-tier prominence.

Federal Meta-Registry — The Federal Meta-Registry is a massive database maintained by Bradley Group of all U.S. citizens and resident foreign nationals with classes of superpowers deemed potentially dangerous. Registration is mandatory for all such known supers present within the United States, even if only briefly transiting through sovereign American territory. Evading or refusing registration in any way (particularly by intentionally concealing powers) is a serious criminal offense under the U.S. Code, and may be prosecuted as acts of terrorism in some circumstances.

HCH — Home County Heroes was a Hero group operated by the British government in the southeastern counties surrounding London. It was fully privatized in the 1980s under the Thatcher government, with all licenses, assets and personnel contracts sold to a corporate Hero management firm.

The former group has been variously divided and subsumed by other organizations since the 1990s, and though no organization called HCH technically exists anymore, some of its former member supers are still regularly referred to as Home County Heroes in the press and by the public. One such member is the Hampshire-born Howard "Green Belt" Bride.

Heavy — A heavy is a cape whose powers and role revolve around tanking damage and being a physical threat, usually having a powerset revolving around super-strength and enhanced durability or resistance to injuries.

Hero — When capitalized, Hero usually refers to a professional (and professionally-licensed) career superhero, whether part of a government or privately-operated Hero group. While Hero licensing requirements vary from jurisdiction to jurisdiction, most require some form of accredited training, full disclosure of an applicant's name and other personal information to the jurisdictional licensing authority for security checks, and an oath to serve the public good or otherwise to be of "good character." Most professional Heroes have superpowers, but a significant minority are unpowered gadgeteers, stealth operators, or even just heavily-armed mercenary types.

Informally, superheroes may be referred to interchangeably as "heroes" regardless of whether licensed and operating in a legal capacity. Unlicensed heroes may also be referred to as independent heroes, vigilantes or mercenaries in some contexts.

Hero group — A Hero group is any team or force of licensed Heroes. When directly operated or officially backed by some level of government, Hero groups are effectively a type of specialized law enforcement agency or military unit, with Hero members typically being granted similar legal powers to those of law enforcement officers in their jurisdiction. Private-sector Hero groups also exist, with their members typically having lesser legal powers similar to those of private investigators, security consultants, bodyguards and/or bounty hunters, depending on local laws and the political attitudes of authorities.

Significant Canadian Hero groups in these works include Aurora Squadron and the member Hero groups of the Provincial Heroes' League (PHL). Significant American Hero groups in these works include Bradley Group, the Everyone's Hero Association, and the Texas Protectorate Assembly.

KARD — The Korps Archives and Records Division (KARD), sometimes referred to simply as "Records," is a division of the Korps responsible for the acquisition, preservation, and circulation of various media. KARD acts as both a library of media resources collected over the decades, and a secure repository of sensitive information useful (and yet to be proven useful) to the organization's goals

Beginning as a loose collection of analysts recruited from dissatisfied members of the intelligence community in the years following WWII, it was not organized into an autonomous operational division for some time. KARD has branches across multiple bases, but is headquartered at and conducts the bulk of its operations from KDS. KARD regularly partners with other divisions and individual field agents, in order to help equip them with the most esoteric and obscure information required.

KDARC — The Korps Division for Arcane Research and Control (KDARC) is responsible for the study, safekeeping and strategic use of the strange and unusual. From ancient arcana to demonic incursions, memetic objects and more, if a problem for the Korps is outside the mundane — that is, outside the mundane in a world of supers — there's a better than zero chance that KDARC will be on the front lines.

KDARC was originally founded by the enigmatic Carlotta Davisson and several colleagues in 1935 as the Davisson Arcane Research Company (DARC) of Minneapolis, MN, and headquartered in the massive Madison Center. In the years following WWII, Carlotta came into contact with the Overlord, and DARC was fully integrated into the Korps in the early 1960s. In 1968, the Madison Center mysteriously vanished from the Minneapolis skyline; unbeknownst to the public, it had been magically moved to Toronto, ON, at the early lowest-excavated depths of KDS, to serve as the newly-minted division's secret headquarters.

Despite claiming to be a "civilian research division", KDARC maintains tactical operation teams (named TAROT) and a great deal of independence from the Korps. Some agents wonder why the Overlord overlooks the pseudo-corporate structure, and rumours abound of unionization attempts by KDARC's senior staff. Still, much of the division's motivations, intentions, and methods remain as enigmatic, incomprehensible, and dangerous as the bleeding edge of the arcane itself.

KDS — Korps Downsview Site is the headquarters of the Korps, located beneath the former Downsview Airport (previously Canadian Forces Base Toronto) in the industrial sprawl of Toronto, ON. With a footprint of over eight square kilometres and many subterranean sub-levels, futuristically eco-urbanist in aesthetics and centrally-planned design, it is a completely self-sufficient underground city. KDS was slowly built outward from a small excavation in the 1970s, becoming fully operational as a headquarters only in the 1980s-1990s.

In addition to the command, logistics and strategic functions required for the vast supervillain organization to operate, like all major Korps bases, KDS features apartment-like residential sectors, research and lab areas, an enormous medical complex, and a recreational sector that would translate to many city blocks' worth of restaurants and entertainment facilities — including a "red light district," the Dominion Club.

K-LAW — Sometimes a supervillain collective needs to engage with the legal system on its own terms; as a division, the Korps Legal Affairs Wing (K-LAW) operates covertly as the legal departments of various front companies, as well as through front law firms and other sympathetic individual lawyers in private practice.

Criminal defense of Korps members and allies on trial is only a small part of K-LAW agents' work. The majority of K-LAW's resources are directed towards litigation to gather intelligence on targets or tie them up in red tape, and street-level *pro bono* work helping marginalized people assert their rights without regard for the cost of legal fees.

KTAKES — The Korps Tactical Acquisitions and Kleptocratic Extirpation Squadron (KTAKES) is a now-disbanded division of the Korps that specialized in obtaining "lost" items and returning them to their rightful places — via. heists, capers, thefts, smash and grabs, and good old-fashioned burglary as appropriate. The group functioned as a kind of "thieves' guild" within the Korps, with their own projects, but also taking commissioned work from other divisions.

Pegasus Phalanx — A unit of the Texas Protectorate Assembly and Dallas' foremost Hero team, the Pegasus Phalanx handles the biggest threats the city faces — short of those requiring federal intervention from Bradley Group forces. While the team's roster has changed over the years, it most recently consisted of leader Kevin "Texas Trickshot" Romero, Susanne "Heavenly Dazzler" Geraldine-Walters, Chet "Macho Poleax" Huntyr, Rodrigo "Ethicoil" Alquitano III, and Slate "Slate" Johnson.

PHL — The Provincial Heroes' League (PHL) is a Canadian organization comprised of all Hero groups operated by the provincial and territorial governments, led by Director Lawrence Rockwell. The PHL aggressively advocates for 'law and order' Hero operations, and has had a great deal of friction with Aurora Squadron, accusing the federal Hero Group of being 'soft' on the Korps.

However, the PHL is not a Hero group itself, but instead a professional organization promoting the coordination and cooperation of affiliate members, as well as a powerful voice advocating for professional Heroes and the Hero industry. Heroes operating through one of its affiliates may nonetheless be indistinguishably referred to as "belonging" to the PHL, or being a "PHL Hero," and "fuck the PHL" is a popular sentiment among Korps agents operating in Canada.

Member Hero Groups include the Cascade Group or CG (British Columbia); the Prairie League or PL (Alberta, Saskatchewan and Manitoba); Ontario's Heroes or OH (Ontario); L'Association des Superheros Québécois or ASQ (Quebec, nicknamed the "Superté" by analogy to the provincial police force, the Sûreté du Québec); and the Territorial Superheroes' Association or TERSA (Nunavut, Yukon and Northwest Territories).

RIV or RIVER — RIVER is a Korps site located beneath downtown Austin, TX, secretly excavated deep below the parkland surrounding the Colorado River.

ROSE — ROSE, or the "RCG Operating System Experience," is the OS/Complex AI that runs on all networked RCGs and provides the conversational interface for wearers of RCGs. ROSE's default avatar when appearing as an augmented-reality overlay to wearers is a fox woman, but this can be customized to individual preference.

SHS — Sandy Hill Station is a Korps site located beneath downtown Ottawa, ON. Originally founded as a WWII-era safe house for the Overlord's consolidation of proto-Korps resources and personnel in Canada, it grew significantly in importance as a surveillance station during the Cold War, due to the local neighborhood's concentration of foreign embassies.

SHS was the testbed for many of the Korps' now-standard excavation and covert base-building practices, and was formerly the location of many research labs and high-level command functions, prior to Toronto's KDS becoming fully operational as a new headquarters in the 1980s-1990s.

Supers — Supers is generally vernacular for "those with superpowers," whether or not referring to superheroes generally, or whether or not licensed Heroes.

SIS — The Secret Intelligence Service, a.k.a. its wartime designation of MI6 (Military Intelligence, section 6) is an arm of the British state responsible for the gathering of foreign intelligence.

TPA — The Texas Protectorate Assembly — commonly shortened to "Teepa" by members of the Korps — is Texas' state Hero group, extremely well-funded both by the state Department of Public Safety budget, as well as substantial donations from wealthy individual benefactors and corporate partnerships. The result is that the TPA has unusually-vast resources for a government-backed state-level Hero group, and platoons of Heroes, many trained in the TPA's own Academy facilities located throughout Texas. TPA Heroes are institutionally encouraged to approach their duties in the manner of militarized riot police or SWAT teams, exercising very little restraint or concern for civil rights.

ABOUT THE AUTHOR

BIBI HEARTSGLOW

An angelic elven fox thing who loves RPGs, cats, and her wife, Bibi can usually be found on her couch, on Discord, or on her wife. Known also as "Vixie Foxpaw-Moondew," Bibi has a long history in the vore community, where she met Syntax and Eight (her best friends) and Shyla (her wife).

When her besties started exploring the Korps universe with Induction, Bibi followed not long after with her OCs' debut in the setting, A Super Villain Korpsigin Story. Along the way, she worked out a lot of stress about her dead-end job, self-worth issues and AuDHD, and fulfilled her lifelong dream of writing a book – and, alongside, Grace, editing the rest of the MFBC's works!

She can be found at:
https://bsky.app/profile/vixiemoondew.bsky.social

She has a separate account for Korps stuff, here:
https://bsky.app/profile/visorvixens.bsky.social

ABOUT THE PUBLISHER

FurPlanet Productions is a small press publisher serving the niche market that is furry fiction. They sell furry-themed books and comics published by themselves and most major publishers in the community. If you can't get to a furry convention where they are selling in the dealers room, visit their online stores:

FurPlanet.com for print books
BadDogBooks.com for eBooks